Advance Praise for Plain Haven

"…combines gentle romance with a fascinating look into the inner workings of Amish society." ~Dana Mentink, Bestselling Author, www.danamentink.com

"…chockful of lovable characters, action, and Amish ambiance."~Kelly Irvin, Blogging at www.kellyirvin.com, *The Saddle Maker's Son*, ECPA bestseller

"…an exciting tale with just enough humor and romance to touch your heart!" ~Amy Lillard author of the Wells Landing Series

"Fans of Amish fiction will enjoy Simpson's debut novel, *Plain Haven*, set in Maryland. A page-turner!" ~Suzanne Woods Fisher, bestselling author of *The Imposter*

"…Amish and romantic suspense combined into one fast-paced, action-packed story!" Mary Ellis, author of *Magnolia Moonlight*

"…heartwarming characters, a satisfying sweet romance, and plenty of suspense to keep Amish fans turning the page until the very end." ~*Ruth Reid, Bestselling author of the Heaven on Earth and Amish Wonders series.*

Plain Haven
Plainly Maryland-Book 1

Susan Lantz Simpson

Vinspire Publishing
www.vinspirepublishing.com

Copyright ©2017 Susan Lantz Simpson

Cover illustration copyright © 2016 Elaina Lee/For the Muse Designs

First Edition

Printed and bound in the United States of America. All rights reserved. No part of this book may be reproduced or transmitted in any form or by any means, electronic or mechanical, including photocopying, recording, or by an information storage and retrieval system-except by a reviewer who may quote brief passages in a review to be printed in a magazine, newspaper, or on the Web-without permission in writing from the publisher. For information, please contact Vinspire Publishing, LLC, P.O. Box 1165, Ladson, SC 29456-1165.

All characters in this work are purely fictional and have no existence outside the imagination of the author and have no relation whatsoever to anyone bearing the same name or names. They are not even distantly inspired by any individual known or unknown to the author, and all incidents are pure invention.

ISBN: 978-1545466292

Published by Vinspire Publishing, LLC

To Rachel and Holly,
Love Always

Prologue

Virginia

The mid-August morning already promised another hot, sticky day, even though pink fingers of sunrise were just beginning to write across the gradually brightening sky. Lilly panted and reached a hand to dislodge the tendrils of pale hair that had escaped the elastic band holding her high ponytail and glued themselves to her neck. She was nearly at the end of her morning ten-mile run, and a cool shower called to her.

Huff, puff. Huff, puff, she chanted silently as she inhaled and exhaled. Years working as a children's librarian colored her thoughts, even while running. She rounded a curve in the tree-lined country road and stopped mid-stride. A chill shot down her spine.

The rear double doors of a white, over-sized Chevy van parked on the shoulder of the road had been flung wide open. Two men grunted as they dragged a large canvas bag toward the opening. Each man hunched under the weight of the odd-shaped bag they carried between them as they shuffled to the guardrail.

It wasn't, it couldn't be—*please, God, not a body.*

Afraid she would draw attention to herself if she turned and ran, Lily abandoned the road and darted behind a thick oak tree. She crouched down, hoping to hide, though it would be hard to blend in with the foliage while wearing a bright pink t-shirt. Her heart thumping and breaths erratic, she trained her gaze on the men as they swung the bag back and catapulted it down the embankment beyond the guardrail.

"Whew!" the taller of the two men gasped. He snatched off his faded green baseball cap and swiped it across his forehead, surveying the area as he did so. "What the — she saw us!" he yelled.

Adrenaline surging, Lilly shot from behind the tree. *Run! Run! Run!* her brain screamed. Fear, smelling like perspiration and damp earth, nearly choked her. She panted. Her ears were clogged with the sounds of her thumping heart and pounding feet. Were they following?

She chanced a look over her shoulder. Her eyes connected briefly with the eyes of the taller man. *Keep moving!*

Lilly ran harder, faster. She feared her heart would explode, but she had to keep moving. If they came after her in the van, she wouldn't have a chance. She ducked down a narrow side street. If she could make it to the houses at the end, she could get help.

Tires squealed. An engine roared to life. *Dear God, help me*! Lilly pushed herself harder until she realized the engine sound grew fainter. They were driving in the opposite direction.

Why in the world were they abandoning the pursuit? Maybe she had been wrong. Maybe that bag they heaved over the guardrail didn't contain a body.

She stopped mid-stride, breathing in ragged gasps of air. She bent over to relieve the pain in her side and tugged the lower edge of her shirt up to mop the sweat dripping down her face.

Only then did she notice what her bright pink t-shirt clearly told the world in big, black letters on the front and the back— that she was a library employee. Those guys would have no trouble at all figuring out who she was. All they needed to do was go to the library website where they could view numerous pictures of her reading to children. Her name would be printed in the captions. Her blood froze.

Lilly fumbled in her shorts pocket until her trembling fingers found her cell phone. Where was the ID she kept with her phone? It must have fallen out in her mad dash. Now those guys would know where she lived as well as where she worked.

"Please let me have service," she prayed aloud. She punched in 9-1-1 and waited what seemed like eons for her call to go through.

I think I'm going to be very late for work—if I ever make it there again.

Chapter One

Lilly glanced around the starkly furnished interrogation room at the city police department. A long, wooden table surrounded by uncomfortable-looking wooden chairs dominated the center of the room. A U.S. flag presided over one corner of the room, and a Commonwealth of Virginia flag over the opposite corner. A few scattered pictures of government buildings and scenes of Williamsburg, Portsmouth, and Norfolk speckled the white walls.

"Your life is in danger, Ms. Brandt," the solid man stated. The U.S. Marshal badge on his chest bore the name Marshall O'Brien.

"I understand that. I thought maybe the police could provide security for me and I could continue on with my life until you catch those guys."

"You figured wrong. Those guys know you can identify them. They aren't totally stupid. This isn't the first crime they have committed. Trust me, they *will* come for you."

Lilly shivered. She didn't think it was the air conditioning that made her suddenly long for a sweater or jacket. If only she had had time to go home to change out of her shorts and t-shirt. She thrust her hands into the pockets of her shorts and thought of pulling the elastic band from her hair to let her hair flow down her back and provide an added layer of warmth.

The marshal pulled out a chair. "Sit down before you fall down, Ms. Brandt."

"I-I'm fine." The words barely left Lilly's lips before she sank onto one of the hard, wooden chairs.

"I think you scared her, man," mumbled the young police officer who materialized from the edge of Lilly's periphery. He filled a paper cup with water from the cooler against the wall and passed it to her.

"She should be scared," the marshal snapped.

Lilly's hands trembled so violently she used both to lift the little cup to her lips. She took just a tiny sip, hoping it would slide past the lump in her throat.

"Have a seat, Officer Kade. Detective Bradford will join us any minute as well as your chief. Are you okay, Ms. Brandt?" It sounded like O'Brien added the last question as an afterthought.

"Just lovely." Lilly raised her eyes to meet the marshal's gaze.

The door flew open to allow three more men to enter. *Don't any women work here?* Lilly sure would like to have another female around for moral support. What was the gruff U.S. Marshal doing here anyway? Couldn't the local police handle this case?

"Close the door, Loudon," the oldest of the three men said. His salt-and-pepper hair was cut short in military style, and his brown suit strained to cover his muscular frame.

He crossed the room in two long strides and held his hand out to Lilly. "I'm Chief Adam Marsden. This is Detective Alex Bradford." He paused to nod at the tall, fit, thirty-something dark-haired man. "And this is Officer Doug Loudon." He indicated the uniformed police officer with the pimply face who looked about fifteen. "I see you've already met Officer Tim Kade and Marshal Bill O'Brien."

"Well, sort of." Lilly shook hands with the other men. She looked at the chief. "I was just asking the marshal if it would be possible for you to provide protection so I could continue working. I have bills to pay and things to do."

"Well, life as you knew it is officially over," O'Brien said.

"What?" Lilly's voice came out in a squeak.

"You can lighten up a little," the detective--was it Bradford?--mumbled. He turned kind eyes in Lilly's direction and gave her a small lopsided smile.

"This is serious business," O'Brien boomed.

"I'm well aware of that, but we don't have to terrify our witness."

"Can someone please explain what is going on?" Lilly interjected. "Why is 'life as I knew it' over?"

"Ms. Brandt," Detective Bradford began. "These guys are connected with numerous crimes, and you can identify them. That puts you in grave danger.

We can't protect you if you continue to go about your normal routine."

"Why haven't they been caught if they've committed so many crimes?" Lilly hesitated a moment, fearing the answer, but then asked anyway. "By the way, what else have they done?"

"They're smart and wily. Into drug trafficking. They don't care who they have to, uh, eliminate. But they've gotten a little cocky, a little careless lately. They let you get a look at them. Now that they know they can be identified, they won't stop until they..."

Lilly clasped her hands so tightly together she expected to hear bones snap. The detective looked at her hands and modified his comments. "Well, they won't let you testify against them when we catch them as you've agreed to do. And, trust me, we *will* catch them."

"W-What do I do?" Surely the question came from someone else while Lilly hung suspended from the ceiling looking down on a bad cop show.

"That's where I come in," Marshal O'Brien said. "We want to transfer you to a safe location."

"Like witness protection or something?"

"Yes."

"Do you mean I have to leave? I have to go into hiding? I have to be someone else?" Before anyone could answer she whispered, "I don't want to do that."

"Do you want to live?" O'Brien fairly shouted.

"Can't you all just catch these guys, let me testify, and get this all over with?"

Loudon rolled his eyes. "It's not that easy!"

The chief shot Loudon a dirty look. "We have been after these guys for months. As I said before, they aren't stupid, but they'll be pretty desperate by now."

"I don't have any other choice?"

"I'm afraid not. This is the best chance we have of keeping you safe," Chief Marsden explained as gently as possible.

"You mean of keeping me alive?"

Marsden nodded.

"Oh," was all she whispered. Her eyes filled with tears that she struggled to blink away.

"So who is she gonna become?" A goofy grin spread across Loudon's face. If he was attempting to lighten the mood in the room, he failed miserably as far as Lilly was concerned. His chief shot him a warning look, and the grin rapidly disappeared. Lilly shifted her gaze from one man to another.

"What's the plan, O'Brien?" Chief Marsden gave his attention to the marshal.

"I've been working out the details with Detective Bradford's help."

"Liz will be here any minute. She had to gather up as many supplies as she could on short notice."

"Who is Liz?" Lilly managed to whisper in Bradford's direction.

"My sister-in-law. I hate to involve her in any way, but she's the only one who can help on such short notice."

"Help with what?"

"She'll prep you and teach you as much Pennsylvania Dutch as she can in the few hours she'll have with you."

"Pennsylvania Dutch?"

"Good thing you took German in school. That should help," O'Brien said.

"H-how do you know I took German?"

"I know everything about you."

"He even knows what color underwear you're wearing," Loudon interjected, slapping the table and snorting at his comment.

"What?" Lilly gasped. Her cheeks burned

"That part isn't true," Marsden patted Lilly's hand.

Detective Bradford took up the explanation. "My sister-in-law used to be Amish and grew up in the Lancaster, Pennsylvania area. She worked at her family's market in Annapolis where my brother attended the Naval Academy. Now, he's stationed in Norfolk so they live close by. She's willing to help familiarize you with the Amish culture and customs—as much as she can."

"A-Amish? But why?"

"You, Ms. Lilly Brandt, are now Hannah Kurtz, an Amish lady from Pennsylvania who is leaving her home to live with the Amish in Southern Maryland," O'Brien informed her.

"Me? Amish? Why Southern Maryland?" Lilly vaguely remembered reading articles about the Amish. She knew the women wore dresses all the time. They wore hats and pinned their hair up a certain way. They canned foods and stitched quilts. Her mind snapped back to focus on O'Brien's words.

"There are several groups of Amish and Mennonites living in St. Mary's County, Maryland. It's a small, out-of-the-way place where you should be safe."

"But I have to work."

"The Amish take care of their own."

"I'm a runner. I can't run in a long dress!"

"Don't worry. You'll get plenty of exercise." Loudon snickered, making wood-chopping motions. Marsden scowled.

"I don't know how to quilt or knit or can food. I can barely boil an egg." Okay, that part was an exaggeration, but she was trying to make a point.

"It won't be as bad as you think," Detective Bradford said, evidently trying to be reassuring but failing miserably.

"How do you know?" Lilly jumped to her feet. "Besides, I can't endanger innocent people. I couldn't live with myself if someone got hurt because of me."

"We're reasonably sure that won't happen," Marshal O'Brien replied.

"*Reasonably*! I need better than *reasonably*. And I can't lie to these people about who I am."

"You won't be lying," O'Brien sputtered, obviously near the end of his patience. "You *are* Hannah Kurtz now. Here is your proof." He pushed a birth certificate, social security card, and pictureless ID into Lilly's ice-cold hands.

Lilly looked at the papers through watery eyes and sank back onto the uncomfortable chair. "What about Aunt Vee and Rennie? I have to let them know I'm okay. I can't just disappear."

Lilly thought of her Aunt Genevieve who had taken her in when she was twelve after her parents died in a car accident. Her cousin Renee, a.k.a. Rennie, was her best friend. She couldn't let them mourn. She couldn't cause them that pain.

"The fewer people who know our plan, the better," O'Brien snapped.

"You don't want them to be in any danger—" Detective Bradford began.

"Absolutely not!"

"Then we can't tell them the plan. I know this sounds callous, but we have to let them think you've vanished from the earth." The detective gazed at her with kind eyes that willed her to understand.

A tear slid down Lilly's cheek. She nodded her head. "They have to stay safe," she whispered. She covered her face with her shaking hands and tried desperately to contain the flow of tears. She wanted to drop her head to the table and sob out her fears and frustrations. She wanted to throw something in protest at her situation. She wanted to howl about the injustice of losing control of her life, of losing her freedom when she had done nothing wrong.

Instead she sat, her hands over her face. She barely heard the receptionist at the door announce, "Detective, your sister-in-law is here to see you. She says it's important."

Lilly separated her fingers to peer between the cracks at the young woman hustled into the room by the receptionist. Dressed in a below-the-knee-length navy skirt and long-sleeved white blouse, she carried a large, bulging shopping bag bearing the Old Navy logo. Golden-brown hair hung to her waist. Large brown eyes scanned the room, pausing briefly on Detective Bradford before settling on Lilly's covered face. A small sympathetic smile hinted at camaraderie. Lilly dropped her shaking hands to her lap and clung to that friendly face as a lifeline.

"Liz, thank you for coming." Detective Bradford crossed the room in several long strides to greet the pretty young woman. Liz nodded to each of the men the detective introduced to her. "And this is Lilly—I mean Hannah—the woman who needs your help. I'm sorry to involve you in this, Liz, but we need to hurry and get Hannah to safety."

"'Tis all right Alex." Liz spoke with a slight accent. She turned her attention to Lilly. "Nice to meet you, Hannah."

"Thank you for coming." Lilly's voice sounded strained to her own ears. She tried to moisten her dry lips with her tongue. Her throat felt even drier than her lips. Surely this was some sort of crazy nightmare. Surely she'd wake up soon.

"There's a private room over there where you can talk," Detective Bradford nodded at a closet-sized door in the corner of the room. "I'm sorry you won't have much time."

Liz nodded in understanding. Lilly sat like a stone.

"Ms. Brandt!" O'Brien jerked his head in the direction of the private room, obviously used to people instantly obeying his orders.

Lilly scooted back the wooden chair that suddenly seemed so heavy. She hesitated until Liz Bradford smiled at her. Then she forced her feet to move.

"Thanks, Liz," the detective said.

Lilly squared her shoulders and took a deep breath. She would do her best to learn from this sweet-looking young woman who dropped everything to help her. She followed Liz into the small room with no windows, knowing when she came out she would have left the old Lilly behind.

Three hours later, Lilly Brandt emerged from the cell-like room a different person. A long-sleeved, loose-fitting, royal-blue dress topped with a black cape and apron swallowed her petite body. Her long, pale blonde hair, parted in the middle, was now twisted back into a bun. A white *kapp* perched atop her head, the ties dangling over her shoulders.

She put one black sneaker-shod foot hesitantly in front of the other and glanced over her shoulder at Liz.

Liz barely nodded her head, smiled encouragingly, and whispered, "*Jah*. You can do it." Lilly took the Old Navy bag from Liz and turned back to face the roomful of men. She shifted her khaki slacks and midnight blue blouse to her other hand.

O'Brien marched across the room and planted himself in front of Lilly. He held out his right hand. "I'll take those."

"W-What?"

"Those clothes."

"My clothes?"

"Is there an echo in here? Yes, Ms. Kurtz. You can't very well keep those clothes. Do they look like something an Amish woman would wear?"

"I-I suppose not." For some reason, relinquishing her clothes was the final straw. Lilly fought off the threatening, maddening tears and clutched her clothes tighter.

Liz laid a hand on Lilly's arm. "It's okay, Hannah."

Lilly drew in a ragged breath and dropped the clothes across O'Brien's outstretched arm. Giving up her clothes meant relinquishing the last hold on her life—her previous life. She pulled her hand back, sniffed, squared her shoulders, and looked O'Brien in the eye. "They'll look lovely on you," she said in a combination of her school-learned German and the smattering of Pennsylvania Dutch she'd just acquired.

Her forced smile turned into a nervous giggle when behind her, Liz burst out laughing. Lilly prayed O'Brien didn't understand either language. The puzzled look that crossed his face briefly assured her he was clueless.

"How did it go?" Detective Bradford crossed the room in long strides.

"Just fine, Alex. Hannah is a quick learner. She will do fine."

"Good. That's good."

Hannah, Lilly thought. *I've got to start thinking and behaving like Hannah. I've got to start being Hannah.* How in the world was she supposed to do that?

"You can get a little sleep, and then you'll be leaving for Maryland before daylight. The drive is only a few hours, so you should arrive in time for breakfast. Are you ready?"

Lilly — *nee,* Hannah — nodded. "Won't I be waking them up?"

"They've been notified that their visitor from Pennsylvania will be getting in early from her overnight bus and car ride," Alex Bradford assured her. "Besides, they will have been up since before daylight doing chores."

"Won't it be a tiny bit suspicious if I arrive with police officers?"

"They won't be in uniform. Most Amish hire drivers for travelling long distances. Don't worry."

"I'll never pull this off," Lilly mumbled.

"It will be okay." Liz squeezed Lilly's upper arm. "I have a good feeling — here." She pointed to her heart.

Lilly turned and hugged Liz impulsively. "Thank you. I mean, *danki*. I wish we could be friends." Lilly fought tears again.

"Maybe one day…" Liz's voice trailed off.

"Here. Blow your nose and let's get this show on the road." O'Brien thrust a tissue into Lilly's hand.

"Your kindness is overwhelming," Lilly said, again in German, and then bit her tongue. She was pretty sure Amish women weren't so sarcastic.

Liz laughed again. "God bless you, Hannah."

Lilly nodded, not trusting her voice to come out without breaking and not wanting to give O'Brien another reason to make a snide remark. What was up with the guy, anyway? Didn't people in his line of work need to be even slightly sympathetic?

"I'll order in some dinner for you and show you where you can sleep. Would you like burgers, chicken, pizza, or what?" At least the detective showed some compassion.

Lilly had a vision of being offered a last meal before her execution. "I'm a vegetarian."

"Won't be for long," Loudon mumbled.

Lilly's mouth dropped open. Before she could say anything, O'Brien butted in. "Do you know any Amish vegetarians, Mrs. Bradford?"

"Well, no," Liz began, "but there can always be the first one."

"I'll look really out of place and suspicious, won't I?"

"Maybe we can think of a medical reason why you have to avoid meat," Detective Bradford suggested. "So let me revise the menu selection. Would you like a salad, Chinese food, or what?"

"I'm really not very hungry."

"You're going to dry up and blow away," Loudon observed. "That dress hangs on you already."

Lilly looked the pimply-faced cop in the eye. "Are you always so complimentary?" She turned back to Detective Bradford. "Could I just have some fresh fruit and wheat crackers—and maybe some yogurt?"

"Sure. Liz, do you want something? You could eat with Hannah if you like, maybe go over some more information."

"Okay. Jon is on duty, so it will be nice not to eat alone. I'll have whatever you get for Hannah."

"All right, ladies, follow me. I'll show you where Lil—Hannah will sleep. You can eat there as well."

Alex Bradford led the way from the room by yet another side door. "I've had a few other necessities brought in for you, Hannah. Liz gave me a list, and I've done my best to gather everything."

"What about all my belongings in my apartment?"

"Uh...well, what's there will...uh, be put in storage."

"What's wrong, Detective? I get the feeling something happened."

"Your apartment was ransacked."

"Someone broke in?"

"Yes. Actually, it's a good thing you *weren't* there earlier."

"Was everything...destroyed?"

"There was a lot of damage."

"You won't have a need for that stuff, anyway," Marshal O'Brien muttered.

Lilly shot him a nasty look.

"I'm so sorry, Hannah." Liz squeezed Lilly's arm again.

"I guess Marshal O'Brien is right. I won't need the television or computer or clothes anyway." Lilly choked back a sob. She fought hard for control. "And Aunt Genevieve and Rennie and the others will — will think I-I'm dead?"

"I'm sorry, Hannah, but our priority is to keep you safe."

Lilly's shoulders slumped. She felt like one of those giant Macy's Parade balloon characters that had sprung a leak. She expected to crash any moment. Liz reached to clasp her ice-cold hand.

Dear God, please help me. And please don't let Aunt Vee, Uncle Ted, and my cousins grieve for me.

Chapter Two

After being jostled from her makeshift bed at 3:00 a.m., Lilly was hustled into the large, dark sedan waiting at an obscure side door of the building. She slumped into the corner of the backseat. Officer Kade slammed her door shut and slid behind the steering wheel. Officer Loudon climbed into the front passenger seat. Lilly felt slightly uneasy being alone with the two police officers, but she knew she had absolutely no choice. She just wished Detective Bradford and Liz could have been her traveling companions. Kade drove down the street to the Hampton Inn and stopped as close to the entrance as possible.

"What are we doing?" Lilly tried to keep the tremor out of her voice. Could she really trust these two?

"Just play along," Kade replied. "We can't take any chance that we were followed."

"What—" Lilly began, but Kade and Loudon had quickly pushed their doors open. Loudon opened Lilly's door and called out, "We'll see you to your room, Mrs. Lapp."

"I don't want to be a bother." Lilly played her part as she attempted to make a graceful exit from the car while keeping the unfamiliar clothing in place.

"No bother. Thank you for your cooperation in the fire investigation. I'm sorry it took so long at the station." Loudon spoke loud enough for any eavesdroppers or lurkers to hear.

The officers took their positions on either side, towering over Lilly's petite frame. Kade pulled open the glass front door of the hotel and entered before Lilly as though he were her shield. Loudon practically squeezed through the door at the same instant as Lilly, seriously violating her personal space.

The middle-aged man on duty at the desk nodded at the trio but refrained from speaking to them. Apparently, he'd been clued in. The officers picked up their pace as they proceeded down a dimly lit hallway. Lilly didn't dare ask where they were headed. Instead, she concentrated on keeping up with the long-legged men.

Near the end of the hall, they stopped abruptly. Loudon pretended to unlock the door as he said. "Good night, Mrs. Lapp. Thank you again." The door opened magically from the inside.

Lilly gasped as Kade practically pushed her into the nearly dark room and closed the door behind her. Her eyes struggled to adjust to the light or lack thereof, and she nearly jumped through the ceiling when someone touched her arm.

"Come this way."

Lilly let out her breath when she recognized Marshal O'Brien—not her favorite person but at least someone familiar.

"You'll be leaving by this patio door in a few minutes." O'Brien nodded toward the door covered by heavy, dark green drapes. Should she ask what awaited her on the other side?

Lilly's heart thumped wildly beneath the plain blue dress and black cape. She opened her mouth to ask what the plan was but didn't get the question out.

"Let's go," O'Brien ordered. Honestly, didn't the man have a compassionate bone in his body? He was a good marshal, wasn't he?

O'Brien pulled the drapes back only slightly and cracked open the door just enough for Lilly to exit into the unknown. Her breath caught when she felt a firm grip on her arm. She could just barely discern a tall man in jeans, tee-shirt, and baseball cap. She started to pull away. Was she always going to fear men who wore baseball caps?

"Psst! It's me. Loudon," the man spoke into her ear.

"Oh." Lilly allowed herself to be led to the waiting SUV and shoved unceremoniously into the back seat. She took note of Kade behind the wheel, dressed similarly to Loudon. "You guys. How'd—where—"

"We peeled off the uniforms and had these fancy duds on underneath," Louden explained. "O'Brien had this SUV waiting for us. Even has Pennsylvania tags. How do you like those tinted windows?"

"Oh, lovely."

"Well, nobody can see in. That's for sure."

Lilly clicked her seatbelt and squirmed to find a comfortable position.

Once on the road, the lights from Virginia Beach and its outskirts gradually faded so Lilly pulled her gaze from the window. Loudon tuned in a local radio station as Kade studied the road ahead with frequent glances in the rearview mirror. She could sense that even Loudon was on high alert, despite his nonchalant demeanor.

Lilly's eyes grew heavy as the car hummed along the highway. *Hannah, Hannah, Hannah,* she chanted inwardly. She had to get used to answering to Hannah. She had to get used to *being* Hannah. She mentally reviewed as much of the cultural information Liz had provided as she could, trying to fix facts about the Amish in her brain.

Fatigue overtook her with the monotony of the ride. Sleep claimed her mind and body.

Lilly never fully awoke during the coffee and doughnut stop but vaguely remembered mumbling "no" when Loudon offered to bring her something.

When her senses returned, the rising sun reflected pinkish-red streaks across the Potomac River. The Harry Nice Bridge leading into Maryland loomed straight up in the air. Two lanes of traffic merged into a single lane to cross the high bridge.

Lilly sucked in a breath as they began the ascent and wondered when the last bridge inspection had occurred—and when the last head-on collision sent a vehicle careening over the practically non-existent guard rail. To distract herself, she focused on the boats already bobbing in the river, fishermen and crabbers getting an early start.

It really is quite pretty.

She drew to full attention when the SUV picked up speed as it descended the high bridge. They slowed briefly at the toll booth, even though they didn't have to pay the toll on this north-bound side. Then Kade stomped on the accelerator, sending the car zooming along Route 301. Every few minutes, he would glance in the rearview mirror.

Lilly thought her heart would leap from her chest. "Are we being followed?"

"That Toyota could be following us. We'll see."

They made a sudden right turn and slid into the parking lot of the Visitors' Center. Just moments later, the Toyota drove into the parking lot. Loudon reached under his seat to pull out the Steelers cap he had stashed there and plopped it on his head. He threw open the door, jumped out, and turned toward the back seat.

"We ain't never gonna get back if you don't quit hollering to stop at every place with a bathroom, Gertie," he yelled.

"I can't help it," Kade yelled back in a high-pitched voice, his hand covering any movement of his lips.

"What's the driver doing?" Loudon whispered.

"He got out and went inside the Visitors' Center. I got the tag number. Get in."

Loudon barely got both legs inside the car before Kade hit the gas and they flew back onto the highway, blending in with morning commuters making their mad dash to work.

Lilly sat back again and tried to calm her nerves and her pounding heart by checking out her surroundings. *Not much here*, she thought. A lonely, practically abandoned motel or two, a restaurant, and a few roads veering off in either direction. They sailed along until Kade signaled a right turn onto Route 234. A sign promised a scenic route and claimed the road led to historic areas.

A few houses sat in well-manicured lawns along this road, but there were no businesses or motels like there had been along the highway they'd just left. Glimpses of water gave way to marshy land and then woods. Where were communities and stores? Where were these guys taking her? Did they even know or did they just blindly follow the GPS on the dashboard?

After about fifteen miles, she guessed, they turned left onto another road beside a little store with gas pumps. The car travelled slowly now. Lilly sat up straight and tried to smooth her blue dress and apron. She hoped travelers could be forgiven for looking disheveled.

Lilly hadn't even recognized herself when she stared into the mirror earlier. No mascara. No lip gloss. Pale hair pulled back into her version of an Amish hairstyle. Pale face—paler than usual. *Oh, well, I guess I have to stop worrying about my appearance. Amish ladies do not wear makeup. Amish ladies do not worry about hairstyles. I am Amish now. I hope I can pull this off.*

The car slowed even more as Kade and Loudon scanned the dirt roads for signs. *Hannah. Hannah. Hannah.* The chant echoed through her head again. *I'm Hannah Kurtz now. Lord, help me.*

The sun was just beginning to highlight farms and fields on either side of the road. Rows of corn stalks reached for the sky, garden plots boasted green, leafy plants, and gold and rust-colored marigolds, pink and purple petunias, and funny-faced pansies bloomed in pots and flower beds beside big white houses.

"Lookee there—a pay phone," Loudon pointed to a phone shanty at the end of a long dirt driveway. "Haven't seen one of them in ages."

Lilly gulped. No home phone. No contact with her world—her former world, she amended.

Kade turned right onto a yet smaller road. Woodley Hill Road, the green sign proclaimed. Kade stomped on the brake. "This must be it," he said, nodding at another long driveway on the right. He turned onto the driveway and proceeded toward the house.

Lilly's eyes travelled up the driveway and focused on the two-story white house surrounded by scarlet and white geraniums. Black and white cows swished their tails in a nearby field. Bird houses hung on the lower branches of several sturdy trees. Lilly's heart pounded beneath the buttonless blue dress. No humans milled about in the yard or fields. A small reprieve. Lilly fought to get her nerves under control. Everyone must be inside.

"They're probably all gathered around the table having a big ol' breakfast of sausage and gravy and eggs and pancakes," Loudon said.

He must have read her mind. Great! She'd have to face the whole family all at once. She had never eaten those foods and didn't think she'd be able to force herself to start now. This was never going to work.

Kade stopped the car beside the house and popped the lock on the rear door so Lilly could retrieve her belongings—such as they were. Loudon jumped out of the car before Lilly could even get her door open.

"I'll help you get your things, Ms. Kurtz," Loudon said in a voice loud enough to be heard through the open door of the house. He reached into the back of the SUV and handed Lilly a small suitcase and a duffle bag. In a lower, conspiratorial voice meant only for Lilly's ears he said, "You've got Detective Bradford's number if you need it. Anything unusual or suspicious, you run out to that phone and give him a call."

Everything about her life was suddenly unusual and suspicious, but Lilly nodded her head. She was a little surprised that Officer Loudon had such a serious side. Maybe he was a good cop after all.

"You take care," the pimply-faced man said.

"I-I'll try. Thank you."

As soon as Loudon jumped back into the passenger seat, Kade shifted the car into gear and turned it in the direction of the road.

Lilly had a sudden urge to cry and race down the driveway in pursuit of the retreating SUV. At least the two officers were somewhat familiar. Nothing about this place was remotely familiar.

"Get a grip," she commanded herself. She took a deep breath and released it slowly, then gave herself a little shake and climbed the front steps. She set down the suitcase and raised her hand to knock. Before her knuckles made contact with the door frame, a deep male voice called out, "*Kum* on in!"

Lilly gulped and depressed the handle on the screen door. The door squeaked open and then slammed shut behind her despite her attempt to gently close it. She dropped both bags to the floor and scooted them out of the way. The strong smell of fried bacon assailed her nostrils, and she fought not to gag.

Think happy thoughts, Hannah, she admonished herself. She choked down the lump in her throat, squared her shoulders, and tentatively followed the sound of forks scraping against plates.

Lilly stopped in the kitchen doorway. Six pairs of hands paused in midair while six pairs of eyes from the brown-bearded young man to the golden-haired baby in the high chair stared unabashedly at her. Lilly's eyes darted around the sunny kitchen, taking in the white walls adorned only with a large calendar with a feed supply store's name printed across the bottom, the big black woodstove, the long oak table around which sat three young children, a baby in a high chair, and the bearded man.

Lastly, her eyes rested on the kind-faced, pretty young woman with the dark-honey hair pinned beneath her white *kapp*. "I-I'm Hannah. Hannah Kurtz," she whispered. Saying it aloud made it real. She had to be Hannah now. No more Lilly Brandt.

"*Wilkom*," the man said. "I'm Samuel Hertzler. That's my wife Rebecca and our *kinner*. Jonas there is eight. Eli is six, and Emma is four." He nodded briefly at each child. "And the baby is Elizabeth."

"I-it's nice to meet you. Thank…uh…I-uh…I'm grateful for your hospi-uh—for-for having me." Hannah mentally smacked herself. She sounded like a complete idiot. She hoped they thought she was merely nervous.

"We're glad you're here." Rebecca's voice had a slight accent very much like Liz's. She rose quickly from her chair. "*Kum* sit. Let me get you a plate. You must be hungry after your drive."

"Please don't go to any trouble. I-I'm not really hungry."

"*Nee*? How about some *kaffee* or tea?"

"Tea would be nice." Hannah pulled out a heavy oak chair beside the little girl.

Emma peered at her with big, green eyes identical to her mother's before dropping her gaze and smiling into her plate.

"*Danki*," Hannah murmured, trying out her Pennsylvania Dutch as Rebecca set the mug of tea in front of her. She slid the sugar bowl and honey jar within reach. Lilly always used artificial sweetener.

She held in a sigh when she realized *Hannah* would probably not find such a thing here in Rebecca's kitchen. She raised the steaming mug cautiously to her lips.

"No sugar?" Jonas, the older boy, burst out, making a face.

"Mind your manners," Samuel scolded.

Jonas quickly stuffed a piece of obviously homemade brown bread into his mouth.

Hannah inwardly agreed with the boy, though. Hot tea without sweetener was less than desirable. She guessed she'd have to develop some new tastes.

Samuel bowed his head again and all but the baby followed suit. He pushed back from the table. "*Kum, buwe*. There's work to do."

Jonas and Eli at once jumped from their chairs, retrieved their straw hats—miniatures of Samuel's—and followed their father to the door.

The little boys were clones of Samuel. Blue shirts were tucked into broadfall trousers held up by suspenders. All had dark brown hair that hung just below their ears.

Hannah wondered if Rebecca had positioned a big mixing bowl on their heads and trimmed around the edges. In unison, the three Hertzler males plopped the straw hats atop their heads, almost as if they had been practicing to do this in sync.

Rebecca reached for the empty plates.

"Let me help you," Hannah offered.

"Emma can help, but you're welcome to keep me company while I *redd* up the kitchen."

Even a four-year-old has work to do, Hannah marveled. The little girl carried her brothers' cups and silverware to drop into the sink Rebecca had already filled with sudsy water. Rebecca handed Emma a red checked dishcloth and asked her to wipe the table.

"She likes to help," Rebecca explained. She lowered her voice. "Of course, I have to go behind her to wipe the table thoroughly, but she'd be heartbroken if I didn't let her help." Baby Elizabeth played with the bread crumbs on the high chair's tray and then reached out to plunk Emma on the head.

"*Kum*. I'll show you your room." Rebecca dried her hands on a dishtowel after the last plate had been stacked in the cabinet and the big oak table had been re-cleaned. She wiped Elizabeth's hands and face and deposited her in the playpen near where Emma played with her faceless doll. Then she led the way to the stairs.

Chapter Three

"Here we are," Rebecca stopped at the first room at the top of the stairs. She set Hannah's suitcase on the polished wood floor and pushed open the bedroom door. "You're next to the girls. The boys are across the hall. Mine and Samuel's room is on the other side of the bathroom. I hope the room is okay, Hannah."

Hannah's mind was a million miles away. Somehow, it registered that Rebecca had just spoken to her. "Um...oh, I'm sure it will be fine, Rebecca. *Danki.*"

Her brain chanted, *Hannah, Hannah, Hannah!* She had to remember when someone spoke to Hannah, they were speaking to her. She was glad she threw in a little Pennsylvania Dutch. She set the duffle bag just inside the room.

"Oh, the room is perfect." Hannah took in the bright room where sunshine streamed in through the two curtainless windows.

"What a beautiful quilt." Hannah crossed the room and stroked the blue, purple, and black fabric artistically arranged in a pattern Hannah couldn't recall.

Her mind sorted through the pages of the quilt book Liz had shown her, but she just hadn't had time to commit names to memory. She was rather impressed she even recognized having seen the pattern before.

"It's a Log Cabin I made shortly after Samuel and I were married." Rebecca supplied the missing quilt name. This time, Hannah would remember.

"You do nice work."

"I enjoy quilting. I'm sure you do fine work, too."

"I wouldn't count on it," Hannah mumbled and then amended her answer. "I haven't had a lot of opportunity to learn many domestic things—I don't think."

"Samuel said something about your having to go to work at a young age—"

"Um, my parents died when I was young. I...uh, suffered a memory loss recently after an accident. I'm trying to remember how to do things." It wasn't entirely untrue. She *was* trying to remember all the things Liz had told her.

"I'm so sorry, Hannah. I'll be happy to help you learn anything you need to know. I hope you'll be content here." Rebecca patted Hannah's arm and smiled. "I'll let you get settled. If you'd like a nap after your long drive, feel free. Just come downstairs whenever you're ready."

"*Danki.*"

Hannah looked around the room. The white walls were bare except for another feed store calendar depicting a meadow full of wildflowers and a row of wooden pegs for clothes. She was glad Liz told her there would be pegs instead of closets. The windows let in abundant light and, she was sure, abundant heat as the day wore on. She hoped she wouldn't suffocate without air conditioning. And six people sharing one bathroom? How would she manage that?

"You're spoiled, *Hannah*," she whispered.

Hannah pulled out the few dresses, the cape, and the black bonnet Liz had rounded up for her and hung them all on pegs. It was a good thing Liz had never discarded the clothes from her former life.

She placed her other meager belongings in the solid cherry dresser drawers. Should she remove her shoes and stockings? Rebecca and Emma were barefoot. She decided to leave them on for the time being.

What do I do now? Hannah found herself picking at her nails—a habit she thought she had long since broken. She had dozed in the car so wasn't sleepy. Maybe she could help Rebecca with something. She had a feeling it was going to be a long day—probably the first of many long days. She prayed those two criminals would be caught soon so her life could return to normal.

Relieved the Hertzlers had indoor plumbing, Hannah freshened up a bit in the old-fashioned bathroom. She hung up the towel and tiptoed to the edge of the stairs, unsure what she should do. She gulped in a breath, squeezed back the tears that seemed a constant threat, and bravely descended, managing to avoid the creaky step near the top.

Hannah rounded the corner to the kitchen and stopped in her tracks. A tall, broad-shouldered young man lowered an obviously heavy bushel basket full of peaches to the floor beside the sink. Taut muscles rippled beneath the rolled-up sleeves of his blue shirt.

Out of the corner of her eye, Hannah caught sight of a large silver pot on the stove, steam rising from the open top. Glass jars and metal lids floated in another steaming pot.

Rebecca stood barefoot at the sink, a knife in one hand and a peach in the other. The ties of her prayer *kapp* swung as she turned to face her visitor.

"Thank your *mamm* for me, Jake. These peaches look *wunderbaar.*" She nodded in the direction of the big basket. "Ach, Hannah!" Rebecca caught sight of Hannah in the doorway. "*Kum* in."

The young man turned abruptly, his blond hair falling across one brilliant blue eye. "Hello." His deep voice sounded almost musical.

No beard. Must be unmarried, Hannah mused. "Hello." Her voice came out whisper-soft.

"Hannah, this is Jacob Beiler. His family's farm is over off of Ryland Road. We'll take you around soon and point out homes and businesses. Jacob is a *wunderbaar* furniture maker." The young man's face colored slightly at Rebecca's praise. "Jacob, Hannah has just come from Pennsylvania to stay with us a while. Samuel may have mentioned it to you."

"*Jah*, he did. Nice to meet you, Hannah."

"N-n-nice to meet you, too," Why did she feel she was drowning in those eyes? She averted her gaze.

"Guess I'd better get to work." Jacob retrieved his straw hat from the table and twisted it in his hands.

"*Danki* again for bringing the peaches," Rebecca said. "My trees just didn't produce enough."

"No problem." The big man seemed suddenly ill-at-ease. "See ya, Hannah. See ya, Rebecca."

Hannah nodded, unable to force any words out of her dry mouth. Jacob glanced in Hannah's direction and smiled before heading for the door.

"Samuel and the boys should be at the barn."

"I'll say hello to them." With that, Jacob Beiler slipped out the screen door.

Hannah struggled to voice a normal sound. Why did this stranger have such a profound effect on her? She couldn't get involved with these people. She couldn't endanger them in any way. Besides, she wouldn't be here that long, would she?

"Can I help you with…something?" She turned her attention back to Rebecca. "You'll just have to tell me what to do."

"It's peach-canning day. If you feel up to it, I'm sure I could use your help."

"What would you like me to do?"

"I've got my jars and canner ready. I'll wash and dip the peaches in the boiling water if you cut and peel them."

"Uh, okay, uh…"

"I'll show you first and then you try." Rebecca picked up the paring knife and demonstrated. She wiped her hands on a dish towel and handed the black-handled knife to Hannah. Her smile gave Hannah the courage Hannah sorely lacked.

Hannah took the knife in her hands. She could do this. She'd cut up fruit before, just not so much fruit. *I hope I don't amputate any fingers.* She picked up a warm, fuzzy peach and turned it around in her hands.

Hannah was sure she must be the slowest peach preparer Rebecca had ever seen, but Rebecca never chided her or seemed to lose patience. They worked in silence for a long while, each concentrating on the task at hand.

What I wouldn't give for an air conditioner or even a fan! Hannah blew at the wisps of fine, pale hair that escaped the bun she thought she had securely pinned. The damp tendrils didn't move but instead, adhered to her face and neck. Only the ribbons of her *kapp* danced with her exhalation.

Beads of perspiration dotted her forehead as rivers flowed down her back. She needed to distract herself from focusing on this stifling, steamy room.

"Tell me about the community here." She might as well learn as much as she could about her temporary home.

"We're a small group. Nothing like Lancaster or Sugar Creek or any of those places."

Sugar Creek? That was in Ohio, right? Hannah strained to remember Liz's brief history lesson but quickly tuned back in to Rebecca's words.

"We live much the same as the others, though I suppose we each have some differences." Rebecca went on to describe where various families lived on various side roads that Hannah would probably never remember the names of.

"Does everyone farm?"

"Oh, *jah*. I guess most do, though many run businesses as well."

"What about the women? Are there any jobs? I may need to think about earning my keep."

Rebecca laughed. "You are welcome here as long as you like. You don't have to get a job. To answer your question, most women are busy at home. We do sell our produce at markets. Many sell baked goods or crafts. Barbara has a quilt shop, Esther has a greenhouse and nursery, Sophie sells herbs and medicinals and such. Oh, and Miriam runs the general store with her husband Levi. We'll visit them all soon. We don't have the restaurants and tourist places like some of the bigger Amish communities, and we don't work in the local stores."

Hannah nodded. She didn't know if she felt glad or sad about this revelation. She supposed it would keep her safer not to mingle much with the *Englisch*, but it would also further isolate her.

She suppressed a sigh. As Rebecca had shown her, she ran the handle of a long wooden spoon gently between the sliced peaches and the edge of the last jar to release air bubbles.

Rebecca wiped the top of the jar, popped on the lid, screwed the metal band on tightly, and set the jar in the canner. She added a little more hot water to cover the jars an inch or so before placing the lid on the canner.

"Whew!" she exclaimed. "That's done. I didn't have enough to make jam or jelly. I guess that will be another day."

Thank you, Lord. Hannah didn't think she could possibly cut up one more peach. Her back ached and her hands cramped. She wiggled her fingers and winced with pain.

"You'll get used to it," Rebecca assured her. "Now we have to clean up and think about supper."

Hannah wanted nothing more than to run outside and try to catch any possible breeze. They had fed the children and Samuel a quick lunch of sandwiches and cookies so they could continue canning, but a proper dinner would be expected. *Can't order a nice vegetable pizza!*

Hannah began washing dishes and cleaning up the peach mess while Rebecca peeled and cut up potatoes and carrots to slide into the oven with the roast. She was grateful for running water and the gas-powered stove, but a fan sure would be nice. She couldn't wait to peel off these hot clothes and take a shower or bath or whatever.

"Why don't you take a break?" Rebecca suggested. "I sure appreciate your help today."

"Maybe I'll check on the girls for you." Hannah had heard Elizabeth fussing a bit earlier.

A few minutes later, Rebecca stepped to the doorway of the living room and found Elizabeth on Hannah's lap and Emma snuggled up to her side. Hannah was animatedly telling them a story that held the girls awestruck.

"You're a *wunderbaar gut* storyteller," Rebecca observed.

"I love *kinner.*" Thank goodness she had memorized many of the stories she had read to children during the library's story hour. Being a children's librarian might come in handy here after all.

After practically dozing off in her dinner of plain vegetables, fruit, and bread—she had told Rebecca she was too hot to eat anything other than tomatoes, cucumbers, and cantaloupe—she summoned up just enough energy to help clean up the kitchen, clean up herself, and crawl into bed. Only a faint breeze made its way through her open, curtainless windows, but she was too tired to care.

Loudon might be right. She might not have to worry about running to stay in shape if her first day as an Amish woman was any indication. She also might have to tweak her diet a bit since she probably wouldn't get much mileage out of cucumbers, tomatoes, and cantaloupe. Her stomach gave a rumble of agreement.

Despite the fact that every bone and muscle in her body groaned with either achiness or fatigue or both, she rejoiced that today she didn't worry about a lunatic in a baseball cap or a paunchy, balding maniac putting a bullet into her and rolling her body down a ravine. She wanted to say her prayers. She really tried. Just before sleep claimed her, a vision of a tall, blond-haired, blue-eyed Amish man danced across her brain.

Chapter Four

Jacob had found himself whistling all afternoon as he sanded the cherry dresser he'd constructed. He paid little attention to the conversation floating around the supper table or, sad to say, to the passages of Scripture Daed read from the big family Bible.

The tune he'd whistled softly on his way upstairs to bed died in midair as a dose of reality shot through him. What was wrong with him, staring at the newcomer, Hannah Kurtz, like some lovelorn teenager?

Sure, she was probably the prettiest woman he'd ever seen with that pale blonde hair and those big blue eyes. The tiny brown freckles sprinkled across her nose only made her look more adorable. And she was so tiny. It just made him want to protect her.

Stop it! Jake wanted to slap himself. He would *not* let himself fall in *lieb* ever again. Not after that fiasco in Ohio. His heart had shattered into a million pieces, and he was still trying to glue them all back together. Thanks to Anna Lapp, he couldn't—wouldn't—trust another woman.

Jake let his mind wander as he prepared for bed. He needed to remind himself why he could have no romantic notions about Hannah or anyone else for that matter. Maybe the sweet young woman with the magnificent dark-lashed cornflower-blue eyes would return to Pennsylvania soon and be out of his life forever. But would she be out of his thoughts?

"Remember, Jacob, my man," he said aloud. "Remember the heartache." His visit to Ohio two years ago started out on a positive note. He planned to stay with his mamm's cousin Abe to learn some finer carpentry techniques. He wanted to know as much as possible before starting his own business or taking over his daed's. Abe was a master of the trade and a fine teacher. Jake had been satisfied with all the skills he acquired under Abe's tutelage.

Naturally, Jake participated in church and other gatherings while living with Abe's family in Sugar Creek. If he'd just never gone to any of the singings, maybe he would never have gotten caught in Anna Lapp's snare. But, no. He had to go to the singings and respond to Anna's flirtations. Who wouldn't have been flattered by a charming brunette with big brown eyes that she shamelessly batted at him from across the room. He should have known better.

By his third singing, Jake had worked up the courage to ask Anna if he could escort her home from the singing. She had snuggled up beside him in the courting buggy he'd borrowed from his cousin and chattered the whole way home, which was probably a good thing since he tripped all over his tongue whenever he opened his mouth to speak. He was content to just let Anna prattle on, even if he didn't know the people she chatted about.

Eventually, Jake could string together enough syllables to form coherent sentences around Anna. She talked enough for the two of them and never seemed to notice if Jake spoke or not. And he, like a lovesick fool, had been content simply to be in Anna's presence. Looking back now, Jake could see the shallowness of the relationship. Funny how hindsight was so keen.

It wasn't long before Anna began to talk about *their* home and about the celery her family would plant in the summer, hinting at a fall wedding. They would drive home from singings and sit on her folks' front porch, holding hands.

When she leaned up to kiss his cheek, Jake thought he was in *lieb* for sure. But he wasn't in a rush to get married. He wanted to master his furniture-making skills first, and he really wanted to return home to Maryland to set up housekeeping.

"There are so many more people here," Anna had argued. "Business would be a lot better."

"Not necessarily," Jake countered. "We have lots of people who want fine handcrafted furniture."

Anna had pouted prettily, shrugged her shoulders, and said, "I'll think on it." Then she was off, talking about her friends who were getting married the next wedding season or about things she saw in the *Englisch* stores she wanted to buy for their house. She seemed to spend a lot of her time visiting *Englisch* establishments. Jake should have been concerned—if he hadn't been so trusting. Maybe he could have saved himself some heartache.

Then one Sunday evening, Anna didn't show up as usual at the singing. She hadn't mentioned at the after-church meal that she had a change in plans. If Jake had been more observant or more experienced or more *something*, he might have noticed that Anna hadn't been as talkative or bubbly. He might have noticed that she seemed almost reluctant to go for a walk or that she pulled her hand from his and put some space between them when they did walk.

Jake still kicked himself for being so naïve. He had asked Anna's best friend where Anna was. Martha had hung her head and shrugged her shoulders, not daring to look into his eyes. That should have been a dead give-away that something was amiss.

The next day, he took Cousin Abe's buggy into town for supplies, pondering Anna's strange behavior as he drove. He absentmindedly loaded materials, retrieved the few groceries Abe's wife asked him to pick up, and decided to visit the ice cream shop. A nice chocolate milkshake to drink on the way home should cool him off and lift his sagging spirits.

Jake tied the horse at the post and hopped down before looking at his surroundings. He shoved his hands into his pockets jingling the coins there, and turned toward the shop. He could already taste the icy, thick shake. Hopefully, it would soothe his nerves while filling his belly.

He glanced toward the shop's entrance, blinked his eyes twice, shook his head, and squinted at the people milling about. If he hadn't seen it with his own eyes, he would never have believed the scene unfolding in front of him. Unwittingly, his feet propelled him forward to check out the situation.

The woman with the messy brown braid wearing skin-tight jeans and a midriff-bearing top clung to a tall, scruffy-looking man in sore need of a comb and a shave. His mind didn't want to register what his eyes witnessed, but the fluttery big brown eyes left no doubt.

Jake's heart plummeted to his feet. He was no longer interested in a milkshake. It would probably sour in his stomach now. He untied the horse and put one foot up to hoist himself into the buggy when a hand touched his arm.

"Jacob, wait."

Jake didn't want to look at her. He didn't want to see this…this *Englischer* with her hair down and her revealing clothes. He wanted to pull away and ignore her, but he couldn't disregard the good manners his mamm had instilled in him.

He turned slowly. The only thing he could think to say was, "Why?"

"I-I don't want to be Amish."

"What about all the talk of marrying and our house, Anna? What about our plans?"

"Oh. That." Anna flipped her braid over her shoulder.

"*Jah*, that."

"That was just talk. You know me. I like to talk."

"*Nee*, actually, I don't think I know you at all. I guess I never did." After a brief pause, Jake added in a near whisper, "You never really cared about me, did you?"

"Hey, Annie. Come on, babe," the scruffy-looking *Englischer* called out. Anna waved her hand at him.

Jake again turned to go. His shoulders slumped. He suddenly felt old and used up.

"Don't be mad, Jake. We had fun while it lasted."

"Fun? Is that what it was?" Jake fought to push his anger, his hurt back down inside. "I was just a distraction? Someone to fill your time until something better came along?" Jake bit his tongue to keep from spewing out words he would later regret.

"I-I was confused."

"And you aren't anymore?"

"*Nee*. I mean no. I never really fit in as an Amish woman. I thought maybe I could. But I want to be free. I want to do what *I* want to do, not what the Ordnung tells me to do."

"You fit in here? This is what you want?" Jake jerked his head in the direction of the young man lighting a cigarette and tapping his foot tapping his foot on the blacktop.

"*Jah.* I mean yes. I had to wait for the timing to be right."

"And is it right now?"

Anna nodded her head. "I'm sorry." She flounced away, ran over to the man stamping out the cigarette, and threw her arms around him. The last image that burned in Jake's mind was of Anna planting a kiss smack on the man's mouth.

He heaved himself into the buggy and clucked to the horse to get moving. He couldn't get out of town fast enough. The sound of Anna's and the man's laughter echoed in his ears, and his face burned in embarrassment, shame, and dejection. He vowed to leave Ohio as soon as he could and to guard his heart from any future abuse.

Once home in Maryland, his mamm tried to get him to go to singings and activities. She sang the praises of Esther Stauffer—who was too involved with her plants—and Sarah Fisher—who only had eyes for Zeke Esh—and every other *maidel* in the area. But Jake stood firm. He would not allow his heart to be shattered again.

"And here you are, thinking about a tiny blonde-haired angel with sparkling blue eyes you could drown in. You need to stop this right now, Jacob Beiler! She'll just break your heart, too. Besides, she'll go back home, and you'll be left alone again."

He had to talk some sense into himself fast. He had to forget about Hannah Kurtz and steer clear of her for however long she stayed in St. Mary's County. He had to protect himself. He was happy with his life as it was, even if he ended up like old Silas. He did what he wanted, when he wanted, all by himself. He was…lonely, that's what he was.

Chapter Five

Somewhere in the recesses of her subconscious mind, Hannah sensed the household awakening. She ventured to open one eye. Darkness still clothed the room. She rose up on an elbow but even squinting, she could not discern where the hands on the wind-up clock pointed.

She had always been an early riser—after all, she usually ran just as the sun climbed into the sky—but now she rose practically in the middle of the night. No self-respecting Amish woman would lie in bed as her household came to life, she mused, so she slid to the edge of the bed and struggled to get her bearings. *Get dressed, wash your face, and get downstairs!*

Tucking an errant strand of hair beneath her *kapp* and smoothing her dress and apron, she tried to look presentable before entering the kitchen. Rebecca's hair behaved so well, staying pinned beneath her *kapp* even in the steamy kitchen. Her hair, however, had a mind of its own. Rebecca has had a lot of years of practice, Hannah reminded herself. She hoped she didn't look too unkempt.

"*Gude mariye*," Hannah called so softly she didn't know if Rebecca heard her.

"Ach, *gude mariye*, Hannah. You could have slept later. I think I worked you too hard yesterday."

"*N-nee*, Rebecca. I want to do whatever I can to help out."

Rebecca nodded and turned back to the pot of oatmeal she stirred on the stove. Good, Hannah thought, no bacon today. She didn't think her empty stomach could handle the pungent odor of grease right now. "What can I do?"

"If you would, please, you can hand me the bowls on the counter there. Samuel and the boys will be along in a minute. They've been tending to the animals."

Hannah retrieved the ceramic bowls and handed the first one to Rebecca.

"*Danki*." Rebecca scooped out a ladle full of thick oatmeal. It made a plopping sound when it hit the bowl.

No instant oatmeal here. Hannah could usually tolerate the oatmeal she concocted from the little packets to which she added boiling water. She wasn't sure she could get this pasty-looking stuff down. She wondered if it would form cement in her stomach. When she reached for the next bowl, she spied a large box of cornflakes. *Oh, thank goodness. I can eat those – maybe for three meals a day.*

As soon as Hannah set the bowls on the table, the rest of the family, except for Elizabeth, appeared if by magic.

"Oatmeal, Hannah?" Rebecca set a bowl of sliced strawberries on the oak table next to the bread and homemade strawberry jam and apple butter.

"Um, could I just have some cornflakes?"

"Sure."

Rebecca set a carton of milk on the table before disappearing for a moment to get Elizabeth. When everyone was seated, all heads bowed in unison for silent prayer. Samuel cleared his throat, indicating the end of prayer time, and Jonas and Eli reached for the strawberries at the same time. Samuel quickly intervened and sprinkled sliced strawberries atop each boy's oatmeal.

Hannah poured cornflakes in her bowl just as her stomach began to rumble. She reached for the milk carton. Whole milk. She usually used skim milk, but she'd have to make do. If she used it sparingly, maybe her body wouldn't go into shock. She hoped her arteries didn't rebel with the extra fat she would no doubt consume.

She reached for a skinny slice of bread and lightly spread a layer of apple butter across the top surface. "Ummmm! This is delicious. Did you make this, Rebecca?"

"*Jah*. We had a great apple crop last year. I'm hoping the apples do as well this year."

"There looks like a lot of 'em, Mamm," Eli, the younger boy, said around his mouthful of oatmeal.

"Don't talk with food in your mouth, son," Samuel admonished.

Eli looked contrite for only a moment. Then excitement lit his face. He might otherwise be a clone of his father, but he had Rebecca's emerald eyes that twinkled and crinkled at the corners. "Me and Jonas are gonna help Daed fix the fence today and then cut hay."

Hannah couldn't understand why those particular hot, dirty jobs would be so thrilling until Eli added, "Then maybe we'll get an ice cream from the ice cream man."

Hannah smiled. Now she understood. Waiting for the ice cream truck used to be a big treat for her and her cousins Rennie and Michael, too. They could hear the tinkling carnival music of the ice cream truck a mile away and start begging Aunt Genevieve for money. Occasionally, she would relent—if they had been extra good or if they had cleaned their rooms.

Hannah used to love biting off the hard chocolate coating and savoring the vanilla ice cream as it dripped from the stick. Sometimes, she would choose an ice cream sandwich. She'd squish the ice cream out and lick it from all around the edges of the chocolate cake-like pieces. Oh, those were fun days. Yes, she understood Eli's enthusiasm.

"You'd best behave then and work hard, ain't so?" Rebecca gave Eli a stern look.

"*Jah*, Mamm. We will."

The boys, copying their father movement for movement, pushed back from the table and strode to the door, pressing their straw hats firmly onto their heads.

Hannah and Emma cleared the table while Rebecca cleaned up Baby Elizabeth. She lifted

Elizabeth from the high chair and deposited her on the floor.

"Emma," Rebecca called. "Go take your *schweschder* in the living room to play." Immediately, the baby toddled across the linoleum floor in pursuit of her big sister.

"I thought I'd show you around a bit after I clean up the kitchen and get this load of laundry hung out. I do my big wash on Mondays, of course, but with all these active *kinner*, there are always extra loads."

Rebecca didn't seem bothered by that fact, though. "I'll clean up the kitchen if you want to hang out the wash," Hannah offered. She figured she should be able to do that without any problem.

"*Danki*. That will help us get an earlier start. I made sandwiches for Samuel and the boys for lunch so we won't have to rush."

Hannah nodded and turned back to the sudsy water to finish washing dishes. She could hear Emma chattering to Elizabeth in Pennsylvania Dutch. She remembered Liz told her children didn't usually learn English until they went to school.

Rebecca retrieved her laundry basket and headed outside to complete her chore. Hannah wondered what discoveries she would make during her tour of Southern Maryland Amish country — a place she never knew existed until a couple days ago.

Since the only clouds in the bright blue sky were the big, white marshmallow ones, Rebecca started to take the open cart but instead opted for the gray buggy with the orange reflective triangle on back so they would have some shade. She expertly hitched up the big brown horse, appropriately named Brownie, and pronounced them ready for their outing.

Hannah had no idea how to get into the buggy gracefully wearing her long blue dress. She mentally shrugged her shoulders and, while Rebecca was momentarily distracted by the little girls, climbed in the only way she could figure. She more plopped than sat on the seat, but at least she did land on the seat. She offered to hold Elizabeth on her lap as Emma wiggled in between Hannah and Rebecca.

Hannah looked around her, worry beginning to creep in. They were actually going out on the paved road? Where cars zoomed by? Was this safe? Hannah offered a quick prayer for safety—and courage—as the buggy jerked forward and Brownie plodded down the gravel driveway.

Neighboring farms on Woodley Hill Road were obviously Amish. A small brown apartment building sat near the end of the road—obviously not Amish. Rebecca turned the cart left onto a larger road that Hannah remembered was Route 236 or something like that. She turned to look at the houses where cars lined the driveways.

"We have some nice *Englisch* neighbors, too. We're all kind of mixed together."

"Oh," Hannah didn't know what else to say.

Rebecca kept the horse and buggy toward the right edge of the road but had to swerve more toward the middle to avoid a bicyclist.

The man, who was practically beside them, pedaled furiously. A baseball cap was pulled low so the bill shaded his face. Hannah sucked in a sharp breath when the man turned briefly and looked into her face.

Even though he didn't quite resemble "the murderer," Hannah's heart flip-flopped. Something did seem familiar about him, but she couldn't quite distinguish why.

The cap shaded his face too much to make his features clearly identifiable. Her stomach contracted in fear and threatened to expel the cornflakes she hadn't yet digested.

The man looked away as Rebecca maneuvered around him. She seemed oblivious to Hannah's strange reaction. Hannah took slow, deep breaths to calm her nerves. She had to stop panicking every time she saw a man wearing a baseball cap or she'd be a total basket case. She would also be compelled to explain her curious response to Rebecca or whoever witnessed her fears.

Several cars slowed before passing them, the drivers obviously accustomed to being on the lookout for Amish buggies and carts. Evidently, the little yellow sign with the picture of a buggy and the words "share the road" was effective. There were a few sharp turns and hills on the road that gave Hannah a fright. Rebecca turned onto Ryland Road and slowed the horse a little more.

On the right, Hannah saw a road leading to big *Englisch* homes. Once past this road, properties were obviously Amish. Rebecca pointed to a house with a barn or workshop slightly behind it. "That's Jeremiah

Yoder's place. Jeremiah repairs engines. He also sharpens blades for saws and mowers and things."

"What beautiful flowers." Hannah pointed to a house a little further down the road.

"Do you like flowers?"

"Oh y-*jah*." Hannah barely remembered to use Pennsylvania Dutch.

"Let's stop and see Esther. You'll like her. She knows all about flowers." A hand-painted sign told visitors this was Esther's Greenery. As on all Amish business signs, "no Sunday sales" was painted below the name.

When Rebecca drove up the gravel driveway closer to the two-story house, Hannah could see two greenhouses situated behind the house.

"Oh, she grows flowers! I thought you meant she just liked them."

"Esther has quite the green thumb. She lives here with her family but the greenery is her business. She's still a *maidel*, too." Hannah tried not to smile. She supposed that was Amish for old maid.

At her advanced age of twenty-four, she must be one of the oldest unmarried women in the community. She wondered just how old Esther might be.

"She sounds...fascinating." Hannah's mind conjured up a picture of a wizened little old Amish woman with dirt under her fingernails.

"*Jah*, Esther is quite a character."

Hannah wondered what Rebecca meant by this but didn't get the chance to ask. Before Rebecca even halted the horse near the first greenhouse, a tall, slender woman in a purple dress covered by a black apron exited the building.

Her hand shielded her eyes to block the sun as she looked toward Rebecca, Hannah, and the children. "Ach, Rebecca. *Wie geht's?*"

"Fine," Rebecca replied.

Esther dropped her hand, and Hannah discovered she couldn't have been more wrong. Esther was a lovely young woman. The front of her deep brown, almost black, hair that was not pinned neatly under her *kapp* gleamed in the sunlight. Her large chocolate-brown eyes made Hannah think of two Hershey's kisses — the dark chocolate ones. She smiled a genuine welcome and reached to take Elizabeth from Hannah's arms.

"This *boppli* is getting so big," she cooed and tickled the little girl beneath the chin, eliciting a giggle.

"*Jah*. She's eighteen months now."

"And Miss Emma is almost a lady."

Emma smiled before ducking her head behind her mamm.

"Ach, Esther, this is Hannah Kurtz who has come to stay with us." Rebecca introduced her.

"I remember you said a guest was coming. I just didn't remember when. *Wilkum*, Hannah. I'm Esther Stauffer."

"Nice to meet you."

While Esther turned to tickle Elizabeth again and Rebecca helped Emma out of the buggy, Hannah scrambled down as quickly and as gracefully as she could manage. Eventually, she'd get the hang of getting in and out of a cart or buggy. She hoped so, anyway.

"Hannah likes flowers, too," Emma said.

"*Jah?*"

"She said so."

"*Jah*, I do, Emma," Hannah gave Emma a brief hug.

"*Kum.* I'll show you my greenhouses if you like. I may just have a peppermint for a sweet girl, too," she added chucking Emma under her chin as she shifted Elizabeth to the other hip.

"Here, give me the *boppli* so you can show Hannah around." Rebecca reached out for her youngest.

Esther hugged Elizabeth before handing her over. "You know I just love *bopplin.*"

"You need one of your own," Rebecca teased.

"*Jah*, and a husband first, I'm thinking."

"You know old Silas is still looking."

Esther slapped Rebecca's arm playfully. "You know I'd sooner marry that bull over in the field than gruff old Silas Bontrager. If he was the last man on earth, I'd stay single! I'm not that old, you know, Rebecca Hertzler."

"You're nearly as old as I am."

"I'll have you know I just turned twenty-five. Just because I'm not married with a dozen *kinner* doesn't mean I'm ready for the grave!"

Hannah burst out laughing. She took an instant liking to Esther Stauffer. This, apparently, was an Amish woman who spoke her mind. Maybe they would be friends—if she stayed here long enough.

"Esther, maybe you and Hannah can go to the singing on Sunday evening," Rebecca suggested.

"Don't you think I might be older than the men there? They're just boys."

"Some older men go, too. You know Sarah Fisher's cousin Andrew from Ohio is visiting." Rebecca continued to tease, winking at Hannah.

"I remember Andrew." Esther shook her head.

"*Jah*, from when we were all *kinner*. People change when they grow up. I'm sure Andrew has outgrown his mischief-making."

"Hmph! Let me show Hannah around. I'm happy with my plants, *danki*."

Hannah entered the first greenhouse behind Esther. The heat and humidity would have been completely stifling if a small breeze hadn't been blowing in through the open doors at either end of the greenhouse. The smell of dirt was strong, but Hannah didn't mind.

Even though Rennie laughed at her, she used to enjoy weeding Aunt Genevieve's many flowerbeds and tending to the garden. Something about working among God's creation soothed her. That may be to her advantage here.

"Oh, you have geraniums, begonias, petunias, snapdragons, marigolds," Hannah named off flowers she recognized as she trailed behind Esther. "But something smells *wunderbaar*. I don't recognize..."

"It's the pinks," Esther said. She led the way to the table where flats of small pink flowers gave off a heavenly scent. "They're actually types of dianthus, but we just call them pinks."

"I don't believe I've seen those before."

"My *grossmammi* used to grow them before she passed. I took cuttings and have been growing them to sell. They are one of my most popular flowers."

"I can see why. I'd fill my yard with those."

Esther moved along the rest of the flowers, naming them as she went. Hannah followed at her heels like a little puppy. It did give her a chance to observe Esther without the other young woman's awareness.

She was almost a head taller than Hannah and quite slim. She walked straight and held her head high, exuding an assurance in her knowledge and abilities. Her rich, dark hair looked thick and sleek, and Hannah imagined it fell to her waist when she loosed it from the bun.

Her voice was soft but not a timid soft. It had a pleasant cadence. That voice now called Hannah out of her reverie as she waited for Hannah at the opposite door from where they entered.

"In the other greenhouse, I have my vegetable plants—tomatoes, carrots, lettuce, and the like."

Hannah peeked into the other greenhouse. "You have quite a lot. You must stay busy."

"*Jah*. Business is good. I have regular customers who come here. I also set up at the farmers' markets. Rebecca, are you going to take Hannah to the markets?" Esther called out.

"*Jah*, sure. We can go to the one at the library parking lot any day—except Sunday, of course—or to the big market on Saturday. We'll see."

"The big market has a lot of junk that *Englishers* sell," Esther explained. "The library market is strictly Amish and Mennonites."

"Oh," Hannah said. She seemed to be saying that a lot. Mennonites? She'd heard of them but wasn't sure how they differed from the Amish.

"We'd better be on our way," Rebecca said. "I want to show Hannah a few other places. *Kum*, Emma," she called to the little girl picking yellow buttercups in the field near the greenhouses. Emma trotted over to the women and thrust her bouquet of small yellow flowers out to Hannah.

"For me?" Hannah bent down to take the flowers.

The little girl nodded, shyness suddenly overtaking her.

"They're beautiful. *Danki* ever so much, Emma."

"Here, let me put them in a little cup of water for you." Esther stepped into the greenhouse for a second and came back with a small paper cup half filled with water. "The poor things will wilt in a minute in this heat without a drink of water."

"*Danki*." Hannah plunked the fistful of flowers into the cup.

Esther helped Rebecca get the children in the buggy while Hannah held up her dress slightly and climbed in. *Hey, I'm getting better at this*!

"Thanks for the tour, Esther," Hannah called. "Nice meeting you."

"Same here. *Kum* back anytime."

"Think about Silas," Rebecca teased.

"Andrew is looking better all the time, though not a lot," Esther quipped.

The three women laughed as Rebecca got the horse moving.

Chapter Six

The sun, now almost directly overhead, beat down on the roof of the buggy, heating up the inside to at least a thousand degrees. Hannah barely resisted the urge to push up her sleeves. Oh, for a pair of shorts and a t-shirt! The big, brown horse snorted and swished his tail as he pulled the buggy down the road.

"Just a little further, Brownie," Rebecca soothed. "Then you'll get shade and water." Hannah could see waves of heat rising from the blacktopped road. Poor Brownie must be miserable. Though not ocean breezes by any stretch of the imagination, the occasional wisps of air brought some small relief.

I'll never take air conditioned cars or houses for granted again, Hannah thought.

A few miles down the road from Esther's place, they turned down a lane that wound its way in between thick fields of tall corn on one side and bushy soybeans on the other.

"Looks like someone is going to have a good harvest," Hannah observed.

"I expect so," Rebecca agreed. "Seth Beiler and his sons have always been successful farmers."

At the name "Beiler," Hannah's ears perked up and her stomach had a funny fluttering sensation. *There are probably a hundred Beilers. Besides, you're not even Amish.*

You are now! The voice seemed to come from the heavens. Did Rebecca hear it? Hannah glanced at Rebecca out of the corner of her eye but her gaze still focused straight ahead, and she gave no indication she heard any voices. *You're losing it, kiddo. You'd better get a grip!*

"I won't be here long," Rebecca said. "I want to thank Naomi for the peaches and then get over to show you the store."

Hannah dragged her mind back from the tall, muscular young man she had met yesterday and forced her attention on Rebecca's words.

"That's fine," she said. Store? As in a grocery store, a department store, or even Wal-Mart? A store should have air conditioning. Maybe she could get a brief respite from this oppressive heat.

The windmill near the two-story white house with a green roof barely turned. The tiny breeze from earlier on must have given up entirely. Yet when Rebecca stopped Brownie beneath a huge oak tree, the temperature seemed a good fifteen degrees cooler. Hannah sighed in relief. She imagined poor Brownie did, too, if horses could sigh.

A boy of about fifteen ran toward them. *"Wie geht's!"* he called. "I'll get water for Brownie."

"*Danki*, Daniel. I won't be long so I won't unhitch him."

"A little treat for him is okay, *jah*?"

"Sure, *danki*. Oh, Daniel, this is Hannah Kurtz from Pennsylvania."

"Hello, Hannah."

"Nice to meet you," Hannah replied.

The boy immediately turned to Brownie, patting the horse and talking softly to him.

Before they could climb down, the screen door opened to allow a middle-aged woman with graying brown hair to emerge. She wiped her hands on her black apron.

"Rebecca," she called, breaking into a huge smile. "And you have the girls."

"*Jah*. And this is Hannah Kurtz."

"*Wilkom*. *Kum* in, please. I'm Naomi."

"We really can't stay, but I wanted to thank you for the *wunderbaar* peaches. Hannah and I canned them yesterday and brought your basket back."

"No need to have hurried with that old basket. I'm glad you could use the peaches. *Kum,* stretch your legs a minute. I'm thinking these wee ones are hungry. Here, I'll take the *boppli*." Naomi reached for Elizabeth.

Everyone always seemed to be eager to help with children, Hannah thought, passing the toddler into Naomi's outstretched arms. She jumped from the cart and turned to help Emma.

"*Kum,* have a bite of lunch. It's almost ready."

"*Danki*, Naomi, but we really can't stay long. I wanted to show Hannah the store before we head home."

The sounds coming from a large warehouse-type building captured Hannah's attention. Hammering and air tools and muffled voices filled the air. Noticing her gaze, Naomi said, "Go have a look at the shop while I at least get you sandwiches. They have all kinds of things in the shop."

Emma scurried over to take Hannah's hand. The little girl seemed to have formed an immediate attachment to her. Hannah was pleased but wary at the same time. She didn't want Emma to be disappointed when she left. Hannah closed her hand over Emma's small one.

"Let's go see." As always, she hoped her attempt at speaking Pennsylvania Dutch was understandable. Emma skipped, pulling Hannah along with her.

Hannah stopped in the doorway, closed her eyes, and inhaled the scent of wood and varnish. She pictured Uncle Ted in his woodworking shop. She loved the smell of wood. She loved playing in the wood shavings and sawdust. Most of all, she loved seeing a beautiful box or toy or shelf fashioned from a lump of wood.

For a moment her eyes filled with tears at the thought of her uncle and his family. Oh, how she missed them in just these few days, and she prayed they weren't grieving for her. Her eyes popped open at Emma's tug on her arm.

"You praying?"

"I suppose I was."

Hannah and Emma crossed the threshold into the furniture shop with Rebecca right behind them. Naomi had taken Elizabeth into the house with her. Hannah ran her hand along the oak hope chests and cherry dressers.

She set a curved rocking chair into motion. "These are—are—*wunderbaar*," she exclaimed.

"*Jah*. The Beilers do nice work," Rebecca agreed.

"Can I help you ladies or are you just browsing?" Jacob teased, brushing sawdust from his trousers as he entered the display area.

"I think I'll take three rocking chairs and a dresser," Rebecca quipped.

"I'd love one of these beautiful chests," Hannah said then bit her tongue. Was it prideful to tell Jacob the chests were beautiful?

"Would you like oak or cherry, ma'am?"

"The cherry, I think."

"That will run you about a million dollars, total."

"Go on with you, Jacob Beiler," Rebecca admonished. "Hannah wanted to see your shop."

"Well then, let me give you the tour."

Jacob wound his way through the maze of finished furniture, Rebecca, Hannah, and Emma following like ducklings trailing their mother.

"Here's where we do our work." Jacob shouted to be heard over the hammering. His voice trailed off as the room quieted. "Daed, Micah, this is Hannah Kurtz."

Both men nodded as Hannah murmured a greeting. Jacob's father was an older version of Jacob, but his brother, Micah, had brown hair and eyes like Naomi.

"What are you working on here?" Rebecca pointed to a chest in progress.

"It's a secret." Jacob put his index finger to his lips. "It's a present for Mary. She turns twelve next week."

"Mary is Jake's sister," Rebecca explained. "She'll be so happy with this, Jake."

"I hope so. Don't tell her." Jacob's smile melted Hannah's heart. *What a nice guy. He must care a lot about his sister.*

"We'll let you get back to work. I've got to find my other *dochder*." She started for the door. "We won't tell Mary," she added.

"*D-danki* you for the t-tour." Why did Hannah suddenly feel so timid and tongue-tied?

"You're *wilkom*. Visit anytime." Jacob flashed that bedazzling smile again. Hannah's heart skipped a beat. She nodded and led Emma hastily from the shop.

"Whew! It's another hot day!" Rebecca exclaimed as they resumed their journey.

"*Jah*, it sure is," Hannah agreed. She was glad Rebecca felt as hot as she did. She was afraid it was just her and she didn't want to be a complainer.

"Maybe we'll have an early fall," Rebecca said.

"That would be nice." *Will I still be here in the fall?* Hannah was sure that having a hot, sleepy toddler on her lap and an equally hot child pressed against her side magnified her own body temperature, but she didn't have the heart to shift either little girl off her.

She had quickly grown fond of the children in just a couple days. In fact, everyone she met had been so kind. She felt accepted and a part of the community already.

"Charlatan!" her conscience cried. If only she didn't feel she was deceiving these wonderful people. Even though she didn't want to lie to them and, in fact, tried to be as vague as possible to avoid misrepresenting the truth, she was often overcome by shame and remorse.

Hannah blew a wisp of flaxen hair off her forehead and forced her attention back to Rebecca who was pointing out various homes to her. "We're almost to the store."

There were no hex signs on barns or obvious tourist attractions here. Rebecca explained that theirs was a quiet community. They interacted with *Englischers* for business purposes and were friendly with their *Englisch* neighbors. Otherwise, they maintained separate lives following their Ordnung.

They stopped in the shade near the entrance of the long white building. Emma and Elizabeth had shared one of Naomi's sandwiches along the way and had bread crumbs on their faces and dresses. Hannah brushed them off before handing Elizabeth down to Rebecca.

Hannah should have known Rebecca meant an Amish store. No hope of air conditioning, but she was surprised and relieved to find the store wasn't as stifling as she had feared. Evidently, an early morning breeze had blown through the open doors and windows, keeping the temperature bearable. After introducing Hannah to Miriam and Levi Esh, the store's proprietors, Rebecca urged Hannah to look around.

Hannah wandered along the close-set aisles, taking in the canning supplies, cooking utensils, straw and felt hats, sturdy black shoes, and bolts of solid-colored fabrics—purple, blue, green, and black. Black wood stoves and accessories and farm implements lined the back wall of the store. The last aisle boasted home-canned goods, hand-stitched quilted potholders, crocheted dishcloths, small toys, and children's books.

Hannah stopped and picked up a faceless Amish doll. She couldn't ask why it had no face. She was supposed to know that. She guessed it had something to do with having no graven images. Even faceless, the doll had charm, and she wished she could purchase it.

"*Englischers* shop here, too. Sometimes, they like hand-made items," Rebecca said catching up to Hannah and holding a child's hand in each of her own.

"Oh."

"If you ever want to sell some crocheted or other hand-made items, Miriam is happy to sell them on consignment."

"That's *gut* to know." Hannah did, at least, know how to crochet. Surely she could figure out how to make the dishcloths if she studied one. She would have to find some way to earn her keep. Reluctantly, she returned the little doll to the shelf. Why did she feel a longing to keep this doll? Maybe losing her own identity was akin to being faceless.

She suddenly felt depressed. Who was she? Was she a faceless, nameless nobody now? Somewhere, a voice whispered, *You're still my child.* Hannah glanced right, left, and behind her. No one stood nearby. No one else seemed to have heard the whisper. This was the second time she'd heard a voice. Either her imagination was working overtime or she truly was losing her mind.

Before heading for the door and the waiting horse, Rebecca purchased one of Miriam's chocolate brownies for the little girls to share on the ride home. The plump brownie was large enough for each girl to have half and be satisfied. They said goodbye to Miriam and Levi, promising to see them at church on Sunday. The tired, hot little girls nodded off to sleep, lulled by the rhythmic clip-clopping of the horse's hooves on the blacktop road.

"I think I could figure out how to crochet those cloths," Hannah mused aloud, "but I'd like to do those quilted items."

"I can show you how," Rebecca offered. "You don't remember how to quilt?"

"Uh…no, I don't think so." Hannah despised her untruthfulness. She tried to justify it by telling herself if she ever knew how to quilt she certainly didn't remember learning it.

"Do you know what happened in the accident?"

"Not—not really. I was told I was hit on the head by a falling tree limb during a sudden storm." That really was what she was told to say. She picked at her fingernails, a bad habit she thought she'd overcome.

"That's terrible. What do you remember from before the accident, if you don't mind my asking?"

"I barely remember my parents. They were killed when a-a truck hit them." Hannah's voice dropped to a whisper.

"I'm so sorry." Rebecca reached to pat Hannah's hands and briefly stilled the nail-picking.

Hannah cleared her throat. "I-I went to live with my aunt and uncle and cousins. I-I think my aunt taught me to crochet. I don't remember much about sewing or canning or…"

Hannah's voice drifted off and tears filled her big, blue eyes. *God, forgive me. You know I don't want to lie.* Her parents did die when she was young and she did go to live with her aunt, uncle, and cousins. She sighed.

"That's okay," Rebecca soothed. "I'll help you. Do you know how you happened to be sent here to Maryland?"

"Everyone felt the stress of trying to remember was too great and that maybe a total change would help me." The last part was true, anyway. The total change was supposed to help keep her alive. Hannah inhaled sharply. "Is that the same bicyclist?" She nodded at the man in the baseball cap pedaling toward them.

"It looks like it."

"Don't they have to wear helmets?"

"I thought so, but I'm not sure. I don't recognize him."

Hannah shivered despite the heat. Had they found her? *No, no.* She tried to calm herself. *Lots of people ride bikes. Some are crazy enough to ride on the road without helmets.*

Chapter Seven

The rest of the week and the next one passed in a blur. Hannah hardly remembered she used to run ten miles per day. Was it just a couple weeks ago? She stayed so busy helping with the gardening the canning, the housework, the cooking, the laundry, the mending, the childcare, and whatever other chores could be crammed into the day, that she dropped into bed at night too exhausted to think of putting one foot in front of the other to run. How did one woman handle all of this alone?

Obviously, Rebecca and every other Amish woman did just that every single day. And that rooster! If she was a meat eater, he would be in a stew pot with a fat dumpling on his head. As for being a vegetarian, Hannah wasn't sure how long she could continue to avoid eating meats. She saw the questioning looks Samuel and Rebecca exchanged every time she passed the meat plate without taking a sliver. And she wasn't at all sure she consumed adequate protein and calories.

She could tell she had lost weight she could ill afford to lose in just this short amount of time—despite not running for exercise. *I'm certainly not sedentary, though.* She did eat slivers of cheese, pour a small amount of milk on her cereal, and eat the eggs she had fought the chickens for. She just wasn't sure her usual diet would continue to sustain her.

Saturday again. Extra work, since Sunday was a day of rest and only necessary chores could be performed. Samuel and the boys would take care of the animals. Rebecca and Hannah would prepare simple meals.

This Sunday would be Hannah's first church experience. Since services were only held every other week, last Sunday had been a no-church Sunday. She had spent the day visiting people whose names Hannah struggled to remember, reading the Bible, playing games with the children, and other quieter activities.

Rebecca flew around the house, cleaning and doing a stray load of laundry, all while keeping an eye on Elizabeth. Samuel took Eli and Jonas to work in the hay or corn fields. Hannah wasn't sure which one. Hannah enlisted Emma's help weeding the garden.

Working in Aunt Genevieve's massive flower beds proved to be useful training after all. At least she basically knew the difference between a weed and a valuable plant, even if these were vegetable plants instead of pansies or petunias or marigolds.

Emma had spent time in the garden with her mamm so she could already distinguish a weed from a vegetable, for the most part. A few carrot tops got discarded by accident, but Hannah didn't scold. She had unknowingly plucked up a few vegetables herself. She felt sure Rebecca would forgive them.

While the girls napped, Rebecca pulled mixing bowls and baking pans out of kitchen cabinets. Canisters of flour and sugar followed. "Let's bake some desserts for the after-church meal. Church is at the Eshes' tomorrow. I told Miriam I'd help with desserts."

"What kind of desserts?" Hannah's eyes darted around the kitchen in search of a cookbook or recipe file. Spying neither, she began to panic. She'd baked cookies from scratch many times but certainly no elaborate desserts. With a recipe she might get by, but without a recipe...

"I've got some blackberries, so I think we'll make a blackberry cobbler. And I still have some peaches for a peach crisp. Which do you want to make?"

Hannah gulped. "Where is a-a recipe?"

"Up here." Rebecca tapped her head.

I was afraid of that, Hannah almost said. *What do I say, Lord?*

"I'm so sorry, Hannah." Rebecca reached over to squeeze Hannah's arm. "Do you remember how to make either one?"

Hannah wagged her head. Shame at yet another fib burned through her. *I don't know how much of this I can take, Lord*.

"Don't worry, Hannah. *Gott* will help you." Hannah relaxed visibly. How did Rebecca know to say words that spoke to her soul? "I'll talk you through the cobbler. *Jah?*"

"Sure." Hannah offered a tremulous smile.

"First, mix the berries with a cup of sugar and let it sit while you mix the dough."

Sounds easy enough. By the time she slid the cobbler into the oven, Hannah and the table sported a dusting of flour. Rebecca's side of the table stayed just as clean as ever. Hannah sighed but busied herself cleaning the kitchen while the desserts baked and Rebecca changed the now-awake Elizabeth.

Hannah tried not to seem prideful, but she couldn't help but feel pleased with the cobbler's finished appearance. She hoped it tasted as good as it looked. She'd find out tomorrow. So would everyone else!

The entire family crammed into the gray buggy. Good thing she was so small, Hannah thought, so she could fit in between Jonas and Eli who both wanted to sit beside her. Samuel clicked his tongue, and Brownie took off in the direction of the Esh home.

She'd only been away from the house a few times so was totally unsure where places were located or which small side roads led where. She planned to go to the market next week to help Rebecca sell some produce and canned goods. For now, she looked over the boys' heads to take in the scenery.

The morning was warm but not yet hot and humid. The world—at least the *Englisch* world—still slept. No cars passed them as they turned onto a narrower road. Only a procession of gray buggies, the sound of high-stepping horses and buggy wheels, and the morning songs of several species of birds Hannah couldn't identify interfered with the morning stillness.

Hannah clutched Emma's hand and followed Rebecca who carried Elizabeth. They entered the front room of Miriam and Levi Esh's house where benches had been set up for the church service. They trailed behind Esther Stauffer and her mother and sat on the women's side. Hannah sat with Rebecca, even though she probably should have followed Esther to sit with other unmarried women

Samuel took Eli and Jonas with him to the men's side of the room. The congregation sang songs from the Ausbund until the ministers and Bishop Sol appeared. Hannah pretended to sing then struggled to find a comfortable position on the hard, wooden bench. No cushioned luxury here!

She tried to focus during the three sermons to decipher any recognizable German words. The sermons were spoken in high German rather than Pennsylvania Dutch, so Hannah's high school and college German studies came in a little handy. She understood every few words and attempted to string these words together to form some meaning. Just when she thought a speaker would be finished, he would take a breath and drone on. Some spoke longer than others.

Her backside practically grew to the bench, and Hannah wasn't entirely sure she'd be able to move when or if the service ever ended. A few children fidgeted but most sat still as stone. Just when Hannah thought she could bear no more, they all knelt to pray and the service mercifully concluded.

The men made quick work of turning the benches into dining tables as the women retreated to the kitchen to ready the meal. Hannah understood they ate in shifts with the women serving the men at the first shift.

Hannah carried bowls of beets and pickles and vegetable dishes to the table. She filled glasses with iced tea or brought cups of coffee to the men who preferred a hot drink on a hot day. Feeling eyes upon her, she glanced sideways and found Jacob Beiler's clear blue eyes fastened on her.

She blushed, feeling the heat rise from her cheeks and forehead and travel up the part in her hair. Why her body responded like mercury rising in a thermometer always baffled her. She looked back at the table just in time to prevent coffee from sloshing over the brim of the cup and onto Bishop Sol. She mumbled an apology and scurried to the kitchen.

"Looks like you caught someone's attention," a voice whispered into her ear.

"What?" Hannah whirled around, nearly knocking Esther off her feet.

Esther grabbed Hannah's arm to steady herself. "Whoa, girl! I'm teasing, you know. But Jake sure seemed captivated."

"You're..." Hannah struggled to find the word. "You're *narrisch*!"

"I don't think so, but you're fun to tease."

"You're rotten!" Hannah had to laugh at Esther's fake pouting expression.

"Do you want to take a walk after we eat and clean up?"

"Uh, sure, if Rebecca doesn't need my help."

"The *kinner* will play or sleep. Let's eat fast. We served so maybe someone else will clean up." Hannah hoped so. Even though it was hot outside, the kitchen had to be a million degrees warmer.

"It was nice of your mother and some of the other women to offer to clean up," Hannah remarked after she and Esther carried the last of the leftover food to the kitchen.

"*Jah*. Let's walk. The Eshes own a good bit of land so we can walk a ways."

"Sounds *gut* to me."

They walked along in companionable silence until they reached the shade at the edge of the woods.

"Ah, shade is good," Esther said.

Hannah inhaled deeply and sighed. The tangy scent of cedar trees and pine needles rivaled the scent of the salty ocean breeze she so loved. The sun danced around the trees, making the shadows sway. Last fall's dried brown leaves crunched with each footstep. Here, serenity reigned and fears were banished. *This is almost as good as the ocean.*

"You didn't eat much. Is our food very different from where you're from?"

"Uh, not really." *What do I say? What do I say?*

"You don't eat meat, do you?" Not much got by Esther, apparently.

"Oh, Esther, I just can't stand the thought of eating animals. I know it sounds *narrich*," Hannah blurted out.

"Not crazy. You're just sensitive."

"Do you think everyone else noticed?"

"Probably."

Hannah's shoulders slumped. "I was afraid of that." A tear slid down her cheek.

"Hey. Don't worry. You won't be shunned for not eating meat. We all have our quirks. Me? I'd rather be outside working with my plants than cooking or sewing. Everyone thinks I'll be an old maid."

"Does that make you sad?"

"I'd rather be alone than with old Silas or married off to some other old man who wants to be waited on."

Hannah laughed. "You definitely speak your mind."

"Another strike against me, for certain and sure."

Hannah had hoped to remain aloof. She didn't want to forge relationships that wouldn't last long since she'd be leaving, but she couldn't resist Esther's friendliness and honesty.

"It must be ten degrees cooler here in the woods." Esther sighed.

"It does feel better in the shade, for sure."

"I imagine it's a bit hotter here than where you're from, ain't so?"

"Pretty close to the same." Hannah caught herself just before she added that ocean breezes usually kept things a bit more pleasant where she was from.

Unless the Atlantic had shifted, she wouldn't have experienced ocean breezes in Pennsylvania. She so missed the salty air. She pulled her wandering mind back to St. Mary's County and her companion.

"So what do you think of this place?"

"It's—it's quiet."

"Probably a lot quieter than Lancaster County."

"Quiet is nice, though." *Safer, too, I hope.*

"Have you been to the markets yet?"

"*Nee.* Rebecca said maybe this week."

"You can come with me to the market at the library tomorrow, if you want. I've got plants and flowers to sell, and mamm will be up early, baking, so I'll have fresh baked goods to sell."

"I'd like that. I'll check to see if Rebecca needs me for anything and…" She stopped speaking in mid-thought when a branch snapped loudly behind them.

She grabbed Esther's arm with one hand and clamped the other hand over her mouth to stifle a scream. Had they found her? Her body shifted into full fight-or-flight mod. She opted for flight and shifted her eyes from side to side to determine which way to flee.

"Probably just a deer, and probably more scared of you." Esther patted Hannah's hand that probably bruised her upper arm. "Ach, Jacob Beiler! You nearly scared poor Hannah to death."

"Sorry, Hannah." Jacob was instantly contrite. "I just needed to walk off that meal and the *wunderbaar* blackberry cobbler I ate too much of." A grin lit his face as Jacob winked at Hannah.

"Hannah made that, ain't so?" Esther nudged the silent girl beside her.

Hannah nodded, waiting for her heart rate to slow and her breathing to return to normal before attempting to speak. Would she always be scared of every sound? She probably looked very foolish to Esther and Jacob.

She finally ventured a look into Jacob's smiling face and beautiful blue eyes. "I'm glad you enjoyed the cobbler." Her voice was just above a whisper.

"Are you ladies coming to the singing?"

"I-I-don't think Rebecca and Samuel planned on that." She knew the young unmarried people participated in singings on the Sunday evenings they had church services.

"You know I haven't been to a singing in a coon's age," Esther said.

"Might be fun. You should come." Jacob's gaze took in both young women before settling on Hannah. She lowered her eyes. She could *not* feel an attraction to Jacob Beiler.

"Hope to see you later." Jacob sauntered off whistling one of the songs they had sung in church.

"I think you would have a ride home from the singing." Esther elbowed Hannah and nodded in the direction Jacob took.

Hannah felt the heat rise to the top of her head. "Don't be silly," she said. "He doesn't even know me."

"That's the point of the singings and the ride home."

Hannah didn't want to acknowledge the butterflies that took flight in her stomach when Jacob looked at her. She tried to ignore the way her heart raced when he winked at her. She could not get close to anyone here, not only because she would be leaving, but also because she didn't want to endanger anyone. Had those criminals been caught? Were they pursuing her?

She couldn't jeopardize anyone else's safety. She couldn't fall for Jacob Beiler—even if he did have the most gorgeous blue eyes and charming dimpled grin she'd ever seen. She couldn't think these thoughts. She wasn't even Amish. She was an imposter. She should remain faceless like the little doll.

"Maybe if you attend the singing, you'll get a ride home," Hannah teased.

"I doubt it."

"Don't you want to get married and have children?"

"Doesn't every Amish woman?"

"Probably, but what about you?"

"*Jah*. Sure. But I don't think that will happen. I'm different. I tend to be too outspoken."

"Honesty is a good thing, ain't so?"

"Except if you're supposed to be obedient." Esther laughed. "I'll probably always be a *maidel*. Or maybe I'll marry when I'm old like Sophie Hostetler."

"Sophie. Sophie." Hannah snapped her fingers. "The herb woman?"

"That's the one. She knows all about which herbs and plants help which ailment. We usually visit Sophie before we seek out the doctor."

"She's a fascinating woman. And she's not so old, Esther Stauffer." Sophie was a wiry woman as Hannah recalled, in constant motion. She was average height and build, and her brown hair sported a bit of gray around the edges.

"*Older* then. She's Miriam Zook's older sister. She's been our medicine woman for as long as I can remember so I think of her as old. Have you been to her shop?"

"*Nee*, but I'd like to go there."

"We'll go, then."

Hannah sensed a camaraderie quickly growing between herself and Esther. She knew she needed to put on the brakes to spare them both, but she wasn't sure she could. She'd formed an instant bond with Esther — almost like her instant attraction to Jacob.

She was getting caught up in being Hannah Kurtz, in being Amish. She wasn't sure she was play-acting so much anymore. She was beginning to really care for these people and to think of them as her people. Lilly Brandt had practically vanished from the face of the earth. How did that happen so quickly?

"Tell me about the singings." Hannah changed the subject. "Do a lot of people go?"

"Like I said, I haven't been in a while. Usually all the young unmarrieds go." Esther rattled off names that Hannah was unable to put faces with. Noticing Hannah's blank look, Esther smiled. "I guess that's too many people for you to place right now."

"I'm trying to put it together, but it's not happening very fast."

"Give it some time. You remember Sarah Fisher, though? She sat beside me at meal time."

"She's the schoolteacher?" Hannah actually did remember her.

Sarah came across as gentle and quiet. Her silver-rimmed glasses needed a serious adjustment or else she had a nervous habit of constantly pushing them up on her nose. She seemed like a pleasant young woman, maybe slightly younger than her own twenty-four years. She was pleasingly plump but not fat.

"*Jah,* Sarah will be at the singing and, as usual, will wait for Zeke Esh to ask to drive her home. She may be waiting until the cows come home." Esther clamped her hand across her mouth. "There I go, spouting off again."

"Zeke. He's Miriam's and Levi's son?"

"That's right. Tall, lanky guy."

"He sat next to Jacob at the table?"

"So who didn't notice Jacob?"

Hannah blushed. "Well, he's one of the few young men I know so I—"

"Uh huh. Don't explain."

Hannah knew her cheeks burned brighter.

"Don't mind me, Hannah." Esther reached out to touch Hannah's arm. "I like to tease. I don't mean any harm."

"No offense taken."

"Back to Zeke Esh. He joined the church but can't seem to be serious about marrying or anything. Sarah's *in lieb,* though, and is willing to make the supreme sacrifice to wait for Zeke to notice her," Esther finished with a flourish.

"Zeke seemed nice enough. I mean, he was certainly polite when I served his lemonade."

"Oh, for sure. Zeke is a nice enough fellow, just *befuddled*. I guess he'll settle down sooner or later — sooner if his mamm and Sarah have their way."

"I hope things work out for Sarah. If she gets married, she can't teach, can she?"

"Normally teachers are *maidels*. Hey, if Sarah hooks Zeke — I mean if Sarah and Zeke ever marry — you'd be a good teacher. That is if *you* don't up and marry."

"Not likely. What makes you think I'd be a good teacher?"

"You have that tender touch. I've seen you with Rebecca's *kinner*. And you seem smart, too."

"It doesn't look like teaching will be even a remote possibility if Zeke's as marriage-shy as you say."

"You never know. Sarah may get him to come around. Her folks planted extra celery."

Hannah heard families planted extra celery when they believed a daughter would marry in the fall since celery was a mainstay of wedding celebrations. Maybe Sarah would marry soon.

What am I thinking? I can't teach school here. I won't be here. I'm not even Amish. But the seed had been planted. She would love to teach. Her fellow librarians always told her she should have been a teacher. The seed germinated.

Chapter Eight

The children shouted goodbye to playmates as they clamored into buggies. Most families had gathered up dishes and children and prepared to head home. Hannah once again squeezed in between Jonas and Eli who both wanted to sit beside her. Not to be left out, Emma plopped down on Hannah's lap for the ride home. Elizabeth dozed in Rebecca's arms.

Samuel scooped his youngest child into his arms so Rebecca could climb into the front seat and then gently deposited her on her mother's lap. He hopped in on the opposite side of the buggy, released the brake, and snapped the reins.

"Would you like to come back to the singing?" Rebecca turned slightly and looked over her shoulder. "Samuel will bring you back after the animals are cared for."

"*Nee*, but *danki*. I-I-don't think I'm ready for that yet."

"It's a good way to get to know the other young people."

"Maybe next time." Hannah didn't want to appear standoffish, but she couldn't become any more involved. Would there be a next time? Would she still be here? She'd had no word from the authorities so assumed the criminals were still on the loose. She suppressed a shudder. She wished she could call Detective Bradford for an update. She wished she could talk to Liz and learn more about how she was supposed to act. She felt like she was making up her life as she went along.

"Will you tell us a story?" Eli asked.

"Of course. After we get home." Home? Now she thought of Rebecca's and Samuel's house as home?

"After chores," Samuel reminded.

"*Jah,* Daed," two voices replied in unison.

Hannah racked her brain for a story. It wasn't that she didn't know plenty of stories. As a children's librarian, she'd read so many books at story times that she had many of them memorized. She just wasn't sure which ones were appropriate or allowed for Amish children.

Besides, her memory was supposed to be faulty. How was she going to justify remembering children's stories but not how to preserve foods or quilt? She'd have to think of something. Fast.

The sun did not shine as brightly now so Hannah was not quite as miserable packed into the buggy between squirming children. Emma seemed to be growing sleepier after having played hard with the other young children. Her head bobbed, and Hannah expected it to crash against her chest at any moment.

Close to home, Emma jerked and her eyes popped open when Hannah clutched her tightly and sucked in a shaky breath. The same bicyclist in the red baseball cap pedaled toward them. He peered into the buggy. Hannah drew back so her face remained shadowed. The cap shaded his face again, obscuring any identifiable features.

"Ach!" Emma cried.

"Sorry, Emma." Hannah whispered, loosening her grip.

"*Was ist letz?*" Rebecca called.

"N-nothing." Hannah let out the breath she just realized she had been holding. "Th-that bicyclist startled me is all. D-do you know him?"

"*Nee*, I don't think so. Do you, Samuel?"

"I don't believe I do, but lots of *Englischers* come and go."

"I guess so," Hannah mumbled. She felt pretty sure that Samuel was savvy to people and activities usually common to the area. Hannah tried to turn nonchalantly and look out the back of the buggy.

The bicyclist chose that very moment to turn and look as well. Hannah quickly returned her gaze to the front and unconsciously hunched a little lower in the seat. At least the man hadn't made a U-turn and followed them. Was he a threat? She wished she knew.

Though glad to be able to get out of the buggy and stretch her cramped legs, Hannah hesitated, afraid she'd see the bicyclist following the gravel driveway to the house. After Eli leaped from the buggy, Hannah passed a groggy Emma into Samuel's waiting arms. She climbed out slowly, glancing down the driveway as she did so. No bicycles in sight. She breathed a sigh of relief. *This is ridiculous. I have to stop being afraid of everyone and everything.*

Fear not I am with you; be not dismayed I am your God. I will strengthen you and help you. The Bible verse she had memorized years ago spoke to her jangled nerves. *Trust. I have to trust.*

Samuel and the boys changed into choring clothes while Hannah and Rebecca prepared a light supper. Hannah didn't think she'd be able to eat anything but figured she'd better make at least a half-hearted attempt to avoid Samuel's scrutiny or Rebecca's concern.

The children, Rebecca, and Samuel ate cold meatloaf sandwiches using up the leftovers from last night's dinner. Hannah sliced peaches for everyone, and of course, the perpetually full cookie jar would supply dessert. Hannah toyed with peach slices.

"I'm still full from the earlier meal," she claimed.

"You didn't eat that much after church. Are you feeling all right, Hannah?"

Hannah, touched by Rebecca's loving concern, quickly assured her she was fine. "I guess my appetite has been off lately."

"That's okay," Rebecca soothed. "I just don't want you to get sick or lose weight."

"You'll blow away in a gust of wind," Samuel remarked. "We'll have to tie rocks to your apron to hold you down."

Hannah laughed. "I'm not that small."

"Like a little bird," Samuel said. "You've got to eat like me." He reached into the cookie jar for a handful of oatmeal raisin cookies.

"We'd be as big as the barn if we ate like you," Rebecca said playfully, slapping Samuel's full hand.

"Can we have cookies, too, Mamm?" Levi scooped the last of his peaches into his mouth.

"You may each have one," Rebecca replied.

After cleaning the kitchen, Rebecca and Hannah joined the family in the living room where Samuel read from the big German Bible. Hannah actually understood some of the reading and tried to appear as though she comprehended completely. After prayers, the children clamored for stories.

"You can remember stories, ain't so?" Samuel observed when Hannah finished her story.

"*Jah*. Some things from the past are as clear as day." She hoped that would satisfy Samuel's curiosity.

"All right, *kinner*, it's bedtime," Rebecca announced.

Levi, Eli, and Emma rose obediently from their spots surrounding Hannah.

We used to protest going to bed and prolong the inevitable as long as possible. These children apparently know from a young age to listen to their parents without balking.

Hannah hugged each child and had to stifle a yawn herself. She didn't want to remain in the room alone with Samuel for fear he'd ask her more questions.

"I'm pretty tired myself." She stood and arched her back to stretch. "I think I'll get ready for bed, too. *Gut nacht*, Samuel."

"*Gut nacht*. Sleep well."

Hannah followed Rebecca and the children, climbing the stairs behind them. Hannah hated all the pretense, albeit necessary. Her fatigue, however, was genuine.

"No!" Hannah's scream ripped through the house, shattering the silence.

The man in the red baseball cap tightened his grip around her neck. Gagging and coughing, she clutched at the hands cutting off her air supply.

Tears splashed down Hannah's face as consciousness returned. She fought the twisted bed sheet to sit up and pushed tangled pale hair off her face. She looked at Rebecca's frightened but concerned face and vaguely registered Samuel speaking softly to the children outside her door.

"I-I'm so sorry," she gasped. "B-bad d-dream." More tears poured from her eyes.

Rebecca dropped to the edge of the bed, pulling Hannah into her arms. She patted her back to comfort her as she would have one of her children.

"You're safe here, Hannah."

Was she? Would she ever feel really safe again? She couldn't voice her fears. She couldn't share her burdens with another living soul. She shivered and Rebecca tightened her embrace.

"Do you want to talk about it?" Rebecca stroked Hannah's hair. "*Kinner*, go back to bed. Everything is okay." Rebecca directed them toward the door.

"I-it's silly. I d-dreamed s-someone was trying to ch-choke me. I'm so sorry. I-I w-woke everyone." Hannah sniffed and struggled to staunch the flow of tears.

"Here." Rebecca thrust a tissue into Hannah's hands. She continued to pat Hannah's back. "You're okay," she soothed. "We won't let anything happen to you."

Please, God, let Rebecca be right. And please don't let me bring harm to these good people. Hannah shivered again.

"You're quivering. Lie down. I'll sit with you a while." Rebecca pressed Hannah gently back onto the pillow and drew the sheet up under her chin.

"You don't have to stay. I'll be okay."

"Shhh. I'll just stay a few minutes."

Sunrise teased the sky when Hannah awoke. She glanced quickly around the room. *Alone.* She didn't even know when Rebecca left her room. She threw back the covers and jumped from the bed. She should have been up long before now to help Rebecca. After all, she was the one responsible for everyone's lack of sleep. She should try to make it up to them somehow.

Hannah pulled the nightgown quickly over her head and stuffed it in a dresser drawer. She grabbed a dark green dress from the peg. She'd have to see about getting other dresses since it looked like she was going to be here for a while. Only she didn't know how to sew these buttonless, zipperless dresses. Rebecca probably sewed by hand and without a pattern!

She coaxed her baby-fine hair into a bun and hastily pinned the *kapp* into position. *If Rennie could see me, she'd probably double over laughing,* she thought as she rushed from the room.

Hannah stumbled into the kitchen to find Rebecca bustling about, frying eggs and stirring oatmeal. Her eyes looked tired, but she apparently didn't let lack of sleep interfere with her normal duties.

"I'm sorry I overslept. You should have awakened me."

"You had a rough night. I thought I'd let you sleep."

"I caused us all to have a rough night. I'm so sorry. I can't remember when I've had such a vivid nightmare."

"No need to apologize. It's not something you could control. We're none the worse for a little lack of sleep."

Hannah nodded, appreciative of Rebecca's understanding and compassion. There didn't seem to be much about her life she could control these days.

"Here. I'll stir the oatmeal while you finish the eggs."

"*Danki.*" Rebecca yielded the big wooden spoon.

It took a little strength for Hannah to stir the thick oatmeal. She wondered if she'd ever develop a taste for the pasty mixture. It reminded her of the lumpy mud pies she and Rennie concocted as children, just a different color.

Maybe if she thinned it with a little milk or water and doused it with a liberal coating of cinnamon, she'd be able to choke down a small bowl full. It would certainly stick to the stomach — and anywhere else along the way, most likely.

She wondered if there were any cornflakes left or if she had already consumed Rebecca's supply. If she could get to a grocery store, she could pick up some food more palatable to her. But she didn't want to hurt

Rebecca's feelings or appear any odder that she already did. She may have to retrain her taste buds. She gulped and removed the pan from the stove.

As if on cue, the back door opened to admit Samuel and his two little clones just as Rebecca slid the eggs onto plates. All three males removed their straw hats and washed up for breakfast.

Hannah's heart went out to the two little boys. They looked so tired, but they didn't complain even a smidgeon. They shuffled to the table and took their seats, their stomachs alternately emitting loud rumbles.

Hannah smiled at them as she set steaming bowls of oatmeal in front of them. She returned to the kitchen and rummaged stealthily about for a box of cereal—any cereal, at this point. Even plain bran that looked like rabbit pellets would do.

"Do you need something?" Rebecca returned to the kitchen for bread while Hannah still searched.

Caught red-handed. "Um, is there any more cereal?" Hannah ventured.

"*Nee*. It's all gone. I'll have to put it on my next grocery list."

"Okay." Hannah picked up a bowl and tried not to make a face as she ladled a small amount of oatmeal into it. The plopping sound almost made her return the glob to the pan, but she steeled herself and forged ahead.

She turned on the water and let it trickle into her bowl to make the mixture a bit thinner. Spying cinnamon on the spice shelf, she quickly dumped some into her bowl and stirred. She tentatively raised a tiny spoonful to her lips and tasted. "Tolerable," she pronounced softly before joining the family at the big oak table.

Hannah helped Rebecca clean up the kitchen and get the laundry washed and fastened to the line to dry in the early morning sunshine. She was just fastening the last pair of broadcloth trousers onto the line with a wooden clothespin when the clip-cop of a horse heralded the arrival of a visitor.

"*Gude mariye*," Esther called, stopping close to the house.

"*Gude mariye*." Hannah snatched up the big wicker basket and hurried to greet Esther.

"Mamm wanted to come sell her own goods that she's been baking since three this morning—"

"It was four, Esther. Don't exaggerate," her mother called out from the buggy.

"Anyway," Esther continued, "I thought we'd help her set up and stay at the market a little while. Then I can show you where some other homes and businesses are located. Daed will pick her up later."

"Sounds *gut* to me." Hannah felt a certain excitement at getting out to do something different with another single woman. Dare she say "friend?"

You're getting too attached. She promptly ignored the warning.

"Just let me check and see if Rebecca needs me to do anything. Be right back unless you'd like to come in."

"*Nee*. We want to get set up as soon as possible."

"I'll only be a minute. Rebecca!" Hannah practically ran over Rebecca in her haste.

"Whoa! I heard. I'm fine here. You need to get out."

"*Danki.* I'm sure we won't be too late for me to help with supper."

"Don't worry. Enjoy your day."

Hannah raced up the stairs to freshen up quickly and to stuff some money in her pocket, just in case she needed it.

She hugged Emma and Elizabeth on her way to the door and scurried to the waiting buggy.

Leah, Esther's mother, slid closer to Esther to make room. *I'm getting better at crawling into and out of buggies,* Hannah thought as she settled in beside Leah.

It didn't take long to reach the Cherry Hill library parking lot where other Amish vendors were already setting up in the shaded area to the right of the library's entrance. Hannah and Esther helped Leah display her cinnamon rolls, cookies, and cake slices.

"You baked all these things this morning?" Hannah mentally tallied all the baked goods.

"*Jah.*"

"She's just a busy little bee," Esther teased as she arranged some potted plants on one side of the table and nearby on the ground. They were positioning themselves behind the tables when cars began pulling into the parking lot.

"Lots of people come early before it gets too hot." Esther explained. "If you need a break or a restroom, the library opens at nine."

Hannah nodded and felt a tingle of excitement. How good it would feel to enter a library again. Even if she couldn't work there, maybe she could obtain a card and check out books. Somehow, she'd have to determine the type of books appropriate for an Amish woman to read.

When business slowed a little, Esther informed Leah that she and Hannah would take their leave. They visited the library first to use the restroom before setting out.

"What kind of books do you like to read?" Hannah hoped her casual question would settle her book quandary

"*Kum*, I'll show you where I usually look." Esther led Hannah to shelves marked "inspirational fiction" and let Hannah browse for a few minutes. Hannah selected two books and approached the desk to acquire a library card and to check out.

"You look like a *kind* with a new toy," Esther remarked, taking notice of Hannah's excitement over the new card and the books.

"I — it's just I-I think it will be fun to read made-up stories."

"I like to read, too. It's better than sewing." Esther rolled her dark eyes, causing Hannah to laugh.

"That reminds me," Hannah said. "I need some material. Rebecca said she'd help me sew some dresses."

"New fabric you shall have then. I know just the place."

Esther and Hannah explored the countryside, Esther acting as tour guide. Their last stop before heading home was Esh's store so Hannah could purchase dress fabric. They had visited Barbara Zook's quilt shop, but she had strictly quilting materials and beautiful ready-made quilts.

I hope I have time to learn how to quilt before I leave.

The realization struck her that she thought less about leaving these days as she settled more into the daily routine. She had still received no word from Detective Bradford or Marshal O'Brien. She couldn't believe those guys had not been captured yet.

She thought the detective and Chief Marsden were pretty smart, surely smarter than two criminals. Kade, whatever his title was, seemed pretty intelligent. Loudon, she wasn't so sure about. He must have passed all the tests he needed to get as far as he had, so he couldn't have been totally inept. Hannah pushed these thoughts aside as she entered the store with Esther.

The little faceless doll still sat on the shelf, beckoning to Hannah. She crossed the creaking wood floor to pick up the doll.

"A toy to go with the books?" Esther teased.

A slight smile played about Hannah's lips. "I don't know what there is about this doll, but she calls to me. Silly, I suppose."

"*Nee.* Maybe she reminds you of something from your past," Esther offered.

"Maybe." Hannah couldn't tell her new friend that she was fairly certain no Amish dolls played a part in her past. Still, there was something about this doll. Reluctantly, she nestled the doll carefully back into her spot on the shelf.

"*Wie geht's*, ladies."

Hannah jumped and felt a flush creep up her face. Her heart as well as her ears recognized that deep soothing voice.

"Jake Beiler. Fancy meeting you here," Esther said. Hannah had yet to find her voice.

"I came to get more canning lids for my mamm. She's up to her ears in tomatoes." He twisted his straw hat in his hands then reached to push an unruly lock of blond hair off his face.

"Hannah needs fabric." Esther elbowed Hannah.

"*Jah*, fabric," Hannah echoed. Why were her thoughts scrambled around this big man with the brilliant blue eyes?

"*Gut* to see you again." Jake's gaze fastened on Hannah. "Uh, both of you," he amended, shifting his eyes to include Esther as well.

"Uh huh," Esther said, trying not to laugh. She poked Hannah. "The fabric?"

"Oh, *jah*," Hannah whispered and pulled her gaze away from the penetrating blue eyes.

"See ya!" Jake called as the women moved to select fabric. He chuckled.

"Your face is red," Esther whispered.

"Is not."

"You can't see it. I think his face is red, too. Hmmm!"

"You're *narrisch*! Here, I like the blue and purple material. I'd better get thread so I don't have to use Rebecca's."

Hannah endured Esther's good-natured teasing all the way home but returned the banter with ease. "Don't be spreading any rumors, Esther Stauffer," she admonished clutching her books and fabric to her after exiting the buggy.

"I'm not a gossip so don't worry. I just like to tease. Here." Esther held a tissue-wrapped package out to Hannah.

"What's this?" Hannah pulled away the tissue and squealed with delight as she freed the faceless Amish doll from the wrapping.

"I saw how much you liked the doll. If I could sew halfway decently, I'd have made you a doll, but something tells me you wouldn't want a doll with three arms and one leg."

Hannah laughed and reached up to squeeze Esther's hand. "*Danki.*"

"I'm glad to have you as a *friend.*" Esther dropped her gaze, suddenly looking embarrassed.

"You are a true *friend.*" Hannah squeezed Esther's hand again. "I'll treasure this gift." Hannah shifted the books and fabric to one arm and hugged the doll with the other arm. A tear rolled down her cheek as she watched Esther drive away.

These are truly wonderful people.

Chapter Nine

Hannah jabbed pins into her hair to keep it in a bun and fumbled to get the *kapp* positioned on her head. Darkness still shrouded the corners of her room this Saturday morning. The oil lamp turned low illuminated only the dresser where it sat. She didn't need much light to get ready for the day. She had no make-up to put on, no fancy hairstyles to arrange, but she did need to hurry downstairs to help Rebecca with breakfast preparations so they could gather items to take to the market.

They were heading to the big market a little further away across the county line. Hannah had been to the small Plain market next to the library several times, but this would be her first experience at the big market that was only open on Wednesdays and Saturdays. A finger of fear ran up her spine when she thought how she would be exposed to many more *Englischers*. She had begun to feel some measure of safety secluded with the Amish. Now, she'd have to leave her self-constructed cocoon and interact with a whole host of people.

Hannah reached for the little doll sitting beside the oil lamp. The family also used battery-powered lamps, but Hannah had been trying to become proficient in using the oil one.

She could discover no rationale for her attachment to this faceless doll, but she hugged it briefly to her chest. She was certain she was being totally ridiculous—a grown woman with a doll. A grown Amish woman with a doll. She probably shouldn't even have it displayed on her dresser.

The Amish would call her *narrisch* or at least *befuddled*, but she didn't think she was crazy or mixed up. Having lost all contact with her family, she felt a kind of kinship with the faceless doll.

But she was not faceless to God. She knew in her heart it was His voice she heard when she first saw the doll in Esh's store, the voice that told her she was His child. She returned the doll to the dresser and mentally asked God's blessing on Esther who seemed to recognize Hannah's need for the doll.

Hannah blew out the lamp and counted her steps to the door. She had this maneuvering in the darkness down to a science now. She heard pans rattle, letting her know Rebecca already worked in the kitchen.

She was finally growing used to eating thinned oatmeal or bread spread with apple butter or an occasional magnificent bowl of store-bought cereal for breakfast. She still missed her morning run, but her body told her all the walking and hard physical work she performed sufficed.

Her baggy dresses from Liz had grown baggier, and Hannah feared she was losing weight she could ill afford to lose. She may have to partake of some of the sweet treats the Amish so loved to bake.

Hannah entered the kitchen as Rebecca cracked eggs into a glass mixing bowl. The smell of bacon frying still upset her stomach but not as much as it had the first day she walked into the Hertzler home.

I must be adjusting.

Nevertheless, she still couldn't imagine herself actually ingesting bacon. Hannah picked up the wooden spoon to stir the thick oatmeal. This task always seemed to fall to her. She spied the box of cornflakes on the counter and silently blessed Rebecca for purchasing the cereal on her last store trip.

The family trooped in to take their places at the table. After the silent prayer, the boys and Emma chattered excitedly. Apparently, going to the big market was a special treat. They ate more quickly than usual and struggled to wait patiently while Rebecca and Hannah restored the kitchen to order.

The buggy had already been loaded with the produce and baked and home-canned goods the family planned to sell. They were going to share a booth with Esther's family, and Esther had promised to take Hannah on a tour of the market when they could wrangle a break.

Samuel steered them onto the main highway. Hannah, sitting between Eli and Jonas, clasped her hands so tightly her knuckles ached. Cars zooming by in excess of the speed limit caused the buggy to sway in their wake. She tried to gulp down her fear, loosened her fingers, and wiggled some feeling back into them. The children continued their chatter, oblivious to any possible danger—or accustomed to it. Hannah wasn't certain which.

Hannah exhaled with relief when Samuel maneuvered the buggy into the market parking lot.

She hadn't realized how shallowly she'd been breathing during the ride. Her lungs now demanded deep breaths of air. The children waited for their daed to give them the word to exit the buggy but quivered in anticipation beside Hannah.

Finally, Hannah climbed out on shaky legs and took a moment to steady herself before reaching for Elizabeth. She looked around at the busyness of the farmers' market. Cars already filled the parking lots, and numerous buggies and wagons were tethered to posts. A hint of a breeze promised some measure of relief from the already warm day.

Hannah passed Elizabeth back to Rebecca and reached for Emma's hand. Samuel pressed the boys into helping him unload their wares from the buggy.

"We'll meet you at the Stauffers' booth," Samuel called over his shoulder.

"All right," Rebecca answered.

Hannah glanced around. The first vendor she noticed sold assorted trinkets and market souvenirs. Various colors and types of t-shirts swung in the gentle breeze from a rope stretched above the booth.

A nearby trailer boasted steamed crabs. Hannah caught the scent of Old Bay seasoning as they strolled by. The almost sickeningly sweet smells of funnel cake and cotton candy transported Hannah back to carnivals she had attended as a child.

Produce stands lined the entire front of the market. Local farmers, *Englisch* and Amish, sold melons, corn, peaches, and tomatoes. Non-locals sold trucked-in kiwi, bananas, and pineapples. Booths along the sides of the market displayed signs advertising jewelry, clothing, pottery, movies, toys, and other assorted items Samuel termed "junk."

A small restaurant with limited indoor seating and an outdoor ordering window claimed to sell the best breakfast and lunch in Southern Maryland. Hannah had her doubts if the strong odor of grease was any indication.

Most of the Amish vendors occupied booths to one side of the market and sold everything from home-baked or home-canned food, quilts and other needlework, and wooden toys and furniture, to live chickens, roosters, and ducks.

Hannah stumbled slightly, almost throwing herself and Emma off balance when she spotted Jacob Beiler helping an *Englisch* couple with their oak rocking chair purchase.

Jacob chose that very instant to look up. He broke into a wide smile as he made eye contact with Hannah. She ventured a small wave in his direction before dropping her gaze. She couldn't encourage him. A quick peek told her he had returned to his conversation with the *Englischers*.

Samuel, Eli, and Jonas arrived at the booth just ahead of Rebecca and Hannah. Samuel lifted Elizabeth into his arms and instructed the boys to hold hands and stay right beside him. As promised, he would take them to see the animals and just maybe buy them cotton candy.

Rebecca arranged jars of jams, pickles, and canned fruits and vegetables on the wooden counter beside Naomi's baked goods. Esther's flowering and vegetable plants and small pots of herbs occupied the far side of the booth.

Hannah let Emma help her position the quilted potholders and crocheted dishcloths she had finally learned to construct. Maybe she could earn a little money and help buy groceries. At least she could buy cereal since she seemed to devour all of Rebecca's stash in her attempt to avoid greasy bacon and thick oatmeal.

Most of their customers were *Englisch* since the majority of the Amish here worked at their booths. There were some Amish patrons, though, mostly adults on a break or parents with young children who were browsing the different booths. Hannah soon found herself swept up in the carnival-like atmosphere and even got the hang of the bartering that was sometimes part of a sale.

She looked down when Emma tugged on her apron to whisper she needed to use the restroom.

"Do you mind taking her?" Rebecca turned to Hannah.

"Um, I don't know where…"

"I'll come along and show you," Esther offered. "Will you mind the plants, Mamm?"

"*Jah*, of course. Off with you before this sweet little one has an accident."

The small break actually felt good to Hannah. They walked past a kennel full of fluffy, yapping collie pups. Emma stopped and almost reached to pet the closest small sable and white head. Hannah grabbed the little hand before it snaked its way through the wire. "*Nee*. They may bite."

"Pretty puppies," Emma said.

"*Jah*, but they will grow to be very big dogs. *Kum*, let's find the restroom." Hannah tugged the reluctant little girl away from the adorable puppies. Emma scooted her feet, kicking up a cloud of dust, but obeyed.

Thankfully, they didn't have to wait in line at the restroom. They decided to bypass more animals on the way back to the Stauffer booth.

"*Wie geht's?*"

Esther and Hannah turned to locate the owner of the voice. "Ach, Sarah. You look *froh*," Esther called.

Happiness did shine in Sarah's face. Her eyes sparkled behind her wire-rimmed glasses. She practically skipped to catch up with them—not at all like a prim and proper school teacher.

"You look like the cat that ate the canary," Esther observed. "Spill!"

"Ach! It's just that a certain person has started working for Jeremiah Yoder. He really has a knack for taking things apart and putting them together." Sarah's face took on a dreamy expression as she talked.

"We wouldn't be talking about a certain young man by the name of Zeke Esh, would we?" Esther poked Sarah's arm with a finger.

"Shhh!"

"Well, maybe he's finally ready to settle down and take a *fraa*."

"Shhh, Esther, someone will hear!"

"They won't understand," Esther said. They had been speaking in Pennsylvania Dutch, and the only people close by were *Englisch*.

"That's *wunderbaar!*" Hannah squeezed Sarah's arm with the hand that wasn't clasping Emma's small, moist one.

"We may need a new school teacher after all," Esther teased.

"Esther, you're impossible." Sarah made a face at Esther.

Esther and Sarah both turned to Hannah when they heard her inhale sharply. Hannah whirled around, pulling Emma with her, and pretended to be fascinated by a display of pottery. She hoped the man in the red baseball cap didn't see her.

"*Was is letz?*" Esther had followed Hannah's gaze before she had tugged Emma over to the ceramic flower pots and bowls. "It-it's n-nothing," Hannah stammered.

"Does something about that man chaining the bicycle to the post bother you?" Sarah glanced in the man's direction.

"*Nee*. I...uh...who is he? He always seems to show up. H-he makes me *naerfich*, that's all."

"I don't know him. He seems harmless. Do you know him, Esther?"

"*Nee*, but he's off to some of the *Englisch* shops."

"Are you ladies okay?" a soft masculine voice intruded on their conversation.

"*Jah*," Hannah whispered, looking up and up to stare into Jake's blue eyes. Now, she wasn't sure if her heart pounded in double time because of the man on the bike or the handsome man standing in front of her. She prayed he wouldn't hear the thumping that echoed so loudly in her own ears.

"Hannah just got a little *ferhoodled*, that's all," Esther explained.

"I'll walk you back." Jake reached to touch Hannah's arm then drew his hand back as though he had picked up hot coal.

"*Danki.*" Hannah worked hard to get her voice out.

"I have to go," Sarah skittered off in the opposite direction. "See you soon," she called over her shoulder.

"There you are, safe and sound," Jacob announced as they reached the Stauffers' booth.

"*Jah*, safe and sound," Hannah echoed as Jake left to return to his own booth.

Was she?

"*Kum*," Rebecca said to Emma. She sat the little girl in one of the two chairs at the back of the booth and handed her half of a peanut butter and jam sandwich. "Sandwich, Hannah?"

"*Nee, danki.* I'm not hungry just yet." As she straightened some of the dishcloths that had escaped the pile, her fingers brushed a scrap of paper that fluttered to the ground. Bending to pick it up, she noticed dark lettering. She unfolded the paper and read the words.

"Little man by the window stood." Her forehead wrinkled as she pondered the cryptic message. "What in the world?"

"*Was ist letz?*" Rebecca moved to peer over Hannah's shoulder.

"Is this yours?" Hannah shook the paper.

"*Nee.* It doesn't make sense. Where did it come from?"

"It was under these dishcloths. Did you see who put it there?"

"*Nee.* We were busy. Let's see. I do remember an *Englischer* rummaging through the stack of cloths shortly before you came back."

"A man or a woman?"

"A man, actually. At first I thought it a little odd, but I figured he was looking for a gift for his *fraa*."

"Did you see him leave this paper?"

"*Nee.* I turned to help someone with canned goods. Why do you ask?"

"N-no reason. I j-just wondered about the strange note."

"People do all kinds of strange things," Rebecca assured Hannah, patting her arm.

"I suppose so." Hannah crumpled the paper and tossed it into the trash bag. Those words seemed vaguely familiar somehow. Hannah straightened and brushed her hands together as though to remove residue from the note.

Out of the corner of her eye, she caught the man in the baseball cap looking at her before unchaining his bike and riding out of the market parking lot. Could he have left the note? What did it mean?

Her hands trembled as she tucked an errant wisp of hair beneath her *kapp*. Her knees grew weak, and her heart skipped a beat.

"Are you okay?" Concern laced Rebecca's voice.

"*Jah.*" Hannah spoke barely above a whisper. She retreated to the shadows at the back of the booth where she stayed until Samuel and the boys came to help pack up items that hadn't sold.

Chapter Ten

Summer melted into fall with only marginal relief from the heat and humidity. Hannah sorely missed digging her toes into damp sand as she ran barefoot along the shore, waves licking at her legs and spray blowing into her face. If she closed her eyes, she could almost taste the salty air and feel the ocean breeze tangling her long ponytail. *It's all in the past,* she reminded herself.

She had settled into the routine of the Southern Maryland Amish community at last. Though far different from Virginia Beach, the area had a beauty and charm all its own. Lush green farms, untouched by modern machinery, stretched out for acres, one farm running into the next, interrupted occasionally by an *Englischer's* property.

Horses grazed among black and white cows. Impeccable yards boasted an array of colorful geraniums, begonias, and petunias. Birdhouses on poles or swaying from tree branches beckoned to the bluebirds, robins, martens, and other birds Hannah didn't have names for. Log Cabin and Lone Star quilts hung out to dry lending brightness to yards. Purple, black, blue, and green shirts and dresses flapped on the clothesline, forming a patchwork design of their own. Men, women, and children worked hard but played, too. And they cared, really cared, about each other. They had welcomed Hannah with open arms, and they cared about her, too.

Hannah took her place daily beside Rebecca, assisting with whatever chores the day demanded. She had about mastered the wringer washing machine and could clip pants, dresses, diapers, sheets, and towels on the clothesline almost as quickly as Rebecca. She had gotten the hang of baking bread and many other Amish treats. She swept, polished, dusted, and scrubbed as though the house was her own. And she loved the children as though they were her own.

One thing she still had trouble with, though, was hitching the horse to the buggy. The big, brown horse still frightened her at times. Thankfully, Jonas always volunteered to help her with the horse. There was something humbling about an eight-year-old helping her with this huge beast, as Jonas was doing right now. The little boy showed no fear of the huge animal. As far as horses went, Hannah supposed Brownie was a pretty gentle creature.

She knew she'd probably regret it, but she had let Sarah talk her into attending a Sunday evening singing. Church services had been held in the Beilers' big barn so they were hosting the singing. Sarah had told her that Daniel and Micah Beiler always attended singings but that Jacob hadn't put in an appearance since he returned from Ohio two years ago.

With that tidbit of information, Hannah felt pretty confident she wouldn't have to be afraid she'd make a fool of herself around Jacob. Her heart always seemed to pound around the soft-spoken, deep-voiced man, and, to her dismay, she always reverted to a pre-teen girl with a huge crush. Maybe she'd get to know some of the other young people since it looked like she would not be leaving Maryland any time soon.

Unfamiliar with most of the songs, Hannah hoped she gave a good impression of singing along. She moved her mouth at what she thought were appropriate intervals. She heaved a sigh of relief when the songs died off and people began to head for refreshments. Seated beside Sarah, she had observed and been amused by the silent exchanges between Sarah and Zeke who sat across from them. She supposed the pair thought they were being subtle.

Hannah rose from her seat and nodded greetings to people as she picked her way across the barn. A cup of juice or cider or whatever was available would feel heavenly on her parched throat. The singing—or imitation singing—had dried her mouth considerably.

She stopped in her tracks when she saw a tall, blond man standing in a dimly lit corner near the refreshments table. How long had he been there? Hannah's face grew warm. With any luck, the dim lighting would hide the flush that spread across her cheeks and up her scalp. She wiped her suddenly clammy hands on her apron before attempting to smooth the wrinkles from her purple dress.

I thought Sarah said he never attended!

Jacob shuffled over to Hannah as she inched toward him, drawn to him like a bug drawn to a lantern. He held out a cup filled with homemade root beer and cleared his throat twice. "Are you thirsty?"

"*Jah*, I am. *Danki*." Hannah accepted the offered cup in both hands since her fingers were trembling too violently to trust one hand to do the job. Why did she feel so nervous or shy around this man? She was a grown woman!

She raised the cup to her lips and took a tentative sip. She had never tasted root beer that hadn't come from a store-bought bottle or can.

"This is good." She licked the foam from her lips.

Hannah noticed that many of the young people had paired off and were engaged in private conversations. She smiled when she caught Sarah and Zeke slipping out the door.

"What are you smirking at?" Jake teased.

Hannah nodded toward the doorway where a laughing Sarah and Zeke had just disappeared.

Jake's eyes and lips crinkled. Hannah liked that his whole face smiled.

"Sarah sure seems happy," she said.

"*Jah*, I guess she'll finally get ol' Zeke to grow up. Maybe all that celery the Fishers planted won't go to waste, after all."

Hannah nudged Jake playfully. "Maybe." She ventured a gaze into his amazing eyes made even bluer by the blue cotton shirt he wore.

"How do you like our community?"

Jacob seemed seriously interested, not just making idle conversation. *Nice as well as good looking.* He waited patiently for Hannah to formulate an answer. Hannah knew Jacob didn't realize she often had to do quick translations in her head before she could make a sensible reply. She hoped her delay in answering was not thought too odd. After all, she was supposed to be recovering from a head injury.

"I like St. Mary's County just fine. It's small but quiet. I like quiet."

"Me too. I was in Sugar Creek for a while. It's nice there, too, but way more people. And lots of tourists. Good for business but not good if you like peace and quiet."

"So, you're glad to be home?"

"Definitely. This is where I'll stay."

Hannah observed a fleeting sadness creep across Jake's face. She wondered if he'd had a bad experience in Ohio. "Is everything all right?" She reached to tentatively touch his arm but quickly withdrew her hand, fearing the gesture would be too forward.

"Just some…uh, unpleasant memories."

"I think we all have those."

"For sure. How is your recovery coming along? I heard you had an accident."

"I'm doing better. I still have some forgetfulness." *That's not totally an untruth.* She didn't remember everything Liz told her or everything she read. Jacob's next question pulled her out of her reverie.

"You don't have family in Pennsylvania?"

"My parents died when I was young. I lived with my *aenti* and *onkel* while I was growing up. Now, I...I don't have them either."

"I'm so sorry, Hannah." This time, Jacob reached out to pat her arm in sympathy.

Her heart lurched at his touch. She couldn't tell him her relatives were alive but she was dead to them. She felt the same sort of sadness as if they were lost to her forever. It looked like they may very well be, the way the investigation was—or wasn't—going. She pasted a small, tremulous smile on her face.

"*Danki*, Jacob, for your concern. I appreciate it."

"That's what *freinden* are for, ain't so? I hope we're *freinden*."

"Of course!" Hannah's smile widened, matching the broad smile on Jake's face.

"Would you like some cookies or snacks?"

"Maybe so." They walked side by side to the table laden with cookies, brownies, and chips. Hannah ignored the inner voice warning her to put on the brakes. *Now!*

Jacob was not like the *Englisch* men Hannah had had the misfortune of dating. Most of them had been friends of friends and had not been anything like she had expected. Had it been too much to ask for someone like-minded in beliefs, someone to share good conversation with, someone who enjoyed similar activities and had no ulterior motive? She had yet to find such a man.

Now, here before her, stood a young man rooted in his faith, with strong family ties, and a genuine concern for others—even for her, a stranger in his midst. He was hardworking but quick to smile. He was tall and strong and terribly good looking.

"You're smiling again." Jacob handed Hannah a paper napkin. "You have a nice smile."

"It's easy to smile around you." The words left Hannah's mouth before she could snatch them back. What had happened to her filtering system? She quickly scanned the table and selected two cookies, an oatmeal raisin and a chocolate chip.

"Those are my favorites, too." Jacob took two of each as well as a chocolate brownie.

"Hungry?"

"Always. Looks like you could use a few more treats," Jacob retorted then looked instantly contrite as if fearing he had offended the woman at his side. "Oops! Sometimes I tease too much. Maybe I should fill my mouth so I don't say anything else stupid." He quickly stuffed a huge bite of oatmeal cookie in his mouth. His cheeks puffed out as he tried to chew.

Hannah burst out laughing. "Looks like you've bitten off more than you can chew." Jake could only nod. "And you're right. Either my clothes are growing, or I'm shrinking." Hannah looked at her loose dress.

Jake took a gulp of root beer to wash down the cookie. "I wouldn't want you to disappear." His face reddened all the way up to his ears that were mostly covered by his bowl haircut.

Hannah and Jacob continued to talk and laugh. All the while, Hannah tried to squelch the niggling inner voice telling her to run far away from Jacob Beiler. When Hannah finally took notice of her surroundings and removed her focus from the young man at her side, she gasped in astonishment.

"Where are all the people?" The crowd had noticeably thinned. "I-I didn't see them leave."

"Neither did I. I guess many couples have paired off."

"I hadn't planned to stay so late. I'm not terribly comfortable with Brownie and the buggy yet, especially in the dark."

"I'm sorry I kept you so long, talking your ear off. I don't usually do that. In fact, I haven't been to a singing since…since…since I came home." That somber expression claimed his countenance again.

"It's not your fault, Jake. I'm glad I stayed. I really enjoyed talking to you."

"I can't remember when I've had such a fine time. I'll help you hitch Brownie. In fact, I'll drive you home. It isn't far for me to walk back."

"Oh no, Jake. That's nice of you to offer. I will accept your help hitching Brownie, but I should be fine driving. It isn't too great a distance."

They walked side by side to the buggy, still chatting. Jake had the horse hitched before Hannah could even help. He made sure her lantern worked and held her arm as she climbed in.

In the semi-darkness, a white scrap of paper on the buggy seat appeared as bright as a neon sign. Hannah unfolded the paper as Jacob checked out the buggy's battery-operated flashers.

"Saw a rabbit hopping by," she whispered.

Just five words scrawled in black marker across the paper. Hannah stifled a cry. The other note *had* been meant for her. It wasn't merely some random piece of paper that fell out of someone's pocket. Someone was targeting her specifically.

How did they know she would be at the singing tonight? How had they slipped onto the Beilers' property and left the note in the right buggy? How was this note connected to the first one? What did it all mean? Hannah shivered. Now, she really was uneasy about driving alone in the dark.

"Hannah, are you okay? You're trembling."

"Uh...uh, I-I guess I am a little nervous," she finished lamely.

"Let me drive you." He started to climb into the buggy, apparently unable to let a frightened woman drove home alone in the dark.

"I-I'll be okay." She couldn't endanger Jake in any way or any of these people for that matter. Perhaps it wasn't wise, but she had come to care a great deal for Jake and all the Amish community. Yet her present fear was almost palpable.

"Slide over," Jacob ordered.

"*Nee*, Jake. You don't have to—"

"I know I don't have to but I *want* to make sure you get home safely."

Against her better judgment, Hannah scooted over to make room for Jacob. She breathed a sigh of relief when he took the reins and clucked to Brownie.

"*Danki*," she whispered, drawing further back into the shadowed buggy, the scrap of paper scrunched in her hand.

"Are you okay? You seem *ferhoodled*," Rebecca observed as she and Hannah tided the kitchen after breakfast.

"*Nee*. I mean, *nee* I'm not *ferhoodled*, but *jah*, I'm okay." Hannah fingered the scrap of paper in her pocket then drew her hand back as if touching some vile object. What should she do with it?

Her first inclination was to thrust it into the woodstove and watch the flames lap it up. But then the detectives may want it for evidence. What sort of DNA could they possibly lift from it now, though, after being wadded up in her pocket? Her DNA would probably be all they'd find.

"I know a certain someone was late getting home and didn't come home alone." Rebecca had a mischievous glint in her eyes as she turned from making a final swipe across the kitchen counter with her dishcloth.

"So you've become a spy now?"

"Let's just say I'm observant. Maybe there is romance in the air?" Rebecca smiled and winked.

"Go on with you! You like to weave stories."

"I only know what I saw."

"And what exactly did you see in the dark of night?"

"Ach! I saw a certain tall, blond man hop out of the buggy, unhitch Brownie, and lead him into the barn, and head down the road, whistling as he walked."

"You saw all that? And heard whistling too? You *would* make a good spy. You'd best be keeping your tall tales to yourself, my *freind*. I was nervous about driving the buggy in the dark. Jacob was kind enough to drive me home. That's all!"

"Ach, Hannah. You know I won't spread any gossip. I'd be happy if you found someone and settled here. You're family now."

"I know you're teasing, Rebecca. I think of you as family, too. I am so beholden to you and Samuel for putting up with me. I wish I could repay you."

"No talk of that. It's been *wunderbaar* having you here. It's like having a sister living with me, and the *kinner* love you."

"*Danki*, Rebecca. I love them, too. I don't know what I'd do without you."

Truly, Hannah didn't know what would have become of her if Samuel and Rebecca hadn't opened their home to her. If she had stayed in Virginia, would she even be alive now?

How could she contact Detective Bradford to tell him about the notes? How was she going to keep herself and the community safe? Could she find a way to sneak off to the phone shanty?

The morning flew by. Hannah had fought with the hateful washing machine and hung two loads of laundry on the line to dry in the fresh air. The temperature had dropped several degrees, so it was actually rather pleasant outside. Hannah had lingered as long as she dared at the clothesline, enjoying the beautiful day and the faint whiff of fall in the air.

She took a final deep breath before returning to the kitchen to help Rebecca with the baking. Hannah found she really enjoyed baking and discovered she was actually quite adept at it. A hidden talent, she surmised. "I'll finish with this last loaf of bread if you want to fix lunch."

"That's a great idea. With the work done early, maybe we can enjoy some of this beautiful day. Lunch is a little quicker with the boys in school now."

Jonas started second grade and Eli began his first year at the one-room school. Sarah must have her hands full with teaching children from first through eighth grades under one roof. Hannah thought such a set up could be fun but challenging, too. It reminded her of Laura Ingalls of the *Little House* books she had loved to read while growing up.

Samuel gave Rebecca a little hug and returned to his outdoor work after a lunch of thick roast beef sandwiches, pickled beets, sliced cucumbers and tomatoes, and assorted cookies.

Hannah had finally confessed to Rebecca that she could not bring herself to eat meat. Instead of chastising her, Rebecca made sure Hannah had a supply of lentils and beans to go with all the vegetables and fruits. Hannah felt relieved to have finally revealed her secret. This secret, at least.

Rebecca wiped Elizabeth's hands and face and lifted her from the high chair. She let the girls play for a few minutes while she and Hannah once again cleaned the kitchen and then led the girls toward their bedroom for a nap.

"I'll just go for a little walk and get the mail," Hannah said. "Then I'll help with whatever you need done."

"Take your time and enjoy the sunshine. The work won't go anywhere."

Hannah nodded and smiled. Rebecca was always so understanding and so patient and loving with her and with her *kinner*. Hannah hoped she, too, would be a good a mother one day.

Hannah practically skipped down the gravel driveway, reveling in the cooler but bright, sunny day. She mentally scolded herself and forced herself to slow down to a more appropriate fast walk.

This would be a great day for a run, but it looks like my running days are over. I've probably lost all my endurance for running, but at least I'm getting plenty of other exercise.

The magnolia tree continued to sport big white flowers whose sweet fragrance permeated the air. Hannah breathed deeply. Geraniums still bloomed and green leaves trimmed with a hint of yellow or red still clung to the trees. The whole earth was on the fringe of fall.

At the end of the long driveway, Hannah wondered if she could surreptitiously slip across the road to the phone shanty. She had dropped some change into her pocket when she first dressed this morning, figuring the phone was an old-fashioned pay type. Hannah glanced right and left and behind her.

Seeing no one, she skittered across the road and squeezed into the phone booth. She held the receiver to her ear and jiggled buttons when she heard no dial tone. She dropped coins into the slot but still got no beeps or buzzes. She jiggled more buttons. Silence. Great! Dead phone. Hannah pressed the coin return and waited for the machine to spit the change into her hand. Now what?

Hannah quickly surveyed the area before darting back to Samuel's property. She shuffled along the driveway, trying to devise a way to inform the police of the notes.

She double backed to the mailbox when she suddenly remembered she promised to retrieve the mail. She pulled out the latest edition of *The Budget*, the Plain newspaper Samuel and Rebecca received weekly but found no letters. Maybe they had slid to the back of the box. She stretched to reach the far corners of the big metal box and pulled out three letters.

"What in the world?" *Hannah Kurtz* had been scrawled across the top envelope. Who would be writing to her? After the cryptic notes she'd received, she was skeptical about opening the envelope.

"The postmark is Pennsylvania. I don't know anyone in Pennsylvania," she murmured.

She chewed her bottom lip, summoned up her courage, and slid her finger under the loosened corner of the envelope. She pulled out a smaller envelope and thought of those stacking dolls, one inside the other. Why were there two envelopes? Should she open the second one?

Fingers of fear snaked up her spine and prickled her scalp. She took a deep breath, tore the second envelope's flap, and shook out the papers inside.

Before reading the content of the letter, she turned to the last page, seeking a signature. *Liz*. Whew! Hannah relaxed her shoulders and tilted her head from side to side to relieve the tension that had built in her neck and shoulder muscles. She turned back to the first page and began reading.

Hannah smiled at Liz's quaint phrasing and was touched by her concern. Liz wrote she had been thinking of Hannah and had been praying for her. In a roundabout way, she let Hannah know the criminals had not yet been captured and the investigation continued in earnest. Another murder had been attributed to the same men.

Why hadn't those guys been caught yet? They hadn't seemed particularly intelligent. In fact, the taller one didn't seem to care that she got a pretty good look at him. It was almost as if he wanted her to see him.

Hannah sucked in a ragged breath. *Did* he want her to see him? Was she the mouse in his cat-and-mouse game? Had he intended for her to be the next victim all along? Surely not. Why would they target a poor librarian?

Hannah shivered and glanced nervously over her shoulder, half expecting to see an unkempt man in a baseball cap and a short, burly, balding man lurking in the shadows. She knew Liz only meant to update her and not add to her fears.

Liz mentioned her Amish cousins in Lancaster County who were willing to forward letters back and forth between them if Hannah wished to correspond.

Hannah did wish to correspond. Maybe somehow, Liz could find out if Aunt Genevieve and Uncle Ted, Rennie, and Michael were safe and well. Maybe she could get more news about the investigation. Maybe she could tell Liz about the two notes and have her pass the information along to her brother-in-law. Yes. That's exactly what she would do.

Tonight, she would compose a letter to Liz and reveal her suspicions. She wished the letter could go directly to Virginia rather than to Pennsylvania first. If she tied a note to a pigeon, it would probably reach Virginia faster. She stuffed Liz's letter and the small envelope inside the larger envelope as she approached the house.

"Any *gut* news?" Hannah jumped at the sound of Samuel's voice. She hadn't noticed him standing outside the barn.

"Huh?"

Samuel nodded to the newspaper in Hannah's hand. "In the paper?"

"I don't know. Would you like to see it?" Hannah held out the papers. So Samuel had seen her reading.

"*Nee*. I'll read it tonight."

"I got a letter from Pennsylvania," she said. She didn't want Samuel to think she had been reading his or Rebecca's mail and snooping into their business.

"*Gut. Gut.* Everything okay there?"

"*Jah*. I'll take your paper and mail inside." Was he suspicious, or did she just have a guilty conscience because of her pretense?

"*Danki*."

Hannah couldn't explain why she felt nervous, like a school kid who got caught cheating. It seemed perfectly reasonable that she would receive a letter from home — if indeed Pennsylvania had been her home.

Life is too confusing.

"Rebecca," Hannah called, entering the house. "I'll put the mail here on the table." Hannah peeked into the family room.

Rebecca's head lolled back on the chair. Her eyes were closed. Eli's pants she had been mending had dropped to the floor. Hannah rushed across the room and touched Rebecca's arm gently.

"Rebecca, *was is letz?*"

Rebecca's eyes snapped open as she jerked upright. "Ach! I fell asleep. I've just been tired lately. That's all. I guess I'd better think of starting supper."

"I can do that. You can rest longer. Are you sick?"

"*Nee.* Just a little tired. I'll feel better when I get moving."

"Are you sure?"

"I'm sure." Rebecca retrieved the pants from the floor and returned them to her mending basket before pushing to her feet.

"I got a letter from h-home." Hannah stumbled over the word. "I'll just run it up to my room and be right back to help."

Hannah bounded up the stairs. She hadn't seen Rebecca nap before. She hoped she wasn't ill. Maybe Elizabeth had awakened during the night, disturbing Rebecca's sleep.

For some reason unknown to her, Hannah buried the letter under her underwear in the top dresser drawer. She rushed back downstairs to help Rebecca. As Rebecca browned beef for soup, Hannah cut up potatoes and carrots. Hannah couldn't help but notice the dark circles ringing Rebecca's eyes, but when she asked, Rebecca insisted she was fine. Hannah offered a quick, silent prayer for the young mother she had grown so fond of.

Chapter Eleven

The next morning, Hannah bounded out of bed early and immediately leaped to the rag rug. The mornings were certainly cooler now if the cold wood floor under her bare feet was any indication. She pulled on one of Rebecca's old work dresses and pinned her apron.

Although not a big person, Rebecca must be at least several sizes larger than Hannah. Rebecca had hemmed and altered a few dresses for Hannah, but they still swallowed her. Hannah fumbled to keep her baby-fine hair securely pinned before positioning her *kapp*.

"Too cool for bare feet," she mumbled, pulling on black stockings and shoes.

She wondered what it was like at home. Was the ocean air a lot brisker now? How was her family? Did the library already replace her with a new employee?

Hannah shook her head. "This is home now, and it's really not so bad." Rebecca even planned to hire a driver to take them to Wal-Mart later in the week. Hannah chuckled.

My, how life had changed! She used to visit malls and quaint Virginia Beach shops to at least browse if she didn't have money to make purchases. Now, it was a thrill to anticipate visiting Wal-Mart!

"You've come a long way, Hannah girl," she whispered, bending to tie her sturdy black shoes. She paused as the realization hit her: Hannah.

When had she stopped thinking of herself as Lilly? She really had become Hannah. She tied her second shoe and straightened up. She slipped her reply to Liz into her pocket and, now accustomed to the lay of the house, felt her way downstairs in the pre-dawn darkness.

"*Gude mariye*, Hannah," Rebecca said as Hannah entered the kitchen. No smell of frying bacon or sausage greeted her, for which she was grateful. Instead, Rebecca alternately flipped pancakes and stirred the daily oatmeal. Maybe all the oatmeal gave the Amish healthy hearts and offset the high-fat, high-sugar foods they consumed.

"*Gude mariye*, Rebecca." Hannah tried not to scrutinize, but she couldn't help but notice Rebecca's drawn appearance and her shaky hand that stirred the pot of oatmeal. "What would you like me to do?"

Rebecca slid the frying pan off the heat and practically tossed the wooden spoon at Hannah before racing from the room.

"Rebecca?" Hannah called. The other woman didn't acknowledge her but stayed her course. Hannah stirred, banged the spoon against the pot to dislodge the oatmeal adhering to it, and pushed the pot back. She transferred the pancakes from the pan to the pile of golden brown pancakes already stacked on a plate. Somehow, they looked better than the pancakes she used to help Aunt Genevieve make.

Rebecca shuffled into the room subconsciously rubbing her stomach. Her ashen color emphasized the dark circles rimming her eyes.

"Are you ill?"

Rebecca shook her head but looked about ready to collapse.

Frightened now, Hannah rushed to pull out a kitchen chair and helped Rebecca sit. "Maybe I should dri-take you to the doctor." Hannah bit her tongue. She hoped Rebecca didn't notice her near slip up. She almost said "drive" — how was she supposed to drive anywhere?

"Maybe I should get Samuel?" She began to wring her hands. She wasn't sure what she should do.

"*Nee*. I'll be okay," Rebecca whispered. She spoke again softly as though to herself. "It's never been this bad before."

"What? What did you say, Rebecca? You've had this before?" Did she have some kind of medical condition? Some recurring virus or something?

"*Jah*."

Hannah slapped her forehead. "What a *dummchen* I am! Rebecca, are you, are you…" How did she ask an Amish woman this delicate question? Hannah felt her cheeks flush.

"*Jah*. Another *boppli* is on the way. I just have never felt so sick with the others."

"Have you seen a doctor?"

"*Nee*. I'll ask Sophie for something, though."

"Sophie? The medicine woman? Are you sure that's a good idea in your—your condition?" *Oops! I hope I don't sound too Englisch.*

"'Tis all right, Hannah. Sophie has some natural remedies to help with the queasiness, that's all. They're safe. Just herbs."

"What about a doctor?"

"I'll see the midwife."

"You have an Amish midwife here?"

"*Nee*. Carrie Lawson is a nurse midwife. She has an office out on the main road. She usually delivers our babies. She has a birthing center in her office but will come to our homes."

"Oh." Hannah was relieved Rebecca would see someone with medical training.

Nurse midwives and nurse practitioners had practices at home in Virginia. Her own healthcare provider was a nurse practitioner so she felt reassured.

A home birth sounded a little scary, but Rebecca made it sound like a normal occurrence. She didn't want to be nosey or demanding but couldn't stop herself from asking,

"Will you see her soon?"

"*Jah*."

"You promise?"

Rebecca smiled and patted Hannah's hand as though Hannah were the pregnant woman.

"Birth is a perfectly natural thing, but I believe Carrie is in her office today."

"*Gut*. Would you like me to go with you or stay with the girls so Samuel can go?"

"You may come with me, but we'll take the girls. Samuel has work to do."

"Okay."

"Time, now, for breakfast. Samuel and the boys are coming." As if on cue, footsteps stomped up the steps and inside.

"I'll get the girls," Hannah offered.

"*Danki*, Hannah."

Not a word was mentioned about Rebecca's plan to see the midwife. Breakfast progressed normally. Eli and Jonas grabbed their lunch pails and headed for school. Samuel stroked Rebecca's cheek tenderly, a look of concern crossing his face. Rebecca smiled and patted his hand that cupped her chin. Samuel gave his wife the briefest of kisses and turned to retrieve his hat before following the boys outside. Hannah wondered if she would ever have a husband who showed her such love and concern.

Hannah flew through the kitchen chores, pressing Rebecca gently back onto the chair whenever she attempted to rise.

"I'm not an invalid," Rebecca complained.

"I know. I don't mean to treat you like an invalid. I just want you to rest."

"I've been through this four times and kept up with all my chores."

"I'm sure you did, Rebecca. But now, you have me." Hannah smiled brightly.

"*Jah*, I do but…"

"Then please let me help you. You said you are feeling worse than the previous times, so just rest a bit. Please."

"You win, Hannah. I truly am glad to have you here."

Hannah dried her hands and hung up the red plaid dish towel. I'll go get the buggy ready."

Rebecca could only nod. With one hand on her stomach and the other over her mouth, she charged for the bathroom.

"I'll be right back!" Hannah called.

The door slammed behind Hannah as she headed for the barn. She was thankful that Brownie was a gentle old soul or else she would have been in serious trouble. She hoped her fingers wouldn't fumble too much so she could get Brownie hitched in relatively short order.

Could the **crispness** in the morning air be a harbinger of fall? Hannah hoped so. She relished the end of the hot summer and the promise of cooler weather.

"Ach, Samuel. Were you going to use the buggy?"

Samuel was just giving Brownie an affectionate pat after hitching him to the black buggy. "*Nee*. I thought Rebecca…uh…may need to go out."

Hannah didn't know why she flushed at the reference to Rebecca's "delicate condition." She used to discuss women's pregnancies with ease. Maybe she was becoming Amish after all. *Now there's a thought.*

Rebecca trudged to the buggy where Samuel helped her climb in. He gave her a knowing look and squeezed her arm. Then he lifted Emma and Elizabeth in, admonishing them to be good. Hannah hopped into the buggy with ease now and picked up the reins. "Ready?"

"Let's get this over with," Rebecca answered.

"I just need to stop at the end of the driveway to mail my letter."

"That's fine. We don't need to rush. It's not an emergency, you know."

Hannah still fretted over driving a horse and buggy in traffic, but the midwife's office was only about a mile or so down the more heavily travelled highway. Hannah believed she could at least handle that short drive.

She prayed the morning commuters had already passed through. Rebecca seemed to be relaxing a bit and taking in deep breaths of air free of cooking odors.

Breathing easier herself once they arrived safely, Hannah jumped from the buggy to tie Brownie to the post outside the midwife's office. The office was actually a converted white two-story Cape Cod. *Interesting,* Hannah mused.

Emma bounced from the buggy unassisted as Hannah reached to take Elizabeth from her mother's arms. Rebecca's color had improved slightly from the earlier sickly pale color.

"Are you okay?" Hannah snatched Emma's hand before the little girl could take a step.

"Better." She reached out to take Elizabeth who squirmed to get out of Hannah's arms.

"I've got her." Hannah bounced the toddler to divert her attention. "Let's get you signed in or whatever."

They climbed the cement steps and crossed the threshold into a very homey waiting room that looked more like a living room than a medical office waiting room. Comfortable chairs and a sofa replaced standard hard plastic office chairs.

A children's area occupied one corner with a child-sized table and chairs, a busy box, puzzles, books, and toys. Emma looked longingly at that corner but didn't attempt to break free of Hannah's hold. Only one other very obviously pregnant woman sat reading a baby magazine.

Maybe we won't have a long wait, Hannah thought.

Rebecca signed in and carried a clipboard of forms to a chair near the play area. She sank into the overstuffed armchair with a sigh. Hannah steered Emma to the play area and deposited Elizabeth beside the busy box. Both girls began to play quietly.

A nurse in stork-print scrubs called Rebecca back to the examining room. Emma started to follow her mother, but Hannah grabbed her back. She sat on one of the little chairs, thankful she was small enough and lightweight enough to fit.

She retrieved a book from the basket on the floor and began reading aloud softly. Immediately, Elizabeth crawled into her lap, and Emma sat enrapt at her feet. Hannah read one book after another until the door to the examining area opened.

"Now, Rebecca, I want you to take it easy as much as possible. Try to rest when your little ones are napping."

The midwife accompanied Rebecca to the waiting room. Carrie Lawson was probably in her thirties, maybe late thirties. She stood taller than Hannah, but Rebecca's Jonas would soon be taller than Hannah! Carrie's brown hair fell in a short bob that framed her face. She appeared very professional in navy slacks and blue-and-white print blouse covered by a white lab coat.

"I have help at home right now," Rebecca was saying, interrupting Hannah's study of the woman. "*Kum*, Hannah. Meet Carrie."

Hannah shook Carrie's hand as Rebecca explained that Hannah was staying with the Hertzlers.

"You have a lovely waiting room, so home-like," Hannah blurted.

"Would you like to see the birthing center?" Carrie offered. "It seems to be a slow morning so I have time for the tour." Carrie smiled and nodded toward the waiting room devoid of patients.

"*Jah*." Hannah barely remembered to reply as an Amish woman.

Carrie obviously took great pride in her center. Upstairs, she had two birthing rooms that resembled ordinary bedrooms. Beautiful handmade quilts adorned the beds.

"My patients make me lovely presents." Carrie indicated the quilts and wall hangings.

"That's because we appreciate your care and kindness," Rebecca murmured.

A huge tub practically filled another room. Carrie smiled at Hannah's raised eyebrows.

"Some moms like water births or just like to relax in the tub during labor," Carrie explained. Hannah merely nodded. Carrie assured Hannah she had all the appropriate supplies to handle births and that she did not hesitate to transfer women to the hospital if she felt it was necessary.

The little group returned to the waiting room where Carrie gave Rebecca further instructions. "Be sure to make an appointment in *three* weeks and try to rest. You can try the remedies for nausea."

"*Danki*, Carrie."

As they made their way to the buggy Hannah couldn't wait any longer to ask, "Is everything okay? You're coming back in three weeks—she stressed three."

"Everything is fine. Stop fretting. Carrie's lady who does those fancy ultrasounds was there. Carrie wanted me to have one since I feel so different this time." Rebecca held up two fingers.

Hannah's mouth dropped open. Not wanting to say anything aloud around little listening ears, she mouthed, "twins?" Rebecca nodded and broke into a wide grin. Hannah hugged Rebecca awkwardly around Elizabeth and cried, "*Wunderbaar*, ain't so?"

"For sure. Let's stop at Sadie's on the way home. I'm feeling somewhat better," Rebecca continued. "I'll drive since I know you're still a little *naerfich* on the main road."

"Won't Samuel be surprised?" Hannah exclaimed. They had exited the main road and were now heading back along a side road.

Rebecca laughed and nodded her head. "That he will be."

A short distance ahead, Hannah could make out a biker riding on the edge of the road. *Not again*! As they clopped along, closing the distance between them, Hannah relaxed and unclenched her fists.

This was definitely a different person. This man was a serious biker dressed in his black spandex bike shorts and silver helmet, toned muscles pumping the pedals. No baseball cap.

Hannah pried herself from the corner of the buggy where she had retreated and looked forward to the visit with the medicine woman.

Chapter Twelve

Sophie Hostetler's rambling two-story house was situated at the end of a long, winding dirt road. Tall loblolly pine trees lined the road, their long needles appearing soft and fuzzy. Hannah smiled as she inhaled, the strong pine scent, taking her back to Girl Scout camp where she rambled through the woods with Rennie and the whole troop of girls.

"Sophie's husband's parents lived in the *dawdi* house there on the left before they passed." Rebecca pointed out the house as she stopped Brownie on the right side of the house. "This little side protrusion on the right is Sophie's shop."

Hannah nodded, climbed from the buggy, and shook the wrinkles out of her dress before reaching for the girls.

"We won't be too long," Rebecca called to the approaching man whose salt and pepper beard reached his chest. "We don't need to unhitch."

"*Gut* to see you all, Rebecca."

"*Danki*, Gid."

"Sophie should be right inside."

"*Danki*," Rebecca repeated. The door squeaked open before Rebecca, Hannah, and the girls had mounted the steps.

"*Wilkom*." Sophie greeted them as she stepped out onto the porch. Her graying brown hair severely secured in a tight bun looked almost painful to Hannah. No wonder some of these women had thinning hair.

I've got to remember to keep my hair a little loose, which probably won't be much of a problem since it slides out of the hairpins on a regular basis.

Sophie was tall and thin with silver-framed glasses perched on the end of her slightly upturned nose. Her easy smile and almost musical voice contradicted her rather stern demeanor.

"*Gude mariye*, Sophie. *Wie bist due heit?*"

"I'm doing all right, Rebecca. Nice to see you again, Hannah."

"Sophie, I'm needing some herbs."

"Well, you've come to the right place." Sophie's smile broadened. "*Kum* inside and tell me what I can get for you."

The little group entered the mud room and crossed the threshold into the small room Gid had built onto the main house for Sophie's herbs and natural remedies.

The air smelled of lavender and roses and some sweet, spicy mixture. Was it cinnamon and mint and ginger? Hannah couldn't be sure.

She gazed around the long, narrow room, noting the flowers hanging upside down from the ceiling to dry. She recognized the roses and lavender but wasn't certain of the names of the other flowers in various stages of drying.

Shelves along one long wall held tea, vials of powders and oils, and pretty jars filled with spices. A sign in front of a stack of small colorful squares of fabric on the counter advertised lavender sachets to promote relaxation and sleep. Jars of salves and creams occupied shelves across the room along the opposite wall.

There must be a remedy for whatever ailed a body tucked into one of these jars or vials, Hannah surmised. She wondered how Sophie had learned the uses of all these medicinals. Had the knowledge been passed down to her?

As if reading Hannah's mind, Sophie explained. "Those jars there are for skin treatments. Some are for dry skin, some for rashes, and some for cuts or burns." She pointed to each jar and rattled off some of the ingredients to differentiate the products.

She waved at the other shelf. "Over there are things to help just about anything from an upset stomach to joint pain. And they really do help or I wouldn't give them to people."

"This is amazing. You have so many natural ingredients. I'm fascinated." Once again, Hannah hoped she didn't sound too *Englisch*.

"Come by anytime and I'll be happy to tell you more."

"I'd like that."

"Now, Rebecca. What is it you're needing today?"

"Well, now, Sophie. I'm after something to settle my stomach down a mite." Rebecca rubbed her belly as though to soothe the beast.

"A little queasy, are you dear?" A grin spread across Sophie's. "Seems you've had this before."

"*Jah*. Several times."

"Let's see then. Ginger root tea is always *gut*. Some folks also like peppermint or cinnamon, too."

"I might try a little of each. I'll see which one works best."

"Hmm. That stomach must be treating you pretty mean, ain't so?" Sophie's grin widened, creasing her face.

"It surely is."

"Do you think you might need some raspberry tea, too? It's helpful for the morn—uh…sickness and also strengthens…uh, the womb."

Hannah choked back her laughter as she watched the other two women dance around the subject of pregnancy.

"*Jah*, Sophie, I think the raspberry tea will be right helpful."

Sophie chuckled and practically tapped a little jig. "I'm so happy for you, Rebecca."

"Now, Sophie, this is our little secret right now, okay?"

"For sure and for certain, Rebecca. I won't breathe a word."

"I appreciate that."

"Now, let's get those teas. I'm going to throw in a lavender sachet, too. No charge. Put it under your pillow to help you relax. I'm giving you one, too,

Hannah, just in case you have any bad dreams and can't rest."

Was the woman a mind reader, too?

"*Danki*," Hannah accepted the blue-and-white calico print sachet. "That's so thoughtful of you."

"Wait just one second. I have some fresh snickerdoodles for the girls." Sophie whisked through the door and returned promptly with two heavenly smelling, cinnamon-covered cookies for each child.

"*Danki*, Sophie." Rebecca pulled money from her purse to pay for her purchases and handed the napkin-wrapped cookies to Hannah for safe keeping.

"Ach! Before I forget. Would you mind terribly taking these herbs to Naomi Beiler? When her rheumatism acts up, these seem to give her relief," Sophie said.

"No problem at all. I think I'll wait until after lunch and the *kinner* have a nap, if that's okay."

"Sure. No rush. I'm thinking maybe you need a bit of a nap yourself, Rebecca. You look a mite peaked."

"I do feel pretty done in. A nap would be right nice."

"I can take Naomi's herbs to her later. It's a nice day for a walk, ain't so?" Hannah still sometimes struggled using the word "ain't," but she knew the word was part of the normal Amish vocabulary. Other phrases she uttered with relative ease. This was the only one that stuck in her throat.

"Tis a *gut* day for a walk," Sophie agreed. "Here, I'll put the vials in a separate little bag for you."

"I appreciate your offering to take Naomi's herbs, Hannah," Rebecca said with a sigh. "It's been a long morning."

"I don't mind at all. I think Sophie is right. You need to rest this afternoon. I can finish the chores and start supper when I get home." Amazing! Now she thought of Rebecca's house as home.

Hannah transferred Naomi's bag to her left hand as Emma reached for her right hand. She and Rebecca bid Sophie goodbye and hustled the little girls out to the buggy. Rebecca promised they could each nibble on one cookie on the way home and save the other cookies for later.

"Take care!" Sophie called from the porch.

Hannah wanted to be helpful, but now, she questioned her offer to visit Naomi. What if she saw Jacob? What if she didn't see Jacob? What was this magnetic force she felt pulling her toward the handsome furniture maker?

Shortly after they arrived home, Hannah heated up the lentil soup she had prepared the day before while Rebecca assembled ham, cheese, and tomato sandwiches. Samuel didn't complain about the meatless soup as long as he had meat somewhere in the meal.

Rebecca placed two sandwiches on a plate for Samuel who would be ravenous after working to harvest the field corn all morning. She set half of a sandwich at Emma's place at the table and bread with cheese on Elizabeth's high chair tray. Hannah ladled soup for everyone.

"Where is your sandwich?" Hannah didn't see a plate for Rebecca.

"I think I'll just try soup. You may make a vegetarian out of me at the rate I'm going!"

Hannah smiled. "Would that be so bad?"

"*Nee*, just not normal for me."

"What's not normal for you?" Samuel entered the kitchen and looked from Rebecca to Hannah.

"Not eating meat. It just doesn't sit too well in my stomach these days."

"Just try to eat, Becky."

"At least the lentils are good protein for you," Hannah said.

"*Jah*. And I think I can get the soup to stay down."

Hannah shooed Rebecca from the kitchen at the end of the meal and encouraged her to at least rest while the girls napped.

"I'll clean up and then take Naomi's herbs to her. The house will be nice and quiet for you."

"*Gut*. You haven't been sleeping well, Beck. You need rest for yourself and the wee ones." Samuel shook his head. "Two!" he exclaimed.

He apparently took the news of twins in stride and actually seemed thrilled. Hannah wondered how some of the *Englisch* men she knew would accept such a pronouncement.

"Doubly blessed," Rebecca murmured.

"That we are." Samuel kissed Rebecca's cheek before plopping his straw hat on his head and returning to the field. "Rest now." He wagged a finger at his wife.

Hannah took a deep breath as she skipped down the porch steps. The clear, crisp air had a touch of autumn, giving her energy that the summer's heat and humidity had zapped. If she could whistle, she would belt out a happy tune.

No matter how many times her cousin Michael had tried to teach her to whistle, she just could not seem to master the skill. She would purse her lips and blow until her ears popped but never produced a single musical sound. Michael would laugh hysterically.

Dear Michael. How was he?

"It's a beautiful day. I'm not going to think sad thoughts," Hannah said under her breath. She tucked Naomi's package inside her pocket and set off at a brisk pace, humming in lieu of whistling.

At least I can hum.

Hannah studied the phone shanty for a moment, debating whether she should check the phone for a dial tone.

No use. I didn't bring any money anyway.

She wondered how long it would take for Liz to receive her letter and then decided not to think about that either.

Only a few puffy clouds interrupted the brilliant blue sky. The sun shone gave warmth but not scorching heat.

I wonder if I can still run. This would be a great day to run.

Her black sneakers would support her feet. The long dress would be a challenge, though. Once on the road, she glanced furtively right, left, and behind. Just a few squirrels observed her.

She broke into a slow jog to test herself before picking up the pace. *Huff, puff, huff, puff.* She got into her old familiar rhythm and ran until she reached the edge of the Beilers' property where she dropped back to a jog for a moment and further reduced her stride to a fast walk. Her panting subsided as her heart rate dropped. She inhaled deeply.

"That felt good," she told the fat brown rabbit nibbling a tuft of clover. Startled at the sound of her voice, the rabbit hopped into the woods.

"Sorry," Hannah called to the animal. "You don't have to be afraid of me. I won't eat you." Maybe she could figure out a way to sneak out and run a few times per week.

Striding up the Beilers' driveway, Hannah reached to straighten her lopsided *kapp* and tuck stray wisps of fine hair into the pins that didn't quite hold the slippery strands tightly enough. She smoothed her dress and apron. She hoped she didn't smell too bad. She patted her pocket to make sure Naomi's herbs were still safe.

A saw's buzzing grew louder as she neared the house and workshop. She had almost reached the house when the buzzing ceased and masculine voices filled the brief silence.

"So you think you will move back here?"

Jacob's deep voice was unmistakable. Hannah could hear it in her sleep. Best not to think that, she told herself. She would try to sneak into the house undetected.

"*Jah.* I'm surely thinking on it."

The voices grew closer. Hannah feared discovery. Whose owned the other voice? She quickened her pace, hoping to reach the back door of the house before the voices reached her.

She didn't want to see Jacob. She did want to see Jacob. Hannah ground her teeth. She could *not* get involved.

"Hannah!" That deep, soothing voice called just before her hand made contact with the door. Almost made it! She could ignore him, pretend she didn't hear. She could not.

"Jacob." Hannah turned to look at the two approaching men. She felt herself drowning in the sea of Jacob's eye but was powerless, now, to turn away, especially since Jacob stared back into her eyes.

Jacob cleared his throat twice. "You remember Andrew, Sarah's cousin from Ohio?"

"*Jah,* Sugar Creek, ain't so? *Gut* to see you."

"Same here. *Jah,* I'm visiting from Sugar Creek. Jake and I worked together for his Uncle Abe back when Jake stayed in Sugar Creek. I'm leaving for home in a few days."

"Say, Hannah, don't you think Andrew should join us at the singing Sunday before he leaves? There may be someone he wants to talk to." Jacob winked as his face split into a wide grin.

Hannah had only attended one singing so far. Jacob had said "us." Was this his way of saying he hoped she would attend?

"And who might that be?" Andrew elbowed Jake.

"A certain dark-haired *maedel* with—"

"With dirt under her fingernails and a sharp tongue?"

Hannah smiled at Andrew's description. Undoubtedly, Esther's opinion of him would not be a great deal more favorable. They both freely spoke their minds. They'd be perfect together. It might be entertaining to watch them interact.

"I think you'd enjoy yourself at the singing." Mentally, she tried to devise a way to entice Esther to attend.

"Well...maybe."

"Is your mamm inside? Sophie sent something for her."

"*Jah*. Just go on in."

"Okay." Hannah again reached for the door but could still hear the men's conversation.

"You know you have a job here," she heard Jake say.

"*Danki*. When I come back at wedding season—and I'm pretty sure I will from all the celery at Sarah's house—I may just be coming for *gut*. I'll write to let you know."

"*Gut*. But we'll see you at the singing before you go, ain't so?"

"You don't give up, do you?" Andrew called as he walked toward the horse and wagon he had borrowed to make the visit.

Hannah shared a glass of ice-cold lemonade with Naomi who was obviously pleased by Hannah's visit and grateful to receive the herbal preparations she delivered. After her run, Hannah's throat felt devoid of all moisture. The lemonade hit the spot.

"The girls will be getting up from their naps soon, and the boys will be returning home from school. I want to help Rebecca prepare dinner and finish up chores." Hannah drained the last drop from her glass.

"You are a big help to Rebecca for sure and for certain. Please come back when you can stay awhile."

"I surely will, Naomi. I hope these herbs help you feel better soon. *Danki* for the lemonade."

Hannah assumed Jacob would be back at work on some cabinet or dresser or something. Certain she was alone, she felt free to hum a song that hovered at the edge of her memory.

She stepped back out into the sunshine and drew in a deep breath. The scent of the freshly cut wood mingled with the scent of stain or lacquer, Hannah wasn't sure which. It didn't matter. She had always loved these smells. Now, how on earth could she persuade Esther to attend the singing?

Hannah gasped when she felt a hand on her arm. *They found me*! She jerked her arm and got ready to let out a scream.

"Sorry, Hannah. It's just me."

"Ach, Jake! You scared me. I didn't hear you."

"I wasn't trying to sneak up on you."

"I know. I guess I was just lost in thought."

"And singing."

"Humming. You probably wouldn't want to hear me sing." Hannah laughed.

"You probably have the voice of an angel."

"I doubt it."

"What was the song? I didn't recognize it?"

"Hmmm. Let's see. I was humming kind of absentmindedly. It was a song I heard Jonas and Levi sing from school. It is probably a *gut* thing I don't know the words."

"Maybe someday, I'll hear you sing. You're planning to go to Sunday's singing, ain't so?"

Hannah saw Jacob bite his tongue as if the words had tumbled out without his knowledge. He seemed aggravated with himself and looked quickly at his scuffed work shoes to avoid looking at Hannah.

"Well, I was thinking of how to get Esther to go. I'll talk to her later this week. I'm supposed to help her at the little market."

"*Gut. Gut.* Just make sure *you* come to the singing, too." Jacob's face turned the color of the few red roses still clinging to Naomi's rosebush. "I mean, it would be nice if you came, too."

"*Jah,* it might be nice." Hannah knew her cheeks must be glowing with their own shade of red.

"*Gut,*" Jake whispered.

"I-I n-need to get back," Hannah dragged herself from the depths of Jacob's eyes.

"See ya," Jacob said.

"See you," Hannah echoed as she headed down the driveway. *What am I doing?*

Chapter Thirteen

Hannah found herself wedged between Esther and Sarah on the hard, wooden bench at Sunday's church service held in Barbara and Henry Zook's house.

Thankfully, the weather had turned cool enough that it actually felt good to be sitting close together. On the buggy ride to the Zooks' house, Hannah noticed the leaves on the trees had taken on autumn hues of red, orange, and gold. She had been so busy inside the last few days she hadn't had the chance to observe the natural world around her.

Rebecca had been feeling better but not completely herself. Elizabeth had been whiny with a cold but was finally on the mend.

Fall cleaning demanded that quilts be washed and hung on the line, rugs be aired, windows be scrubbed, and the whole house scoured from top to bottom.

Hannah was exhausted and truly glad for this Lord's Day of rest, even if her aching back did have to endure three hours on the cruel, wooden bench.

Hannah struggled to concentrate on the sermons. She had begun to understand them much better and had even memorized some of the songs from the Ausbund.

Briefly, her attention wandered and she wondered why she hadn't received a reply from Liz Bradford. *I guess no news is good news.* She forced her attention back to Bishop Sol.

Sarah squirmed on the bench beside her and picked at her fingernails. Hannah sneaked a peek at Sarah who instantly ceased her motion. The two young women smiled at each other and turned their eyes back to the bishop.

It didn't come as a huge surprise when the bishop announced Zeke's and Sarah's intention to marry. Hannah elbowed Sarah gently but instantly regretted her action when Sarah nearly choked holding back her laughter.

Hannah found it interesting that Amish couples kept wedding plans a secret until they were "published" just mere weeks before the marriage would occur. No agonizing weeks of caterer and florist consultations, dress fittings, rehearsals, or honeymoon planning were involved with Amish weddings.

At the common meal following the church service, Sarah, Esther, and Hannah whispered excitedly as they prepared to serve the men now gathered at the makeshift tables.

"When is the wedding?" Hannah inquired.

"The first Thursday in November."

"Only a few weeks off!" Hannah exclaimed.

"*Jah.* There's a lot to do. I've got to sew my dress, plan the meal, and —"

"Who will teach school?" Esther interrupted.

"I don't know."

"She can't continue to teach?" Hannah wished she could take back her questions. She knew Amish women didn't usually work outside of the home after they married. Her reaction had been purely *Englisch*. She hoped her new friends were too preoccupied to notice.

"Of course not, silly." Sarah giggled. "I'll have to prepare for the wedding and then I'll be busy taking care of a husband and home and *bopplin* when they come along." Sarah's face turned scarlet.

"Of course," Hannah murmured.

"Esther, you could teach," Sarah said.

"Ach, not me! I would not be a good teacher. Besides, I have my business to run." Esther paused for just a moment then fixed her gaze on Hannah. "But Hannah would make a perfect teacher!"

"Me?" Hannah squeaked.

"Of course!" Sarah concurred. "All the *kinner* love you. They flock around you to hear stories. Rebecca's Emma is always hanging on your arm."

"I live with Emma. She thinks of me as family. And just because I can tell stories doesn't mean I'd be a good teacher."

"I've seen your face light up with the little ones. You're a natural-born teacher," Esther observed.

"Do you really think so?" Hannah allowed herself a moment to consider teaching — her secret dream before reality crashed back down on her.

I know nothing about Amish schools. I don't know what the curriculum would be. All the grades are in one room!

"I know so!" Sarah exclaimed. "You just got a dreamy look on your face."

"Kind of like the one you get when you talk about Zeke," Esther teased.

"Ach, Esther!" Sarah made a face at her friend.

"Wouldn't your scholars like to see that?"

Scholars, not students. I'd have to remember that. Wait a minute – I'll never be allowed to teach in an Amish school. I'm not... Before she could finish the thought, her conscience's voice reminded her, *They believe you are Amish.*

"Maybe I can recommend you to the school board," Sarah offered.

"I-I don't know."

"You'd be perfect," Sarah repeated as though she didn't hear Hannah's weak protest. "And I'll help you any way I can. You could even come watch me for a few days, just to get a feel for things. Now, let's see where I can find the school board members. The men have finished eating." Sarah drifted away, still thinking aloud.

"Wait a minute, Sarah," Hannah called.

"Best just to leave her be when she's got a notion in her head," Esther said. "*Kum*, let's refill the plates and bowls."

Reluctantly, Hannah accompanied Esther to the kitchen. Things were getting out of hand.

Hannah smiled in the predawn darkness of her room, remembering last night's singing. She stretched her legs out and withdrew them quickly when her bare feet touched the cold section of the sheet that had not been warmed by her body heat. Mornings were getting frostier.

She snuggled deeper into the covers, yanking the blanket and quilt up to her nose. Since the old rooster hadn't yet thought to crow, she could stay in bed a little longer.

Hannah had finally made peace with the old bird and forgave his rude interruption of her sleep. Many mornings, now, she awakened before him. She no longer cast an evil eye in his direction or threatened him with the stew pot when she fed the chickens or gathered the eggs.

The singing had been fun. As she had reluctantly promised, Esther stopped by to pick her up and take her and had even baked brownies for the refreshment table.

Knowing Esther's avoidance of domestic chores, Hannah had been impressed by the gesture. She had tried to cajole her out of her grumpy mood as they plodded along to the Zooks' barn. Hannah hoped there would be a good turnout for the singing. She feared she may need to light a fire under Esther to get her to prod the horse along since they were clopping along so slowly.

When they finally reached the Zooks' place, Esther had trudged in as if she were facing her execution. Eventually, the scowl had left her face, her forehead smoothed, her hands unclenched, and she actually sang as though she enjoyed it.

Hannah smiled as she watched Esther and Andrew spar after the singing was over. She chuckled aloud, remembering how Andrew had taken Esther's hands to check for dirt beneath her fingernails and Esther had rapped on Andrew's head to see if it was hollow. Those two would make a great couple.

Hannah sighed into the quiet darkness as she thought of Jacob's blue eyes staring into her own, a gentle smile playing about his lips. Her hand still tingled from his clasp as he led her away from the dueling duo and over to the refreshments.

When he asked if he could drive her home, she murmured "yes" before common sense intervened. How could she then go back on her word and hurt the kind man?

She had tried to backpedal without inflicting any pain by telling Jacob she should probably leave with Esther so the other woman would not have to drive home alone. Funny she hadn't noticed that Andrew and Esther had approached the refreshment table and overheard her last comment.

"I'll see that this cantankerous woman gets home." Andrew's mouth had twitched as he tried to suppress a smile.

"I don't need the likes of you babysitting me," Esther had retorted. "I'm perfectly capable of—"

Andrew had halted the tirade by stuffing a snickerdoodle in Esther's mouth and practically dragging the flabbergasted young woman toward the door. Hannah and Jake had both burst into laughter.

The ride home had been terrific. She and Jake sat close enough to absorb some of each other's body heat in the crisp evening air but not close enough to be inappropriate. They had both let down their guard and had chatted easily about all sorts of things. Hannah had been surprised at how quickly they made it back to Samuel's and Rebecca's house.

She wondered how Esther's ride home turned out. She had been stunned when Jacob mentioned casually she might see a flashlight shining into her window one of these nights, so stunned, she could only smile. Jake looked as if he had surprised himself, too, and nervously whispered good night.

Hannah sighed once again, more deeply this time. She had become more and more involved in this community. How would she leave when the time came? Could she leave? Did she even want to leave? What about her life in Virginia? She thought of that less and less.

She didn't want to lead Jacob on, but she could no more stop her feelings for him than she could stop the autumn leaves from turning deep red and burnished gold. She couldn't reason it out in her head, but there was something very special about Jacob Beiler. He wasn't like any man she had ever dated—not that there had been a slew of boyfriends. Jake was so genuine, so honest. No pretense. What he showed to the world was the true Jacob.

Guilt threatened to swallow her. She wanted more than anything to be honest with Jake. How could there be any kind of relationship built on pretense? But she couldn't blow her cover. The fear of endangering the Cherry Hill Plain community was greater than the concern for her own safety. But how did she go about switching off feelings that were growing at an alarming rate?

She flung the covers off, leaped out of bed, and danced across the cold floor to snatch her clothes off the peg. Dressing and winding her hair into a bun in the dark had become second nature. Now she needed to stop the troubling thoughts and get the day underway.

Hannah helped get breakfast on the table, sent Eli and Jonas scampering off to school with full lunch pails, and cleaned up the kitchen in record time. Rebecca did not look as sickly this morning and didn't need to run for the bathroom at all. She only nibbled at dry toast and drank her special ginger tea, but these at least seemed to be agreeing with her temperamental stomach, for now.

Hannah insisted Rebecca take it easy as much as possible and work on her mending while the girls played at her feet. She, on the other hand, would single-handedly fight the beastly wringer washing machine and hang the multiple loads of laundry on the line.

Pants flapped in the brisk autumn breeze as if they had a life of their own. Hannah fought to clip the uncooperative dresses and shirts to the line. She nearly swallowed the wooden clothespin she'd stuck in her mouth when she saw a buggy pull up and Samuel point her out to Bishop Sol and Jeremiah Yoder. Good thing her teeth had a good grip on the clothespin. What in the world could they possibly want with her? Had they somehow discovered she was a phony? Had they come to demand she leave?

Hannah pulled the clothespin from her mouth quickly and jabbed it onto Samuel's wayward blue shirt that attempted to escape from the line. With one hand, she tucked a flapping strand of hair back into her bun and with the other, she smoothed the green dress and black apron. That would have to do. No time to make herself more presentable.

She gulped when the tall, stern-looking bishop and the shorter, plumper Jeremiah Yoder stopped within spitting distance.

Mutt and Jeff or Laurel and Hardy. She fought a smile. She drew in a shaky breath and forced her gaze up to search the bishop's serious brown eyes. It was almost as if he could see into her soul. Hannah resisted a shudder and let her eyes travel to Jeremiah's face instead.

"*Gude mariye*, Hannah," Bishop Sol greeted. Jeremiah nodded.

"*Gude mariye*." Hannah's voice barely surpassed whisper level. She thought about clearing her throat and trying again but decided to wait.

"Hannah, we'd like to talk to you for a few minutes, if this is a *gut* time."

"This is fine. Would you like to come inside?"

"Here is fine."

Hannah nodded and waited, bracing herself for accusations, or reprimand, or whatever. Her mind tried to formulate a defense on short notice.

"Jeremiah and I are two of the school board members," Bishop Sol began. "As you know, Sarah Fisher will be getting married and will no longer be our teacher."

"*Jah*." Hannah nodded.

"She has recommended you, and we—Jeremiah, the other school board members, and I—agreed that we would ask you to teach our scholars."

Hannah's jaw drop. They weren't chasing her out of town! They wanted her to teach their children. They wanted her to stay.

"We know you came here to visit"—Jeremiah apparently found his voice and spoke for the first time—"but we are hoping you will stay."

Hannah felt a smile tug at her lips. "I-I'm honored. I'I haven't taught before, but…"

"We've seen you with the *kinner* at gatherings. We think you have what it takes to be a teacher. Would you consider staying and taking on our scholars?" Bishop Sol's tone softened and his face relaxed. Was it a smile that lit his face or her imagination?

"I-I'd like to stay. I-I'd have to ask Samuel and Rebecca. I don't want to impose on them."

"Of course. We may be able to provide housing for you if need be," Bishop Sol continued. "Sophie and Gid Hostetler's *dawdi* house is empty for one. Can you give us a decision by the end of the week? Don't mean to rush, but we need a teacher soon. This would give you time to work with Sarah a bit and kind of learn the ropes."

"Of course, Bishop Sol. I'll let you know. *Danki* for asking me."

"We'll leave you to your chores, Hannah. We hope to hear from you soon."

"For sure, Bishop. I'll let you know soon."

"Jeremiah, didn't you need to speak to Samuel?" Bishop Sol turned to look at the other man.

"I did. It won't take but a minute." Hannah stared in amazement at the men as they strode toward the barn.

For just an instant, Bishop Sol looked over his shoulder, his mud-brown eyes locking with Hannah's. He nodded almost conspiratorially before looking forward and responding to something Jeremiah said.

What in the world did that look signify? Did it have to do with the job offer or something else? Was it meant to offer support or exert authority?

She halfway feared the bishop, and her body responded to that emotion by producing a healthy crop of goosebumps racing down both arms and legs. Without looking down, she bent and felt around for the laundry basket. She pulled out the last blue shirt and secured it to the clothesline next to the other flapping shirts.

"Was that Bishop Sol?" Rebecca called just as Hannah got herself and the basket inside the house. She left the basket in the mud room and sought Rebecca.

"*Jah*, it was. And Jeremiah Yoder, too." Hannah rubbed her icy hands together. The wet laundry combined with the cool breeze and her ragged nerves left her hands feeling like blocks of ice.

"Were they looking for Samuel? Did they say what they wanted?"

"Uh, they went to see Samuel after they talked to me."

Rebecca remained silent but raised questioning eyebrows at Hannah.

"Th-they want me to teach since Sarah is getting married soon."

"That's *wunderbaar!*" Rebecca jumped from her chair, spilling her basket of thread and needles. She rushed to hug Hannah. "That means you'll stay, ain't so?"

Hannah returned Rebecca's hug. "I haven't given my answer yet."

"Why not? You've wanted to do some kind of work, and you are so good with all the *kinner*, not just my four."

"I surely do enjoy the *kinner*. It's just, well, I haven't taught school, and…uh, I don't want to impose on you and Samuel. You didn't agree to take me in forever." Hannah finished in a rush and stared at the wood floor.

"Hannah Kurtz, you are family now. I'm sure Samuel feels the same way. You've been my lifesaver these weeks I've felt so sick."

"I'm glad I could help you, Rebecca, but Samuel may want his house back for just his family." Before Rebecca could protest further, Hannah continued. "Bishop Sol said if I take the job, there may be a place to stay. He mentioned the Hostetlers had a place. That way, I wouldn't be a bother to you."

"Bother! That's *narrisch*! You have never been a bother. You've been a big help. I don't know how I would have managed without you. With my parents, *bruders*, and *schweschder* living so far away, you have become like a *schweschder* to me."

Rebecca paused to take a deep breath after her speech. She spoke as if Ohio was located on the other side of the moon, but it must seem that way since she certainly couldn't travel by horse and buggy to get there. She would have to arrange for a driver or take a bus, which many Amish did. It would be hard for Rebecca, though, with four youngsters in tow.

"Ach, Rebecca." Tears sprang to Hannah's eyes. She brushed at the one that escaped and trickled down her cheek. "I consider you family, too."

Rebecca hugged her again. "Tears of joy?" Hannah nodded. "Pray on the job, Hannah. You are always *wilkom* here, but if you want your own place, that's fine too. Just stay. Please stay."

Hannah couldn't get a sound past the lump in her throat but nodded against Rebecca's shoulder.

"Mamm, is Hannah sad?" Emma wormed her way in between the two women.

"*Nee*, Emma. Hannah has happy tears."

"Happy tears? We laugh when we're happy." Emma looked thoroughly confused.

Hannah extended one arm out to hug the precious little girl. "Grown-ups are silly sometimes and cry when they're happy." She attempted a reassuring smile.

"You are fine, then?"

"For sure, Emma, I'm fine."

Satisfied all was well with the two adults, Emma dropped to her hands and knees and crawled around, gathering up Rebecca's spools of thread.

"Stay," Rebecca whispered.

Chapter Fourteen

Rebecca's single word—"stay"—reverberated through Hannah's mind all night as she tossed and turned, wrestling with her decision. She wanted to stay. She still missed her aunt, uncle, and cousins and thought of them often, but the ache of separation had disappeared. She had fond memories of her life and work in Virginia, but that's what they were now, memories. She had enjoyed her job as a children's librarian, but now, she had the opportunity to teach. She wanted to teach. Yet how could she accept the teaching position here?

She ticked off the pros and cons in her head.

Pros: A chance to teach—her heart's desire; a way to earn money and help Rebecca and Samuel; a reason to stay in the community; a way to keep Jacob in her life.

Cons: She had never taught school before and hadn't a clue what the Amish curriculum entailed; she didn't want to impose on Samuel's and Rebecca's hospitality and generosity; she didn't know how long she would be here or what would happen when the criminals were finally captured; she didn't want to endanger innocent lives; she feared the repercussions if she was discovered to be the imposter she actually was.

She hadn't received any new ominous notes, so maybe any threat was over. She also hadn't heard from Liz and didn't understand the meaning of this silence.

Quite a lis., Hannah turned over and punched her pillow for the fiftieth time. *Looks like the cons win.* She groaned softly, physically and mentally exhausted. Yet she knew sleep was merely a dim possibility.

Please stay. How could she ignore Rebecca's plea? Rebecca had truly become like a sister to her. Samuel still remained a bit aloof, almost skeptical, but that could be just an Amish male thing. Rebecca and the children were as close to her as any blood kin could be. She knew Rebecca missed her family though she willingly and eagerly moved to St. Mary's County, Maryland, after meeting and falling in love with Samuel during his visit to her hometown. She could be a help to Rebecca who would find herself with *six* young children in a few months.

Who was she kidding? She was not Amish, despite her appearance and her adherence to Amish traditions. Did she want to be Amish? Hannah rolled onto her back and stared into the darkness. *Could I live like this the rest of my life? Could I be an Amish fraa and bear six or eight kinner? I could with Jacob.*

"Stop it right now!" Hannah commanded herself aloud. "A man is not a reason to change my whole life." Her beliefs did mesh with Amish beliefs. She could follow the Ordnung—had been following it as much as she understood it. She could live without cars, computers, television, and electricity. She did not want to live without the peace, love, and faith she had found here.

She bolted upright in bed. "I *am* Amish," she said to the blackness of her room. "I haven't been baptized into the church, but I am Amish. I want to be Amish. I don't want to leave." Tears streamed down her face as she flopped back down. She rolled to her side, curled into fetal position, and sobbed, begging God to show her what to do. What was His will for her?

Hannah must have dozed as night headed for day. Somewhere she heard the cry, "Don't goooo! Don't goooo!" She dragged herself from the deep chasm of sleep and struggled to hear that echoing voice again. All she heard was the rooster crowing. Was that the voice? Was the grumpy old rooster telling her to stay, too? "What should my answer be, Lord?" She hurried to dress.

"You look as though you've been wrestling with a bear all night—for a couple of nights actually," Rebecca remarked two days later as she beat the eggs she prepared to scramble.

"It feels like it," Hannah agreed. "I've had a lot on my mind lately."

"Listen to your heart," Rebecca said softly as Samuel and the boys stomped inside.

"I'll try."

"Fall is definitely here, with winter close behind," Samuel observed. He rubbed his hands together to warm them.

"Do we need to get out the gloves and scarves?" Rebecca asked. She reached to touch Samuel's cheek. "Ach! You are cold! I'd best dig out the winter things soon."

"Real soon, I'm thinking." Samuel kissed Rebecca's cheek before taking his place at the head of the big oak table.

Emma very carefully carried bowls of steaming oatmeal to the table one at a time. Hannah only filled the bowls halfway so Emma could manage them without spilling the oatmeal. Hannah didn't worry too much. No doubt, if Emma accidentally dumped a bowl, the oatmeal would just form a congealed blob that could be easily scraped up.

She still had to thin her oatmeal to get it down, but she was doing better. She no longer gagged when the stuff hit her palate. It had been rather hard to eat anything the past few days, though. Everything seemed to try to crawl back up her esophagus.

After Rebecca plunked Elizabeth in her highchair, the family said their silent grace and began the meal.

"Are you ready to give the school board your answer?" Rebecca and Hannah had finally finished morning chores and sat at the table for a quick *kaffi* break before preparing the noon meal.

Hannah blew across the top of her cup to cool the steaming liquid a bit before taking a sip to wet her dry throat. "I believe so," she whispered into the cup. "I want to stay. I think God wants me to teach."

Rebecca leaned closer to Hannah. "What? Did you say you'll stay and teach? Did I hear correctly?"

"You did." A smile spread slowly across Hannah's face. She deposited her mug on the table.

"*Wunderbaar!*" Rebecca fairly shouted. "I'm so happy. Will you tell Bishop Sol today?" Rebecca squeezed Hannah's arm, making Hannah thankful she was no longer holding her mug. She surely would have received a nasty scalding from the sloshed drink.

"I will." The man intimidated her. She'd rather seek out Jeremiah Yoder but guessed she should inform the bishop first.

"The girls and I will go with you, if you like. It's a nice, crisp day for a little outing." Rebecca seemed to sense Hannah's trepidation.

"I'd like that, if you feel up to it."

"I do indeed. I'll ask Samuel to hitch Brownie right after we eat."

"*Danki*, Rebecca, for everything. I am a little nervous about the meeting."

"The bishop is not really mean, just stern. He takes his job seriously."

"I suppose," Hannah said. She didn't add "if you say so."

Hannah approached the white school building with no small amount of anxiety. At an *Englisch* school, she might experience a mild case of nerves, just one or two butterflies fluttering in her stomach. After all, she'd attended *Englisch* schools—for twelve years, thirteen if kindergarten counted, and sixteen with college—even if she hadn't taught in one. She would have a pretty good idea what to do there.

An Amish school was a horse of a different color. A whole flock of butterflies had taken up residence in her gut, colliding with one another and banging into the walls of her intestines. An all-out panic attack threatened. Now, she questioned the decision she had made. Bishop Sol seemed truly pleased she had taken the teaching job. She might be wrong, but she thought the glimmer of a smile may have briefly crossed his face.

No students were in sight. Hannah arrived early so Sarah could show her around—though it didn't look like that would take long—and to fill her in on the teacher's duties. She looked at the steps leading to the front door and took a deep breath.

You can do this. Now, if she could get her feet out of the cement they seemed to be planted in and get them to mount the steps.

"*Gut*, you're here early," Sarah called, poking her head out the door. "*Kum*. We have a little while before the scholars arrive."

Scholars, not students. I've got to remember that.

Sarah's welcoming smile melted Hannah's fears. She returned the smile as she ran up the steps, letting the enthusiasm for teaching she originally felt take charge again.

Hannah's gaze swept the room. The wood stove already glowed, casting off heat. A little cloakroom of sorts at the back of the room had hooks for holding outerwear, and a long shelf beneath the hooks accommodated lunch pails. The chalkboard on the front wall sported the day's assignments in Sarah's neat penmanship. Maps and children's papers occupied other wall space.

Hannah reined her focus in on the desks in her near vision. Old-fashioned wooden desks with desktop and chair attached by a metal bar were arranged in order of size, ten on one side of the center aisle and eleven on the other side. The girls' side and the boys' side, Hannah surmised. Twenty-one students—*nee,* scholars—of various grades in one room! Could she really do this?

"The smallest desks are for the first and second graders, of course," Sarah explained. "There are four first graders, four second graders, three third graders, and two in each of the remaining grades."

Hannah couldn't suppress a gasp.

Sarah giggled. "It's not so bad. Sometimes, they do things together. And the older scholars are ever so helpful with the younger ones."

"Okay. Show me your lessons." Hannah figured she may as well dive in.

"Well, it's probably very much like when you went to school, if you remember," Sarah said.

"Hardly," Hannah wanted to say but instead, mumbled, "I suppose. Some of my memory is intact and some is sketchy," she added.

That sounded pretty believable for someone who had supposedly suffered a head injury. And to be truthful, some of her elementary school memories really were sketchy now.

"We always start the day with a hymn followed by a Bible reading and the Lord's Prayer." Hannah nodded. "We usually do the harder lessons, like reading and arithmetic, early on when the scholars are fresh and eager. I save things like penmanship and social studies for the afternoon." Again Hannah nodded. "I usually read a story after the long midday recess to kind of calm everyone down and get them back into the work mode."

"That makes sense."

"If you want, you can just watch today and help with the little ones, if you'd like. Then tomorrow, you can teach a class or two. We can go over the lessons after school so you'll be prepared."

"Uh, okay."

"Don't be nervous, Hannah. I know you'll be a *gut* teacher. I'm so glad you took the job." Sarah smiled and reached to squeeze Hannah's hand.

"I hope I can catch on quickly and not fail the *kinner* or the community."

"Don't worry. You're a natural-born teacher. I can tell. And the *kinner* already love you. Ach! I hear some voices. Time to ring the bell."

Hannah swallowed the huge lump of fear that clogged her throat. It hit her empty stomach with a thud and expanded, making her want to retch. She would be completely mortified if she threw up in front of the school children. She should have eaten some of that oatmeal paste to give the ball of fear something to adhere to.

The day passed swiftly once Hannah finally relaxed and enjoyed herself. She helped the first and second graders with their reading and the third and fourth graders with their arithmetic. She even read the post-recess story. After all the story hours at the library, she was able to bring any story to life and to draw the children into the action.

As the children filed out the door at three thirty, Hannah exhaled in relief. Her eyes sparkled, and a satisfied smile curved her lips.

"What did you think?" Sarah erased the day's lessons from the blackboard.

"I-I love it! I think teaching may be my calling. Of course, I only helped today. I may feel totally different when I'm on my own."

"I doubt it," Sarah assured her. "You will be just fine. I feel it here." Sarah tapped her chest. "Here you go." She handed Hannah the chalk. "You write tomorrow's work on the board."

Hannah had to erase the first two lines three times before she got the hang of printing in a straight line on the chalkboard. She walked backwards a ways to survey her penmanship. It wouldn't do for the teacher to have sloppy handwriting. She sneezed as she brushed all the chalk dust from her hands and dress.

"I'm sure Rebecca won't want me to bring all this chalk into her house. There may be more on me than on the board. My writing is still a little crooked." She tilted her head slightly as she read the words she had written and frowned.

"It looks fine. Writing on the board just takes practice."

"Like most things, I guess."

"*Jah.*"

Sarah reviewed the next day's lessons with Hannah before handing the books to her to take home to review. "My nerves will probably cause me to dream about these lessons tonight."

Sarah laughed. "I was *naerfich* at the beginning, too, but it won't last long. I promise."

The two women gathered up their bags and headed for the door. Hannah set out for home, lost in thought. She wanted to believe Sarah's promise. Out of the blue, a verse popped into her mind. "What times I am afraid, I will trust in thee."

I won't be afraid of teaching. I won't be afraid of being found by those men. I will trust. Oh, help me trust, Lord.

Hannah finished out the week, gradually taking over more and more teaching duties as Sarah relinquished them. The following week, the school was all Hannah's. She was officially the teacher with all the responsibilities. She took her job seriously, often staying up late to pore over books and lesson plans until her eyes grew too weary in the dim lamplight.

"How do you like the teaching?" Rebecca asked as she and Hannah worked together preparing breakfast.

Today marked the end of Hannah's first week as teacher. Even if she worked late into the evening, she leaped out of bed early to help Rebecca as much as possible. "I like it just fine. I'm still learning the routine, but I love the scholars."

"I knew you'd be a *wunderbaar* teacher."

"I'm just sorry that I can't help you as much."

"Ach. Don't even think about that. I took care of everything before."

"True, but you weren't expecting twins."

"Hannah, I've been through this four times before, you know. Carrying two isn't a whole lot different, not yet, anyway."

"I just still feel bad. I don't want to live here and not help."

"You help plenty." Rebecca lifted sizzling bacon out of the frying pan strip by strip and deposited each on a paper towel-lined plate. She gently blotted excess grease.

Hannah shuddered. She was doing better with tolerating the smell of meat, but bacon had a pretty strong odor. She quickly carried the plate piled high with pancakes to the table so Rebecca wouldn't see her involuntary, uncontrollable reaction.

She returned to the stove and ventured to ask the question that had nagged at her for some time. "Rebecca, do you think Samuel would rather I live somewhere else?"

Rebecca dropped the spoon into the oatmeal pan with a clatter. "Whatever would make you think that?"

"Well," Hannah forced her hands to stop twisting her apron. "Well, I just thought he'd like to have his home back—you know, with just your family."

"Hannah, you *are* family to us now."

"I'm glad you feel that way, Rebecca. I just don't want to be in the way. You know you'll need a room for the babies."

"That's a ways off."

"I know, but…"

"If it will make you feel better, I'll talk to Samuel, but I'm sure he wants you to stay here."

"*Jah*. Just make sure with him, please."

Rebecca smiled, nodded, and patted Hannah's arm before they joined the rest of the family for breakfast.

After a couple of hectic, nerve-wracking days, Hannah settled into the routine. She walked with Eli and Jonas to and from the little school house. The temperature had taken a nosedive, causing them to pick up the pace a little more each day. The once brilliant red, gold, and orange leaves now crackled beneath their feet. Naked tree limbs scratched the sky.

Hannah occasionally wished for a pair of corduroy slacks and a sweatshirt but had to settle for heavier black stockings and a heavy black cloak over her cotton dress and apron. She tied the black bonnet securely under her chin and tried not to think of fuzzy earmuffs.

Eli and Jonas didn't seem to mind the colder weather as they romped beside her.

"Old Silas said it's going to be a hard winter," Jonas said.

"Really?" Hannah queried.

"*Jah*. Haven't you seen all the fuzzy caterpillars? Old Silas says they have on heavy winter coats."

"Hmm. I have seen furry-looking caterpillars."

"Daed read in the almanac that we could get lots of snow," Eli chimed in. "I like snow."

"I bet you do." Personally, Hannah could do without it except for a dusting at Christmas. She shivered just thinking about snowy weather and subconsciously walked faster.

"Hey, Hannah, I can't keep up," Eli grunted.

"Sorry, Eli. I was just thinking about getting into the school house and making sure it's getting warm before all the scholars arrive."

"Jeremiah Yoder has been starting the fire, ain't so?" Jonas quickened his pace.

"*Jah*, he has. I'm very glad he does that for us."

"Daed said you're such a bitty thing you might blow away in a good puff of wind," Eli reported.

"You ain't supposed to say everything you hear," Jonas reprimanded his brother with an elbow to his side.

"*Aren't*" Hannah corrected. "Not *ain't*. That's okay, Eli." She tickled him under the chin with one gloved hand to erase his forlorn expression. "I am pretty little. I might need a big *bu* like you to keep me from blowing away."

Eli's countenance brightened instantly. He stood straighter and puffed out his chest. "I'll help you, Hannah."

"That's *gut*. *Danki*."

This is a good life. I'm really happy here.

Everything would be perfect if she knew she was safe now. She still wondered why she hadn't received any word from Liz. She had written another letter and still heard nothing. She hoped all was well with the young woman who did so much to help her. She couldn't help but wonder what would happen when the community found out the truth. Most likely they would want her to leave.

I'll worry about that another day. Just like Scarlett O'Hara.

Hannah sucked in a ragged breath and reached out an arm to stop Eli and Jonas.

"*Was ist letz?*" Both boys spoke at once.

"N-nothing. J-just hold up a moment." A sudden movement caught her attention. She squinted in the bright morning sun.

"Just a bicycle," Jonas announced.

"*Jah*" Hannah whispered. Wasn't it a little cold for biking with just a baseball cap for a head covering? Who was this guy, and why did he always appear out of nowhere? Apparently, he wasn't just someone visiting the area for the summer.

"I'm cold," Eli wailed. "Can we go?"

"Okay." The threesome set off again. Hannah practically ran with the boys huffing and puffing behind her. Even at a distance, she could tell the biker turned to look at them. Relief filled Hannah when the school house came into view, smoke belching from the chimney.

"See. Jeremiah got the fire going," Jonas observed.

"He sure did. Let's get inside." *And not just for warmth!*

Chapter Fifteen

Hannah had six weeks of teaching under her belt and felt more and more confident and competent. Teaching eight grades definitely kept her on her toes, but she enjoyed everything about teaching, from planning lessons to teaching classes to grading papers. Weariness often overtook her by the end of the day, but it was a good kind of weariness.

Just the same, she was glad to see Friday arrive. She had dismissed the scholars who had fairly flown from the building. Jonas and Eli waited for Hannah to write Monday's assignments on the chalkboard and to put out the fire. She was gathering up her books and papers when the door burst open.

"Ach! I didn't mean to charge in. The wind got the door."

Hannah smiled. She knew the voice without turning to identify its owner. "It is pretty windy today. If the *kinner* had had kites at recess, they would have soared away."

"Is—has Mary gone then?"

Jacob's sister, Mary, was one of Hannah's two eighth graders and a big help with the younger children. She'd probably be a good teacher herself one day. "*Jah*, Jacob. She bolted out the door at dismissal time."

Jacob laughed. "Sounds like Mary. Full of energy, that one."

"That she is, but she's a good scholar and ever so helpful."

"*Gut* to know." Jacob fidgeted a bit more. "Could—uh...would you..." He hesitated then finished in a rush. "I'd be glad to drive you and the *buwe* home. I just delivered some furniture and have my wagon."

"*Danki*, Jake. That would be nice. It's been a busy day. Let me finish collecting my things, and I want to check that fire one last time."

"Take your time. I'll check the fire."

"I appreciate that." Hannah wondered why Jacob had made himself scarce the past few weeks and why no light had ever shone through her window. She figured it was for the best and tried unsuccessfully to snuff out the disappointment. It really was better for Jacob to forget about her, even though that very thought made her want to cry.

"Ready?"

Hannah nodded. "Let's go, *buwe*." She didn't have to tell them twice. She made sure the school house door was locked as the boys ran ahead to jump into the wagon. Jake took her bag from her, set it in the back of the wagon, and then helped her up onto the high seat. A tingly feeling immediately ran up and down her arm at his touch.

Jacob leapt onto the seat and picked up the reins. "Whew!" he exclaimed. "I've been working night and day to finish a whole cherry bedroom suite for an *Englisch* neighbor. That's what I just delivered."

"I'm sure you're glad to be finished," Hannah murmured.

"I like making the furniture. It's just that this was a rush order, so *jah*, I'm glad it's done."

Silence hung between the two adults while the boys chattered behind them.

"I didn't forget, Hannah." His voice barely broke the silence.

"Pardon me?" Hannah wasn't quite sure if Jacob actually spoke or if the breeze and clopping of the horses' hooves played with her hearing.

"You know. The light."

"The light?"

"Some evening—soon—you may see a light, if you get my meaning."

Hannah's cheeks burned, and she knew they were fiery red. She ducked her head to hide the glow.

Jacob smiled and touched her arm briefly. "Okay?"

"Okay," Hannah whispered. She would kick herself later.

As they drove onto the Hertzlers' long dirt driveway, Hannah asked Jacob to stop so she could check the big metal mailbox. She normally retrieved the mail on her way home from school.

"No problem. Here, you take the reins. I'll hop out and check."

"*Danki*, Jake."

Jacob slammed the metal box closed. "Nothing today," he called.

"Okay." Hannah always felt a little disappointed each day when she didn't receive a reply from Liz. What was going on? Liz had told her to write and had given her mailing instructions.

"You *buwe* want me to let you out by the barn so you can help your daed or do you need to change clothes first?

Before the boys could clamor out of the wagon, Hannah said, "Your mamm will want you to change first. There may be a cookie or two waiting for you," she added when she saw their crestfallen faces. She knew Rebecca had planned to bake today. The boys were eager to run around outside after a day of school, but the thought of cookies appeased them.

"*Danki*, Jake," Hannah said when he stopped the wagon at the house. "I'm sure Rebecca won't mind if you'd like to stay for supper." Hannah bit her tongue. She should not keep encouraging a relationship that could never be.

"*Nee*, I don't mind a bit."

"Ach, Rebecca! I didn't even see you."

Rebecca rose from the oak rocking chair on the porch. "I just came out for a quick breath of fresh air."

"Are you okay?"

"I'm fine. The kitchen just got hot after baking cookies."

"Cookies? Peanut butter? Oatmeal?" the boys called at once.

"Oatmeal raisin. But it will cost you one hug apiece."

Eli and Jonas ran to hug their mother before rushing into the house to claim their cookies.

"Wash your hands. The cookies are already on the table for you."

"I'll see if I can help Samuel with anything," Jacob said, striding toward the barn.

"And I'll just put my things away and help with supper. You can stay outside, Rebecca."

"*Nee*, it's time to check on the girls."

"I can do that,"

"You're my angel." Rebecca laughed and hugged Hannah. "I do need to get inside, though."

Angels don't live a life of lies. She hated the pretense, but what other choice did she have?

In no time, the men and boys stomped inside to wash up for supper. Emma finished setting the table as Hannah set steaming bowls of potatoes, green beans, and corn on the table.

"I got the mail when I went out earlier. I forgot to bring it in before," Samuel tossed the small stack of envelopes on the edge of the table. "Mostly junk mail."

Hannah glanced quickly through the stack, searching for an envelope with Liz's handwriting. A scrap of paper flew from the pile and fluttered to the floor. She bent to pick it up then drew her hand back as though it was a hissing snake.

"Was *ist letz?*"

"I-I don't know, Rebecca. N-nothing, I guess," Hannah replied, letting go of the breath she had subconsciously been holding.

Samuel gave her a searching look before reaching over her and taking the slip of paper. "Before a hunter shoots you dead," he read aloud.

"What in the world is that?" Rebecca shivered.

Hannah fought to control her own trembling. She didn't want the others to see how upset those words made her. "Have you ever gotten something like this before, Samuel?"

"*Nee*. I don't—well, now that I think about it, there was a piece of trash by the mailbox a week or so ago. It said 'Help me! Help me!' I figured someone tossed it out their car window so I didn't pay much attention to it."

Hannah couldn't prevent the gasp that escaped. She locked her hands together to stop their trembling.

"Not to worry. Just somebody pulling a prank or stuffing their trash in our mailbox." Samuel crumpled the paper and crossed to the wood stove to toss the paper in. He glanced over his shoulder at Hannah.

"*Jah*, I guess," she murmured.

If only that's all it was, but Hannah was convinced those words were another cryptic message for her. How could she let anyone know? The phone didn't work, and Liz wasn't responding to her letters.

Hannah mainly shuffled food around on her plate as everyone else ate heartily while conversing. She speared a few green beans with her fork and placed them hesitantly in her mouth. Usually, she enjoyed the flavor of fresh vegetables. This evening, everything tasted like sawdust. She forced herself to chew and swallow and tried hard to act normal.

"Are you okay, Hannah? You're so quiet." Rebecca used her concerned mamm voice.

Hannah felt all eyes on her. She dabbed the napkin at her lips. "I'm fine. Just tired. I'm sorry. I guess I'm just thinking about next week's lesson plans."

"A true teacher." Rebecca smiled.

Hannah smiled back at her and attempted to join the conversation. She hadn't been thinking so much about next week's lesson plans as the note writer's next plans. With great effort, she forced the notes from her mind and winked at Emma who giggled. "And what did you do all day, Miss Emma?"

Jacob teased Eli and Jonas and threw occasional glances and smiles at Hannah when he thought no one observed him. Heat rushed to her face at each of his glances. She quickly concentrated on stirring the food around on her plate. Jacob certainly did get her mind off her troubles. She felt herself begin to relax, tension draining from her shoulders.

He's good for me, but I'm not good for him.

Hannah awoke at her customary pre-dawn hour on Saturday. She scolded herself severely when she reached to pull the covers over her head to get a few more minutes of sleep after tossing and turning most of the night. There was no snooze alarm, and she was afraid she'd sleep until noon, leaving poor Rebecca to do all the work. That thought shamed her into crawling out of the warm bed.

She dressed and pinned her hair up quickly, as much to reach the warmth of the kitchen as to help Rebecca. Southern Maryland's autumn weather was much colder than she had expected. If this was a foretaste of winter, she would surely freeze. She wondered if she could somehow slip long johns on under her dress.

Hannah bounded down the stairs. When she reached the bottom, she stopped, took a breath, and walked slower in order to enter the kitchen in a ladylike manner. Rebecca was just stoking the fire. No breakfast preparations were in the works. Unusual, Hannah thought.

"*Gude mariye*, Rebecca. Are you all right?"

Rebecca jumped, startled. She patted her chest. "Ach! I'm fine. I just had a hard time getting up this morning. I'm getting bigger, so it's a little harder to get comfortable. Her hand slid down to her swelling belly.

"Would you like to go back to bed? I can see to breakfast."

"*Nee, nee*. I need to be up and doing things." She opened the gas-powered refrigerator and removed a carton of eggs. "Would you scramble some eggs, please? I'll get the *kaffi* going."

"Sure." Hannah cracked eggs into a bowl. She added salt, pepper, and milk and beat the mixture. Rebecca had set out the big cast iron frying pan so Hannah added oil and began scrambling a dozen eggs. She knew Rebecca would have used bacon grease from the little canister on the counter instead of oil, but Hannah could not bring herself to dig into the clump of grease. *Good thing they have hens with all the eggs they use.*

Samuel and the boys blew into the kitchen, their noses bright red from the cold early morning air. Hannah almost told them they looked like Rudolph the Red-nosed Reindeer but caught herself just in time. They probably didn't know who Rudolph was and would question her reference to such a thing. Instead she said, "You look about frozen."

"*Jah*," Eli and Jonas replied through chattering teeth.

"We may be in for an early winter," Samuel observed. "I'll cut more wood today, and the *buwe* can help stack it."

Emma stumbled into the kitchen, rubbing sleep from her eyes. Elizabeth trotted right behind her, obviously in awe of her big sister. "Here, Elizabeth, you can help me." Emma handed her little sister the napkins and helped Elizabeth put one at each place.

"She's so good with Elizabeth," Hannah whispered.

"*Jah*, Emma is sure a blessing," Rebecca agreed. "I'm thinking she'll be a big help with the new *bopplin*, too."

By the time Hannah and Emma headed out to gather eggs, the sun had chased off much of the early morning frostiness. Hannah breathed a sigh of relief that the surly rooster was nowhere in sight. Sometimes, the hens were hard enough to deal with if they were sitting on their eggs without worrying about the pesky rooster.

Despite the cold, Hannah saw Samuel pause to wipe his brow as he sawed and chopped wood. The boys gathered up the pieces and stacked them near the back door. The windmill turned silently in the brisk breeze. Hannah could only imagine how the contraption must spin furiously in the strong winter winds.

The day passed quickly with chores, cooking, and preparations for the Lord's Day. It would be a preaching Sunday, which meant Hannah and Rebecca would also need to prepare some food for the common meal after church. Hours later, the baking and meals were over with. The last utensil had been put away, the last counter had been wiped, and the kitchen had been restored to its usual orderliness. Finally, there would be a stretch of time for Hannah to grade papers and work on lesson plans for the upcoming week.

Weariness crept into her muscles and even into her bones as darkness settled outside the window. She strained to focus on her papers. She rubbed each eye and squinted again. No use, she thought. She gathered her materials and tucked them back inside her big quilted tote bag. The battery-operated kitchen clock read nearly eleven o'clock. It truly had been a long, busy day. Everyone else had retired several hours ago. It would sure feel good to slither beneath the covers. She prayed sleep would not elude her tonight.

Hannah held the lamp high and trudged up the steps, remembering to step over the squeaky one lest she awaken anyone. She set the lamp on her bedside table and removed her *kapp*. She crossed to the semi-dark side of the room to place the *kapp* on her dresser and reached to pull the pins from her hair. *Good thing I already had long hair.* She shook her head allowing the strands to cascade halfway down her back. It would have been hard to explain a short hairdo on an Amish woman.

She tossed her head and picked up her hair brush. A glimmer of light from the opposite side of the room halted Hannah's movement. She stopped with the brush poised in midair and turned slowly toward the window. The light seemed to be aimed right at her window. Her heart skipped a beat and then thudded to restore its rhythm.

"What is that?" Cautiously, she crept toward the window. Should she call out for Samuel or investigate on her own? She edged closer to the window, keeping her slight body against the wall. She tilted her head just enough to allow her eyes to search for the source of the strange light. What was it?

Chapter Sixteen

"Jacob," she gasped. "He actually came." Hannah moved in front of the window, her silhouette illuminated in Jacob's flashlight beam. She nodded her head affirmatively, hoping Jacob could discern the movement, then quickly coiled her hair back into a knot and jabbed in the pins. She set the *kapp* back on her head and crossed the room to retrieve the lamp. Stealthily, she slipped back down the stairs and stopped at the bottom, her heart beating erratically again.

What did this mean? What did a young woman do when a man called on her in the evening like this? Liz hadn't told her any of this. No one expected her to be living in Maryland long enough to form or even initiate any serious relationships. All she knew was the bits and pieces she overheard at singings when other young women whispered and giggled together about their late-night visitors. She had to pass through the kitchen and open the back door as quietly as possible. She couldn't let Rebecca or Samuel be awakened by this visit. That much she knew.

"Ach, Jacob!" she said softly pulling open the heavy door. She had set the lamp on the kitchen table so only the big, round moon highlighted the young man who stood twisting his hat.

"Hello," he mumbled.

Hannah touched Jacob's hands to stop the twisting before he ruined his good hat.

"Do-do you want t-to step out to look at the moon and stars? They're beautiful tonight."

"Um, sure. Let me get my cloak."

Hannah closed the door softly and removed her outerwear from the hook. She wrapped the cloak around her and tied the black bonnet securely beneath her chin before tiptoeing back to the door. She pulled the door open slowly to avoid any unnecessary noise and stepped outside. Jacob's hat, not too misshapen given all the abuse it suffered, rested atop his blond head.

"The moon is huge, but the stars are still bright." Hannah turned her head from side to side to take in the heavenly splendor displayed above her.

"*Jah*. I thought you might like to see the sky." Jacob lowered himself to sit on the top step and patted the spot beside him. Hannah sat where he indicated, unable to avoid touching him in the cramped space.

"So many stars," Hannah said. "The Lord *Gott* counts the stars and calls them all by name."

"Psalm 147:4," Jacob said. "I've always liked that verse."

"It's comforting to think if He knows and cares

about all the stars, He surely knows and cares about me."

"For certain He does."

"Look!" Hannah cried. "A shooting star." The star shot across the sky leaving a trail of light.

"Pretty amazing."

"You're pretty amazing," Hannah wanted to say but held her tongue. How many young men in her former life would be content to sit outside on a brisk autumn evening to gaze at the sky? She hadn't met any such men. That life seemed so long ago, like a closed book, a fond memory to revisit in her mind only.

She found she really didn't miss that life anymore. She missed the people, certainly, but not the hectic pace of work and activities. She was happy to be away from snarling traffic jams, irate drivers, and the busyness of the world. The Plain life agreed with her now. After her initial balking at the forced change, she now experienced peace—or she would be if she knew no one planned to come after her to harm her or these people she cared about. She suppressed a sigh.

Jacob looked down at the young woman beside him. He raised an arm as if to drape it across her shoulder but quickly dropped it back down. "How…?"

"Have…?" They both began at the same time. "You first," Hannah said, laughing.

"I was going to ask how you liked living here and teaching school."

"I like both just fine. I love the *kinner* and helping them learn. This is a nice, quiet, peaceful place."

"That it is. A lot quieter than Lancaster County or Sugar Creek or—"

"I like it quiet without all the tourists, though I guess you get your fair share here, and they are good for business."

"*Jah*, but I like the peace here, too. Do-do you think you'll stay here?" Jacob seemed almost afraid to ask the question. Was he afraid her answer would be "no" or was he afraid she would complicate his life?

"Um...well, Jake, I-I think—*nee*, I know I want to stay here." Suddenly, it was absolutely clear to her. If the criminals were put behind bars today and she was given the freedom to leave Maryland right now, she would choose to stay. But would they let her once her deception was revealed? Would they understand? Would they let her be baptized and join their faith?

"*Gut*. I was hoping you would say that." Jacob's words pulled Hannah out of her reverie. "Now, what were you going to say?"

"I was just going to ask if you have lived here all your life."

"*Jah*, except for the months I stayed in Sugar Creek a couple years ago. My great-grandparents were among the first Amish to settle here."

"So the Amish haven't always lived here in Southern Maryland?"

"*Nee*. The first families came here from Pennsylvania in 1939. My great-grandparents on my daed's side moved here in 1940."

"Why did they leave Pennsylvania?"

"They could get the farm land they needed here for a good price, and Maryland let them run their own schools. Some other places tried to force the Amish to stay in school past eighth grade or to attend public schools."

"So Maryland was more lenient?"

"I guess so."

"Did you go to Sugar Creek to work?"

"*Jah*. My mamm's family is from Ohio. I lived with her cousins for a while to learn other carpentry skills. I…uh, decided to…uh…come home before my year there was up."

"You didn't like it there? You sounded a little sad."

"It's a fine place, and I learned a lot, but—" Jacob's voice drifted off.

"But?"

"I had a bad experience."

"I'm sorry. I shouldn't have pried."

"I-it's okay. I should tell you before you hear from someone else. I was courting a girl there. I-I thought things were fine, but, well, she was just pretending. She jumped the fence."

"She turned *Englisch*?"

"She did. She-she lied to me. Honesty is very important, ain't so?"

Hannah shivered and not just from the chilly night air. "*Jah*, "she murmured. He would be devastated if he knew of her lies, even though the deception was out of her hands. She hoped he didn't ask about her family. She didn't want to dig a deeper hole for herself.

"Ach, Hannah, I'm sorry. I've been blabbering on and you're freezing."

"Not freezing, but I am getting cold. W-would you like to come in for some hot cocoa?"

"That would be fine."

They rose together and couldn't help bumping into each other. Jacob grasped Hannah's arm to keep her from falling down the steps.

"Ach, me and my big feet tripping you." Jacob chuckled. "And you're such a tiny thing. You barely come up to my shoulder."

A tingling sensation spread from Hannah's upper arm throughout her body, wrapping itself around her heart. A quick look up into Jacob's face illuminated by the moon told her he must surely feel the same electricity between them. She dropped her gaze quickly and reached to open the door.

They tiptoed into the kitchen lit by the lamp Hannah had left there. Silence reigned in the house, interrupted only by the ticking of the kitchen clock. Hannah shook the kettle to make sure it contained water. Before she could slide the kettle over to the burner on the wood stove, Jacob clasped her wrist. "I'm so sorry, Hannah. Look at the time." He nodded toward the clock. "I didn't know it was so late. I kind of lost all track of time."

Hannah gasped. "Nearly two o'clock! Did we really sit outside for more than two hours?"

"It looks that way. I'm sorry," Jacob repeated. "No wonder you were cold. And I know you must be tired."

"It's fine, Jake. The time flew by. I enjoyed talking to you."

"I enjoyed it, too. I'd better let you get to bed. Tomorrow is a church day, after all. Can I have that cocoa next time?"

"Of course." Hannah's heart leapt. He wanted to see her again! She pushed the kettle back away from the heat.

"Maybe we can take a walk tomorrow after the meal?"

"That would be nice."

"*Gut nacht*, Hannah." Jacob bent to brush Hannah's cheek with his lips. He crept quickly through the kitchen and out the door.

"*Gut nacht*," Hannah murmured, touching her cheek, pressing the whisper of a kiss into her memory.

Hannah knew most of the regular hymns sung from the Ausbund by memory now and had grown used to the lengthy sermons. Only her backside planted on the hard wooden bench gave her cause for concern on church Sundays. She concentrated very hard not to fidget. She sat with Rebecca to help with the girls instead of with the other unmarried *maidels*, just in case Rebecca felt sick and had to rush out.

Other times, she sat with Esther and Sarah. *Old maids, the three of us,* Hannah mused. Wouldn't Rennie dissolve into fits of laughter if she knew Hannah was considered an old maid at the age of twenty-four? She knew Jacob was twenty-five, but men didn't have such a distinction.

At the thought of Jacob, Hannah stole a peek in his direction. He winked at her, and she flushed furiously. How long had he been looking at her? She bit the inside of her cheek to squelch the smile that threatened to erupt and quickly dropped her eyes to Emma who was nodding off to sleep against her.

Hannah scarcely tasted or even saw the food on her plate when it was finally time for the women to eat. All she could think about was walking with Jacob later. Would he kiss her again? Should she let him? She knew she shouldn't encourage him. All resolve left her, though, when she was in his presence or heard his voice or looked into his clear blue eyes.

"Are you sick or in *lieb*?" Esther elbowed Hannah.

Hannah nearly dropped the fork dangling from her fingers. "Esther Stauffer! Whatever are you talking about?"

"You've been playing with that food for the last fifteen minutes and haven't taken one bite."

Hannah immediately speared a pickled beet with her fork and stuffed it into her mouth. "There. Happy?" she mumbled as she chewed.

"You'll have to do better than that if you don't want to dry up and blow away. Besides, men like women with a little meat on their bones."

Hannah nearly spit the beet across the table. She struggled to swallow. "Look who's talking. You're not exactly a heifer yourself."

Esther let out a snort. "At least I'm eating and not mooning over a certain someone."

"Hush! I'm not mooning."

"Uh huh."

"You two will be at my frolic next Saturday, won't you?" Sarah plunked down on Hannah's left side. With her left index finger, she shoved her glasses up into place.

"Wouldn't miss it," Hannah answered.

"*Jah*. It will just be us two old *maidels* left after November. We may as well help you fill your hope chest since it's likely we'll never marry." Esther gave an exaggerated sigh.

"Ach, Esther. Never say never," Sarah said. She chattered on about her upcoming work frolic and marriage as her eyes sought out her intended.

After the meal and cleanup were completed, the men and women mingled and visited. The men gravitated to the barn while the women chatted in the kitchen. The children, who were apparently oblivious to the chilly weather, ran about, laughing and playing. Many of the young people organized a game of volleyball, bouncing around to stay warm.

Hannah spied Sarah slipping off with Levi, their heads close together, most likely whispering about their upcoming wedding. She jumped when a deep voice spoke close to her ear. "Do you want to take a walk or are you too cold?"

Hannah turned to find Jacob standing to her left. A shiver ran down her spine at his nearness. "I'm not too cold, but—" She broke off glancing at Esther. She hated to leave Esther alone.

Esther pointed to the volleyball players. "I think they need someone to keep them in line," she announced. "I'm not a great player so I'll referee." She trotted off to the side yard where the volleyball net had been set up. Hannah suspected Esther might be an excellent player but didn't want to make the team uneven—or be the third party in a twosome.

"Ready?" Jacob waited for her response.

"*Jah.*"

Once they were out of view of any watchful eyes, Jacob took one of Hannah's small, cold hands in his large, rough one. Immediately, the touch of Jacob's hand instigated warmth that travelled from her hand to her arm and throughout her entire body. She knew in her mind she should pull her hand away and put some distance between them, but her heart overruled her brain.

"You're sure you're not too cold?" Jacob smiled down at Hannah, concern etched on his face.

"*Nee.* I think you're blocking the cold air and keeping me warm." Hannah returned the smile. She didn't mention that his very nearness warmed her heart and soul.

They shuffled along, entering the woods and crunching brittle, brown leaves beneath their feet. Even though she continually learned new things about Jacob, on some level, she felt she'd known him forever. Was this what was meant by a soul mate? It was a wonderful feeling.

It was a miserable feeling. Whichever it was, she shouldn't have this feeling at all. What would happen when her dark secret was brought to light? Would Jacob hate her for lying, even though she had no choice? Honesty was very important to him. He stressed that last night. She was betraying the trust he had in her. She wanted to pull away and run screaming into the woods.

"Where are you, Hannah?"

"Ach! I'm sorry Jacob. I'm, uh, just enjoying the walk and the beautiful, brisk day."

"And the company?"

"Especially the company." She knew her flush extended all the way to the black bonnet atop her head.

Jacob squeezed her hand. "I feel the same."

They ambled along, talking and getting to know one another better. Hannah felt so safe with Jacob. All disturbing thoughts vanished.

"Your memory is much better, ain't so?"

The disturbing thoughts raced back to claim their spot in her brain. How should she answer? *Please, God, help me.* "For the most part, I think."

"Do you remember all about how you were injured?"

"I...uh, I—"

"Hannah! Hannah! There you are," Eli yelled as he and Jonas sprinted through the leaves toward them. They drew near Jacob and Hannah, panting hard.

"*Was ist letz?*" Hannah dropped Jacob's hand quickly. She didn't need the boys spreading any tales.

"Mamm...isn't...feeling...good," Jonas gasped.

"'Well ,'" Hannah corrected automatically.

"She...wants...to go home now," Eli finished for his brother.

"Tell her I'll be right there."

"I can take you home, if you'd like to stay longer, Hannah," Jacob offered.

"*Danki*, Jake, but I'd best go help Rebecca. Maybe she can rest if I entertain the children for a while." Hannah turned and jogged at a brisk pace toward the house. *Saved from more lies!*

"We'll talk again, *jah*?" Jacob's long strides easily put him even with Hannah.

"Sure. *Danki* for understanding." When they cleared the woods, Hannah cut across the field in an all-out gallop.

Chapter Seventeen

The week passed quickly. Hannah stayed busy, teaching school and rushing home to relieve Rebecca from evening chores so she could relax a bit with her puffy feet elevated.

Hannah usually prepared lessons and graded papers long after the family had retired for the evening. Though she was often tired, it was a good kind of tired, a satisfying kind of tired. If it wasn't for that little niggle of fear always lurking in the background of her mind, she would be completely happy.

By Saturday, Rebecca was feeling much better. Now in her second trimester, her nausea had subsided greatly. As long as she had a few minutes to rest each day, her ankle swelling remained minimal and her energy level increased. She was looking forward to getting out and attending Sarah's work frolic as much as Hannah was.

"Would you like me to stay home with the *kinner*?" Hannah asked as they tidied the kitchen after breakfast.

"Absolutely not!" Rebecca responded. "You've been excited about this frolic since Sarah invited us."

"*Jah*, but I'd rather make things easier for you."

"Don't worry about the *kinner*. Samuel will keep the *buwe* busy for sure and the girls will come with us. There will be other little ones there to play with. And the older girls will watch out for the wee ones. I'm feeling *gut* so we're all set."

"Okay, if you're sure."

"I'm sure and certain."

Hannah wasn't exactly sure what to expect at this frolic, but Rebecca was right. She was excited. She wanted to learn all she could about the Amish way of life and to participate in as many activities as possible. She believed in making fully informed decisions, but she was nearly one hundred percent sure this was the life for her. This was where she was meant to be. Though her aunt, uncle, and cousins warmly welcomed her into their family, she hadn't felt this complete sense of belonging since before her parents died.

"I've put the pies and cookies in the buggy," Hannah said, returning to the warm kitchen. "It hasn't warmed up much outside."

"At least the drive to Sarah's won't be long," Rebecca replied.

Hannah just began to feel the chill seep into her bones, despite wearing her heavy cape, gloves, and bonnet, as they drove into the Fishers' driveway. Smoke curled from the chimney of the two-story house, promising warmth.

In the living room, women, young and old, sat around a big quilting frame to put finishing touches on Sarah's wedding quilt. Hannah was glad to see only one vacant chair and encouraged Rebecca to sit there. She could probably figure out the quilting since Rebecca and Samuel's sister Barbara had been helping her "relearn" quilting skills, but she felt clumsy and slow. She didn't want to do anything to mess up Sarah's special quilt.

Instead, she felt content to work on smaller projects for Sarah's home—crocheted potholders and embroidered tea towels. These, she could handle. Emma and Elizabeth were all too happy to play with the other young children who'd tagged along with their mothers.

The women chatted nonstop as their needles flew in and out of the fabric. Frolics provided a good opportunity to catch up on news, not just of their own families but also news of kin and friends living in other communities.

Hannah mainly listened, absorbing details and trying to remember facts. She already knew Rebecca's family lived in Ohio, and she hadn't seen them in quite a while. Some families travelled by bus or hired drivers, but Rebecca's family didn't make the trip often.

Sarah's family had cousins in Sugar Creek, Ohio. One of those cousins happened to be Andrew, who Esther dubbed "a thorn in her side." Other families had relatives or friends in Pennsylvania, Indiana, and even Michigan. They stayed in regular contact through circle letters—letters passed around from person to person each adding news — or through the *Budget*, the Plain newspaper.

"Psst!" Sarah whispered, nudging Hannah who sat enrapt, listening to one of Naomi Beiler's stories. "Want to help me?"

Hannah nodded and slipped from the room behind Sarah. "What can I do?"

"Before the others come out to help with the refreshments, I wanted to talk to you."

Hannah waited without speaking.

"I just wanted to tell you that I wanted to ask you to be one of my wedding attendants, but since I can only have two couples, I asked Esther, of course, and felt I had to ask one of my cousins." Sarah spoke quickly, her voice barely above a whisper.

"I'm honored you wanted to ask me," Hannah whispered back. "Esther has been your friend forever. And it's only right you should include your cousin."

"I just wanted you to know that I — well, I think of you as a *gut* friend." Sarah pushed her glasses back into place.

"I think of you the same way." Hannah squeezed Sarah's arm. "I'm happy to help out however I can." She didn't say she was relieved she wouldn't be an attendant because she had practically no idea what functions the attendant performed. She had been a bridesmaid in two college friends' weddings, but she was certain the duties were nowhere near the same.

The days had been growing shorter and darkness threatened as the women gathered up dishes, plates, and sewing supplies to head home. Since they only had a few miles to travel, Hannah knew they would arrive home before daylight completely faded. She still felt a little uneasy outside in the vast darkness with no streetlights to cast a glow.

Rebecca stopped at the end of the driveway so Hannah could check the mailbox. She crossed her fingers, hoping for a letter from Liz. Instead, she pulled out a letter addressed to Rebecca on which rested a handwritten note. Hannah scanned the message, her heart pounding.

Don't bother going inside, little bunny, she read silently. She crumpled the paper, concealing it in her hand. Was someone watching her and waiting for a time to pounce? Were they watching her squirm, a game to amuse them until they moved in for the kill? Were the other victims stalked first? What did these strange words mean?

There had to be a connection between all the notes. It was right there at the edge of her memory, waiting for her to grasp.

The first Thursday in November dawned crisp but bright—a beautiful wedding day for Sarah and Zeke. Hannah and Rebecca hurried to get the family fed and the kitchen tidied before bustling everyone out to the buggy. Hannah was excited and nervous for the bride. She had gone to Sarah's home after school every day the past week to help with wedding preparations. So much cleaning, cooking, and baking had been necessary.

The wedding would be held in the Fishers' barn since the house was not large enough to accommodate the nearly three hundred guests. Out-of-town relatives, including Andrew and his family, had already arrived. Some were staying with the Fishers while others stayed with various families in the community. Hannah felt sure Rebecca and Samuel would have offered to host a family if she wasn't occupying their spare room—a room that would be needed by babies in a few months. Hannah wouldn't visit that topic now.

Gray buggies streamed onto the Fishers' property. Older boys helped unhitch while older girls carried food into the house or minded younger children as their mamms flitted about, helping with last-minute details. Church benches had already been arranged in the barn, set up exactly as they were for Sunday services.

Hannah took her seat with the unmarried women as she usually did for church services while the men and boys filled the opposite benches. Hannah thought Sarah looked nervous, but her eyes sparkled behind her glasses. Her blue dress, though new, was the same style as all other Amish dresses. Hannah had witnessed Sarah finish the last hemming stitches at her frolic. Her white organdy apron and *kapp* were new as well.

Her solemn expression hid the excitement Hannah knew bubbled inside. Across the way, Zeke's pale face and serious demeanor presented a contrast to his usual jovial nature. He sat stiff and straight in his new black suit and white shirt. As the congregation began singing the first song, Zeke and Sarah left to meet privately with the bishop and ministers.

There were no processions, no fancy bridesmaids, no flower girls scattering rose petals down the aisle—all quite different from any weddings Hannah had ever attended. Instead, the day was practically like any other church service. The congregation continued singing hymns from the Ausbund. After about twenty minutes, Sarah and Zeke returned and took their seats as before. Bishop Sol and the ministers entered the Fishers' barn, and the three-hour service continued with the opening sermon, prayer, Bible readings, and main sermon.

The actual wedding vows weren't exchanged until near the end of the long service. Sarah and Zeke promised to care for one another in weakness, sickness, or any similar circumstance. Sarah answered in a quivering but sure voice.

Hannah waited for Sarah to reach up to fiddle with her glasses as she was apt to do when nervous, but she kept her hands at her side. Zeke's response came out loud and strong. They promised to love each other and be patient with each other and to remain together until parted by death. Divorce, Hannah had learned, was a sin and forbidden by the Amish church. Marriage was for life, no matter what.

After speaking their vows, Sarah and Zeke were pronounced husband and wife and then returned to their seats. There was no exchange of rings and no kiss to seal their covenant. Tears pooled in Hannah's eyes at the touching, solemn service. Somehow, without all the *Englisch* wedding hoopla, this simple Amish wedding seemed most reverent. Hannah sniffed as quietly as possible and swiped at a tear before it could roll down her cheek.

She could feel eyes upon her and when she lifted her gaze to the opposite side of the barn, she discovered Jacob's blue eyes fastened on her, He smiled ever so briefly. Heat sprang into her cheeks, but she managed a quick, tremulous smile before looking away.

The service continued with further messages given by church leaders, a few more songs, and a lengthy kneeling prayer. At the conclusion, the congregation filed out of the Stauffers' barn. Finally, smiles broke out in abundance as the post-wedding festivities began.

Sarah, her mother, friends, and other family members had been working for days to prepare food for the huge noon meal. The guests would be served in shifts. Hannah, one of the servers, slipped away from Emma and Elizabeth who had been holding her hands. The men quickly assembled tables using the church benches while the women bustled about the kitchen.

"All that celery Sarah's mamm planted didn't go to waste after all," Esther whispered, nudging Hannah and nodding at the jars of celery decorating the tables. Hannah had already seen the bowls of creamed celery in the kitchen when she dropped off the food she and Rebecca had brought.

Sarah and Zeke and their attendants occupied the *eck*, the corner table where they could see all their guests. Esther wrinkled her nose and made a face when she moved away from Hannah to take her place at the *eck*. She had been paired with Andrew, one of Zeke's attendants, and was not terribly pleased with that arrangement.

Hannah suspected Esther wasn't nearly as upset as she led everyone to believe. She had seen the briefest spark in Esther's eyes when Andrew arrived for the wedding. The other attendants—Grace, Sarah's cousin whose family moved to an Amish community in Delaware several years ago and Adam, Zeke's close friend—were the only other occupants at the *eck*.

When the tables of the first shift were filled, Bishop Sol gave the signal for the silent prayer. All heads bowed in unison to give thanks for the bounteous meal. Hannah helped serve the roast chicken and ham, mashed potatoes, gravy, coleslaw, beets, green beans, and of course, creamed celery, to the hungry guests. After the first group finished eating, she helped wash dishes and reset tables for the second sitting.

Despite the cool November day, perspiration trickled down Hannah's back. She blew a loose wisp of hair from her face and made a mental note to re-pin her hair whenever she got the chance. *It's a good thing the help ate first or we'd never have the energy for all this work.* Hannah suppressed a weary sigh and hurried to bring more food to the tables.

The noon meal lasted well into the afternoon. As guests finished eating, adults visited with one another while young people sang or played games. Everyone seemed to be enjoying the festivities—quite a contrast to the solemn wedding service. Hannah felt she had been scurrying about, toting heavy plates and bowls and washing dishes all her life. She was happy when the married women shooed her out of the kitchen to join the other unmarried folks outside

Hannah finally had the chance to smooth wandering strands of hair back under her *kapp* as she pushed open the back door of the Fishers' house. She inhaled the crisp air, relieved to escape the stuffy kitchen where she had spent much of the past few hours. Children still played, their noses and cheeks tinted a bright red color by the cool breeze. Soon, parents would gather them up and head for home to leave the rest of the evening to the young adults.

From the corner of her eye, Hannah glimpsed Esther waving at her. Before she reached where Esther stood talking to Grace, Adam, Andrew, and Jacob, another movement captured her attention.

The bicyclist in the red cap pedaled down the road toward the Fisher house. Since the house sat closer to the road than many of the other Amish homes, Hannah got a fairly clear view of the man. His cap, pulled down low, shadowed identifying details of his face, as usual, but something seemed familiar about him. Maybe it was just that she'd seen him so many times. He always seemed to turn up out of the blue.

She gasped, her mouth hanging open, when the biker actually rode up the Fisher driveway a short distance before turning around to head back the direction he came from.

"Hey, Hannah!" Esther called. "Are you coming to visit with us?"

Hannah pulled her attention from the road. "Be right there."

"You look pale. Everything okay?" Jacob's voice held concern.

"*Jah*. It's just been a busy day." Hannah glanced over her shoulder quickly. The biker had vanished. She shivered slightly. Who was that guy?

"Hey! You look like you saw a ghost," Esther teased. "*Was ist letz?*"

"N-nothing. I guess I'm just tired."

"But the festivities are just beginning," Andrew said. "What do you know of ghosts, Essie?"

"It's *Esther*! I haven't been Essie in years, *Andy*."

"Okay. Okay. Calm down."

As the two continued to bicker, Jacob whispered, "Do you need to sit down?"

"*Nee*, Jacob. I'll be fine." Hannah managed a weak smile.

Hannah chatted with the others for a while, asking Grace and Andrew about their communities. Though it was nothing new to the others, Hannah found it fascinating that each community had different customs. When Hannah began to shiver—from cold, this time, instead of from fear—the group moved into the barn where other young people had begun singing.

A wedding supper would follow the singing, and Hannah wondered how on earth anyone would ever be able to consume one more morsel of food. As the supper time neared, she was shocked to hear her own stomach rumble with hunger. Apparently, all that lifting and carrying and cleaning and scurrying about burned off the calories from the vegetables she had eaten earlier.

The wedding supper custom, Hannah discovered, was for the young people to sit in couples. Every young man was supposed to bring a young woman to the table. Fine for the courting couples, Hannah thought, but what about everyone else? Some of the younger boys' faces turned tomato red as they forced themselves to approach a girl.

"Will you sit with me?" Jacob spoke into Hannah's ear.

"I'd be happy to sit with you." Hannah felt the flush work its way up her body. She wondered if her face was as red as the faces of the boys she had been watching. The curse of pale skin.

"Will you do me the honor, Miss *Esther?*" Andrew exaggerated a bow.

"Hmmm." Esther tapped her index finger against her cheek as if in deep thought.

"Go on, Esther." Grace laughed at Andrew's antics. "Don't make him grovel."

"Groveling would be good for him, I'm thinking," Esther replied.

"I'll call you Essie the rest of my visit if you don't sit with me." Andrew still bent at the waist in a bow but looked up and wiggled his eyebrows at Esther.

"Ach! You would, wouldn't you? All right, then. Get up!"

"So bossy!" Andrew straightened and reached to clasp Esther's hand. She promptly shook her hand free and marched off toward the supper, leaving Andrew trotting to catch up.

Hannah and Jacob burst out laughing. Jacob held out a hand to Hannah almost hesitantly. *Is he afraid I'll refuse to hold his hand* as *Esther refused Andrew?*

Her brain again admonished her to walk away from Jacob, to guard her heart and his. *Too late,* her heart cried out. Hannah placed her small, cool hand in Jacob's large, warm one and smiled up into his face. Jacob smiled back and, ever so gently, squeezed her fingers.

Cakes, cookies, and pies of every kind followed meats, vegetables, and salads. Any families still lingering now headed for home, except for the married couples who had volunteered to clean up the kitchen. The young, unmarried folks visited and sang until midnight. Hannah thought she would surely fall asleep on her feet. She stifled yawns and struggled to focus on the conversations buzzing around her.

"You look exhausted," Jacob whispered. "Would you like me to take you home now?"

"That would be *wunderbaar*."

Jacob took Hannah's arm to lead her out to his courting buggy. They said good night to the newlyweds and everyone else still lingering in the barn. Jacob practically lifted Hannah into the buggy before climbing in and clucking to the horse. She felt light as a feather in his arms. She felt right in his arms.

Hannah's head bobbed in time to the clip clop of the horse's hooves until it rested against his shoulder. Jacob smiled. He resisted the strong urge to put his arm around Hannah and pull her closer to him. At the Hertzler's back door, Hannah slid out of the buggy into his waiting arms. He helped her walk up the steps and planted a gentle kiss on her forehead.

"*Gut nacht*, Hannah," he whispered into her hair that still smelled like lilacs, even after a long, hard day.

Hannah sighed. "*Gut nacht*, Jacob. *Danki* for-for everything." She squeezed his hand briefly before opening the door and slipping inside. Whistling softly, Jacob returned to his buggy, the scent of lilacs still tantalizing him.

Chapter Eighteen

Hannah had conjured up the mistaken notion that Southern Maryland meant a southern climate. She couldn't have been more wrong. She was accustomed to cold breezes blowing inland from the ocean but not to such downright frigid temperatures—and snow! And it was only late November. Even Rebecca and Samuel were surprised at this early-in-the-season cold spell. Some years, they told her, winters were mild with not a single flake of snow anywhere. Other years presented the direct opposite scenario. Apparently, this was one of those "other" years.

They were constantly filling one wood box with oak and other hardwood and another box with slab wood to burn along with the oak. Hannah dreaded throwing off her quilt and blanket every morning, her feet tingling with cold before they even touched the wood floor. Her slight body felt nearly frozen stiff by the time she and the boys travelled the relatively short distance to the schoolhouse. Samuel had told her repeatedly to "bulk up" for the winter. She assumed he had been teasing. Wrong again.

The Hertzlers had celebrated Thanksgiving with Barbara and Henry Zook and their family. Barbara knew her younger sister-in-law had her hands full with four youngsters and the side effects of pregnancy so had offered to host the meal in her home. Rebecca and Hannah brought side dishes and desserts, but Barbara roasted the turkeys and prepared the mashed potatoes, stuffing, and gravy. Henry's brother Amos and his family joined the gathering with their five children, making for a very full house. Conversation centered around family stories, the unusually cold weather, and the upcoming annual quilt auction scheduled for Saturday.

"It will be my first quilt auction here," Hannah said to Barbara as they washed and dried a mountain of dishes after the sumptuous dinner and dessert. "Tell me about it." She couldn't say this would be her first quilt auction ever.

"Well, this is our biggest fundraising event," Barbara began. "We auction off the quilts we've been stitching all year and sell other homemade items—you know, quilted, knitted, or crocheted things—as well as jams and jellies. The men have furniture and tools for auction, too. Esther may sell some of her herbs and plants and Sophie may sell some of her teas."

"Lots of people come," Anna Zook, Barbara's sister-in-law chimed in. "Plain folks and *Englischers*."

"We use the money for our community funds," Rebecca said from her chair where Barbara made her sit with her feet elevated. "You know, to help with medical costs if someone needs help or for the school."

Hannah nodded. She knew the Amish did not have any kind of insurance—either health or life or homeowners'. They all pitched in to help whoever faced catastrophic circumstances and pulled from this community fund when necessary. At first, Hannah couldn't imagine going without medical insurance when just a simple doctor visit could cost a small fortune. Then she realized *she* had no medical insurance. She sent up a silent prayer, asking God to keep her healthy. Samuel and Rebecca faced the possibility of huge medical expenses if Rebecca delivered the twins early or had any complications that Carrie, the midwife, couldn't handle. Hannah sent another prayer heavenward.

Saturday began frosty but bright. The quilt auction would be held in Levi Esh's big barn as it had been in past years. Since school was not in session on Friday, men, women, and children worked hard all that day, setting everything up for the auction. A local *Englisch* auctioneer graciously donated his time again this year.

Daylight had just taken charge of the sky when buggy after buggy drove up the driveway. Men unhitched horses and turned them out to pasture. Women scurried from kitchen to barn, carrying refreshments. Children generally tried to stay out of the way if they weren't pressed into some sort of service.

Before long cars, trucks, and vans cluttered the driveway and field area designated for parking. Promptly at nine o'clock, the auction got underway.

Having never been to any kind of auction, Hannah was mesmerized by the auctioneer. How could anyone talk like that? She gasped at the high amounts of money many *Englischers* were willing to pay for the quilts. Granted, the quilts were beautiful and flawlessly hand-stitched, but bidding often rose to over a thousand dollars.

From time to time, Hannah felt eyes boring into her back. She hesitated to turn around for fear she'd be staring at the red-capped bicyclist. When she did venture a peak, she found Jeremiah Yoder frowning at her. Why did he have such an unfriendly expression? Amos Zook wore a matching frown. Henry Zook, standing next to his brother, seemed oblivious to everything but the auctioneer.

Bishop Sol caught her eye next. With his full dark beard and heavy eyebrows, she had difficulty interpreting the expression on his face. She didn't see scowl or frown lines, though. Maybe Jeremiah and Amos were upset about some item being auctioned. She was pretty sure she hadn't done anything to offend them.

Hannah's eyes darted around the barn in search of a friendlier face. They paused on Jacob who nodded and smiled at her. She smiled back at him. *That's more like it. I can always count on Jake for moral support.*

Englischers clutching quilts, handmade faceless dolls, crocheted or knitted afghans, dishcloths, and other items made their way to the barn door as Amish men helped *Englisch* men carry furniture to waiting vehicles. Few items remained to be put away since the auction had been so successful.

Hannah sighed in relief that the day had gone so well and that she had had no strange visitors and had received no mysterious notes. She helped clean up the refreshment area which also was mostly devoid of leftovers. Men who weren't helping to load cars and trucks began restoring Henry's barn to order. The auctioneer gathered up his equipment and departed. Final cleanup was all that was left to do.

Full of people, the barn had warmed up nicely — in fact, it had become almost stuffy. Now, nearly empty, the barn's temperature began dropping. Hannah rubbed her hands briskly together before picking up the last food containers to carry into the house. She straightened and turned abruptly, almost crashing into Jeremiah Yoder.

"Hannah, we need to have word with you." Jeremiah's voice was no friendlier than his countenance. He jerked his head slightly at the approaching school board members. Reuben Hostetler and Amos Zook scowled. Henry Zook looked like he'd rather be anywhere else but standing beside his brother. Bishop Sol was unreadable, as usual. In the periphery, Hannah spied Samuel and Jacob.

What on earth could be wrong? Her lessons followed the specifications set forth by the Ordnung. At least she thought they had. No science to speak of, no evolution or any other such atrocities. Reading, mathematics, spelling, handwriting, geography…she mentally ticked off the subjects. Jeremiah cleared his throat, waiting for some response from her.

"C-certainly," she stammered. *"Was ist…?"* Hannah looked from one board member to another.

She suddenly felt like ice water flowed through her veins, and her stomach struggled to hang onto the vegetables and cookies she had eaten throughout the day.

Jeremiah cleared his throat again. "None of the Pennsylvania communities we have contacted knows of you or had any information about an injured woman who suffered some memory loss. Do you want to explain?"

"Hannah Kurtz is a pretty common name," Henry offered in Hannah's defense.

"*Jah*," Amos agreed, "but someone would know of an accident or mishap and the Hannah Kurtz associated with it."

"It doesn't make sense," Reuben Hostetler chimed in. Bishop Sol remained silent. All eyes bored into Hannah's.

"Who are you, Hannah Kurtz?" Jeremiah demanded.

"*Jah*. You've been living in my house. Just who are you?" Samuel had moved from the edge of the group to stand right in front of Hannah. Hannah waited for him to poke an accusing finger at her.

"I-I…" Hannah gulped. Tears sprang to her eyes. She blinked hard and swallowed. What should she say? "I *am* Hannah," she began. "I have an ID at home—at Samuel's house."

"Then where are you really from, *Hannah*?" Jeremiah's cheeks puffed out and reddened. Hannah expected to see his eyes bulge and steam emit from his ears. With effort, he calmed himself and unclenched his hands that had formed fists at his sides. Why wasn't Bishop Sol saying anything?

Hannah remained silent. If she blew her cover, she could endanger the community even more. No one would ever trust her again. They probably wouldn't trust her or welcome her now anyway. Why did she ever accept the teaching job? Then they wouldn't have had a reason to investigate her.

"An answer, please, Hannah," Samuel demanded. "I welcomed you into my home. I trusted you with my *fraa* and my *kinner*. We have all trusted you with our *kinner*."

"I love them!" Hannah exclaimed. "And I love your family, Samuel. I would never do anything to hurt anyone." Hannah's tears were close to spilling down her cheeks.

"Then tell us the truth."

Across the room, Hannah saw Jacob's expression change from shock to hurt. He hung his head and slipped from the barn. She had to talk to him.

"I-I…"

"Maybe she doesn't remember. Have you all thought of that?" Esther moved to stand beside Hannah. She pressed a tissue into Hannah's hand and wrapped an arm around Hannah's waist. Hannah hadn't been aware that Esther was even in the barn. She was probably the only Amish woman who would stand up to an Amish man, let alone the entire school board. Hannah immediately gained strength from her friend's presence.

"How do we know she was even injured and suffered a memory loss?" Amos barely concealed his ire.

"Why would you doubt her now? She has been kind and helpful to everyone, and she's a good teacher," Esther defended.

"How would you know what kind of teacher she is? You don't have any *kinner* in the school," Jeremiah shot back.

"Well, you do, Jeremiah Yoder. Have your *kinner* ever complained? Have you ever visited the school or looked at your *kinners'* lessons? I'll tell you, if I did have little ones, I'd be happy Hannah was their teacher."

"You are bordering on disrespect, Esther." Bishop Sol's quiet comment was his first utterance throughout the entire exchange.

"I don't mean to be disrespectful. I just want you all to think before you cast stones."

"No one is casting stones," Bishop Sol said.

"It sure seems that way to me," Esther sputtered. "Well, just look at this tiny little thing. She couldn't hurt a fly." Esther looked briefly down at the smaller woman beside her and then glared at the men standing in front of them.

"We didn't accuse her of hurting anyone, Esther. We're talking about deception here," Reuben said. "Just what are you up to?" His gaze slid from Esther to Hannah.

Hannah fought not to shrink back or to hide behind Esther. She felt like a child clutching her mother's skirts in fear and peeping out briefly only to withdraw into the shadows. "I-I-only w-want to live here, to b-be part of the community, and t-to teach the scholars. This feels like home to me…" Hannah's voice trailed off. How much more dare she say? "P-please don't make me leave," she added in a whisper. Despite the chill in the barn, Hannah's icy hands felt clammy. She rubbed them down the sides of her purple dress and resisted the urge to tuck them under her armpits to warm them.

"We cannot have a dishonest person teaching our scholars." Jeremiah was emphatic.

"I cannot have a dishonest person living in my house, influencing my *fraa* and *kinner*!" Samuel was even more emphatic.

Hannah gasped. "W-what are you saying, Samuel?" She couldn't believe what was happening.

"I'm saying I think it would be better for you to live somewhere else."

"You're throwing me out? Where will…"

"Samuel Hertzler, I'm ashamed of you." Esther stomped her foot for emphasis.

"Esther, this really isn't any of your business."

"It most certainly is my business. Hannah is my *freind*, and I believe in her. I trust her."

"Hannah, we're still waiting for an answer from you. You could clear this whole matter up," Jeremiah interjected.

Hannah stared at her sturdy black shoes and struggled to gain some semblance of composure. "I-I don't know what—I'm not sure what to say," she stammered. She was so torn. She wanted to tell the truth. She had always wanted to tell the truth. For the community's protection and for her own, she was sworn to secrecy.

Yet these men demanded an answer. They deserved an answer—an honest one. Hannah dragged in a deep, ragged breath and lifted her eyes to the expectant faces. Samuel, Jeremiah, and Amos still scowled. Reuben's and Henry's faces were neutral. Bishop Sol looked—Hannah wasn't sure. Expectant? Hopeful? At some point, Jacob had sneaked back into the barn and planted himself at a distance but still close enough to hear every word spoken.

Hannah prayed silently Jacob would forgive her. Before she could change her mind and before sobs overtook her, she blurted out the gist of her story. The stony faces in front of her now registered shock mixed with anger, all except for Bishop Sol, who gave her a slight nod. Jacob fled the barn as though chased by a demon.

"I knew it!" Esther exclaimed.

"Esther Stauffer, you knew about this matter and didn't tell anyone?" Amos exploded.

"*Nee*, of course not. I meant I knew there was some mystery surrounding Hannah."

"You read too many books," Jeremiah grumbled.

"I can't believe you put my family in danger. My *fraa* and my *kinner* could have been hurt," Samuel struggled to keep his voice beneath a shouting decibel.

"*Nee*, Samuel, I would never cause anyone to be hurt."

"Your very presence could cause someone to be hurt."

"N-no one has hurt me, so I-I don't think anyone else would be hurt." Hannah swiped at a tear. Esther clutched Hannah's arm tighter. Hannah was grateful her friend hadn't run out the door as Jacob had. "Please," she whispered. "I love it here. I want to be part of your community. I want to be Amish. I feel Amish. I'll do whatever you require to be baptized. Even if you don't let me teach, please let me stay. Please." Tears chased each other down her cheeks.

"You can't be a threat to my family," Samuel repeated.

"R-Rebecca n-needs h-help," Hannah tried to reason with him.

"I'm sure some of the women—*Amish* women—will be happy to help if we need help."

"She's not Amish. She can't teach our scholars!" Amos exploded.

"I-I love teaching. I-I love the *kinner*."

"She's a good teacher," Reuben mumbled.

"What's that?" Amos demanded.

"I said she's a good teacher. My boy Caleb actually likes going to school for the first time ever."

"We don't have anyone else who wants to teach right now. Couldn't we let her teach at least until we find someone? Her teaching has been fine." Hannah wanted to hug Henry Zook, but she held her breath and didn't move a muscle.

"Where's she going to live? Samuel doesn't want her at his place," Jeremiah said. Hannah winced. It hurt for Samuel to turn against her.

"With me, of course!" Esther interrupted. "We've got plenty of room."

"You'd better check with your daed and mamm. They don't know the story," Reuben advised.

"Of course I'll check, but I know they will agree with me. They like Hannah, and they are forgiving people, like we are all supposed to be." Hannah shot Esther a grateful, shaky smile.

"Bishop Sol," Jeremiah called. "You haven't said a thing. What are your thoughts?"

Now, I'm doomed. A myriad thoughts whirled around Hannah's brain, none of them comforting. *They all respect the bishop and listen to him. What will be his verdict? I'm not even sure he likes me.*

Chapter Nineteen

Bishop Sol stroked his long, gray-streaked brown beard as if in deep thought. His gaze scanned the expectant face of each man standing around him briefly before settling on Hannah. Hannah sucked in her breath and tried not to cringe as she awaited the bishop's forthcoming condemnation. "I think Hannah can continue teaching."

Hannah exhaled. *What did he say?* Maybe her heart was pounding too loudly for her to hear correctly.

"She's not Amish!" Jeremiah cried. "We need a meeting to discuss this."

"She has been following the Ordnung. Her lessons are good. I've visited the school numerous times." Hannah had only seen the bishop in her classroom a few times. His must have been the presence she felt occasionally while she was involved in lessons and didn't actually see anyone.

"If you wish to meet, we will. I say she continues to teach for now. We will let her know our decision at the Christmas break." Bishop Sol's manner left no room for discussion or argument.

"She lied to us," Samuel said through clenched teeth. Hannah didn't think Samuel would forgive her any time soon, even though forgiveness was the Amish way. She supposed Jacob would feel the same way. Ach, Jacob! She had to talk to him.

"She had good reason." Bishop Sol's voice dropped so low it was barely audible.

"Are you, of all people, condoning lying?" Amos demanded.

"*Nee*. Lying is never *gut*. I don't believe Hannah chose to lie." Hannah stared in amazement. She would never have pegged the bishop as her defender.

"Bishop Sol," Esther began then stopped as if unsure she should continue. She took a deep breath and forged ahead. "Did you know about all this before—before Hannah even came here?" Esther *was* good at ferreting out information. She would make a good detective, Hannah thought.

Bishop Sol looked at his feet momentarily, obviously wrestling with himself, and then looked at Esther. "*Jah*."

"What?" Jeremiah was incredulous. "How could you have allowed our community to be endangered? You jeopardized our lives and our families' lives."

"When? How?" Amos sputtered. "Who proposed this whole idea? How could—" He broke off and shook his head, obviously trying to calm himself.

Hannah's knees grew weak. If Esther hadn't still been clinging to her, she surely would have collapsed at the feet of her accusers. The bishop knew all this time but kept mum? She could have had a confidante. Instead of fearing the man, she could have sought his support and advice. He was an even better secret keeper than she was.

"Can you explain please, Bishop?" Henry, the calmest of them all, obviously tried to keep the peace.

"*Jah*." Bishop Sol paused thoughtfully. "A U.S. Marshal—O'Brien his name was—came to see me to ask for help."

"How did he know about you?" Amos interrupted.

"Let him talk, brother," Henry said.

"Well, I'll tell you," Bishop Sol continued. "A young Amish woman—or formerly Amish woman—gave him the idea of placing Hannah here."

"Liz," Hannah whispered.

"Elizabeth Lapp—or she used to be Lapp. Anyway, she married an *Englischer* before joining her Amish church. Her husband's brother is a detective in Virginia where Hannah is from. This Elizabeth was from Lancaster County but had heard of a smaller group of Amish in St. Mary's County—us. She told the police or marshals or whoever that this should be a safe place for Hannah. The marshal came to see me and said time was tight. I thought about this and prayed. I figured the Lord would want us to help a young woman in trouble through no fault of her own."

"You didn't think to ask the rest of us?" Jeremiah acted as if he had personally been betrayed.

"I suspected the marshal was right. The more people who knew, the greater the chance Hannah would be found out. We will keep this information to ourselves." Bishop Sol looked each man in the eye, even Jacob standing in the corner of the barn. Each man nodded begrudgingly.

"I don't like this," Amos said. "We could all be in danger."

"Not if we all keep our mouths closed," Esther replied.

"What's done is done," Henry sighed. "Now, it is our duty to keep Hannah safe. We can't throw her out to the wolves." Henry gave Hannah a quick wink. She tried to smile but feared she only produced a lopsided grimace.

"But not in my house," Samuel hissed.

"We got that already, Samuel." Esther tapped her foot. "I already told you Hannah could stay with me. We'll come by and get her belongings."

"Are you sure, Esther?" Hannah knew she had no other option but didn't want Esther to feel obligated to uphold her offer after hearing the facts.

"For sure and for certain. We'll go by Samuel's after we leave here."

"*Danki*, Bishop Sol," Hannah whispered as Esther whisked her out of the barn. "I-I need to talk to someone else."

"I suspect so. I just hope he's not mule headed."

Dusk flirted with the sky as Hannah and Esther exited the Eshs' barn. Any other evening, Hannah would have gazed in awe at the streaks of scarlet and pink staining the sky. This evening, Hannah didn't notice the sky. Her only thought was locating Jacob and trying to salvage their budding relationship. They had grown much closer during Jacob's Saturday night visits.

With Jacob, Hannah experienced feelings she had never dreamed possible. She'd thought he had similar feelings for her. Esther elbowed her and nodded toward the figure loosening the horse tethered near the far side of the barn. Esther gave Hannah a little shove in that direction. "I'll talk to mamm."

Hannah's heart pounded as she drew in a shaky breath and hurried toward the lone figure silhouetted against the backdrop of the fiery sky. Even if she couldn't see his features clearly, she'd know Jacob's stance anywhere. As she approached him, she could see the slump in his shoulders. She could feel his dejection, his pain. "Jacob?" Her voice came out as a near whisper.

Jacob looked at Hannah and then back at his horse. "I don't have anything to say to you." He turned his back to her.

"Jacob, please listen to me. Let me explain."

"Do you have more lies to tell me?" She'd never before heard bitterness in his voice, even when he told her about Anna.

Hannah touched Jacob's arm tentatively. At least he didn't recoil from her. "Jake…" she began.

"Who are you? I thought I knew you. I thought I could trust you. I thought you were different from…"

"I'm the same person Jacob. I'm the same inside. I feel the same things. I believe the same things, no matter what my background, no matter how I came to be here."

"*Nee*. You haven't been truthful."

"How could I tell you everything without endangering everyone?"

"You would have kept pretending? When would you have told me the truth? Ever? You must have laughed inside at this dumb Amish man."

"Never, Jacob! I truly, truly care about you. You heard me tell the bishop and the school board that I want to stay. I want to receive instruction and be baptized."

"Is that all a lie, too? More pretending just to take advantage of us?" Hannah detected a tremor in his voice. Even with the approaching darkness, she could see the hurt in his amazing blue eyes.

"*Nee*, Jacob. I never wanted to pretend—ever. I had to. Don't you see? I love the people here. I want to make my home here. I really am an honest person."

"You sure have a funny way of showing it."

"Please, Jacob, try to understand."

"I understand all right. I understand that I was *narrisch* to trust another woman. You're just like Anna!" Jacob spat the name out with disgust.

Hannah felt she had been kicked in the stomach by a mule. The pain started in her belly and rose to squeeze her heart. With great difficulty, she caught her breath and tried to speak past the lump nearly blocking her throat.

"*Nee*, Jacob. I'm not like Anna at all. My feelings for you are not pretend. Don't you see? My life was in danger. The marshal arranged everything even though I didn't want to ever cause anyone any harm or be untruthful. For my safety and everyone else's safety, I had to go along with the story."

"The deception."

"I-I guess you could call it that."

"I do call it that. Deception, plain and simple."

"I really am Hannah Kurtz. My identity has been changed. My parents really did die when I was young, and I really did live with my aunt, uncle, and cousins. They just weren't Amish. This is my life now. I *want* this to be my life."

"It will be a life without me," Jacob muttered and turned to jump into his buggy.

"Ach, Jacob! Please." Hannah reached out to stop him, but he shrugged her hand off his arm. He leapt into the buggy and clucked to his horse. Hannah dropped to her knees in the dirt, sobbing as though her heart was broken.

She stared at the orange triangle on Jacob's retreating buggy. Tears like a waterfall cascaded down her cheeks. Esther rushed to her side, grasped her upper arm, and pulled her to her feet. "That didn't go well, I'm taking it."

"N-not at all," Hannah sniffed. "H-He'll n-never forgive me."

"*Jah*, he will. He's Amish. He'll have to forgive."

"Maybe in words but never in his heart."

"He's a stubborn, pig-headed mule whose brain must have fallen into that watering trough," Esther fumed. "I have a mind to go right to his house this very minute and—"

"Leave him alone, please. I've hurt him badly."

"You did what you had to do, simple as that. You are hurting, too. Doesn't he see that? Let me talk to him. I've known him all his life. I'll..." Esther continued to fume.

"Esther, you are a true *freind*," Hannah interrupted. The tissue Esther had given her earlier was completely sodden now. Hannah stuffed it in her pocket and resorted to wiping her tears on her sleeve. "I'm glad to have you on my side. I'd sure hate to have you against me. You should have seen yourself."

Hannah began to giggle at Esther's previous words and her wet hen attitude. She didn't know if she was just releasing tension or bordering on hysteria. Esther joined in, and soon, they were both wiping tears from their eyes.

"Please don't say anything to Jacob," Hannah begged when she caught her breath. "Give him time to think."

"I'll give him something to think about, all right!"

"Esther."

"Okay. Let's go get your things. Good thing I brought my plants in my own buggy so we don't have to wait."

"What did you tell your mamm and daed?"

"Since Bishop Sol wants us to keep mum, I told them Samuel wishes to have time with just his family before the *bopplin* come. It was kind of lame, I know, but it's as close to the truth as I could get. It sort of gives everyone some kind of motive or alibi or something. Anyway, they bought it, and I heard Samuel give a similar story to Rebecca, who was none too pleased, by the way."

"You do sound like you read suspense novels."

"Shh!"

"You still do?"

"Don't advertise the fact. It's not forbidden. And I only read Christian fiction, but I do like being a sleuth." They both chuckled again as they linked arms and shuffled toward Esther's buggy.

Hannah's thoughts quickly returned to Jacob once Esther turned the horse toward the Stauffer home. His harsh words pierced her heart, her soul. She knew she had lost him forever.

Jacob had wanted to gather Hannah to him and tell her everything would be all right, but he could not—*nee*, would not—go to her. He would not be duped again. He would not make another mistake. Once again, he would have to paste together the fragments of his broken heart.

The crimson glow of sunset had faded, and darkness descended like a shroud over the Hertzler house. The flicker of kerosene and battery-operated lamps beckoned from the windows, but Hannah knew it was not meant as a welcome for her—at least not as far as Samuel was concerned.

Hannah and Esther slid from the buggy and approached the back door of the house. No stars or moon illuminated their way. The sky was a vast, dark emptiness, not unlike Hannah's heart. Unsure whether to knock or simply enter as she always had, Hannah paused at the door closed against the night chill.

Esther, ever bold, reached around Hannah, turned the knob, and pushed open the heavy wood door.

"Rebecca," she called as they entered the mudroom and headed for the kitchen. "It's Esther and Hannah."

"Ach, Hannah!" Rebecca cried, drying her hands on a towel and rushing to embrace Hannah. Her eyes were red and puffy. "I'm so sorry, Hannah. *I* want you to stay. I know you'd never do anything to hurt us."

Obviously, Samuel didn't heed the bishop's warning and told Rebecca more than he should have. Maybe he had to tell her to make her understand his total rejection of Hannah.

"*Danki,*" Hannah whispered "For all your kindness. I'll still help you however I can."

"I know you will. You are like a *schweschder*..."

"*Fraa*, let her get her things." Samuel's disapproval was clear in his cold tone. Hannah hadn't noticed Samuel standing like a statue in a darkened corner of the room, his arms folded across his chest. He clearly wanted her to retrieve her belongings and make a hasty retreat.

"We've had words," Rebecca mouthed.

"*Nee*, Rebecca. Don't let me come between you," Hannah whispered.

"*Fraa!*"

"Just a moment, Samuel. There's no big rush." Hannah had not heard Rebecca contradict Samuel before.

As Hannah moved toward the stairs, Emma flew down them, nearly tumbling head first to the bottom.

"Whoa!" Hannah cried, holding out her arms to catch the child. She swung Emma up to perch on her hip, hugging her hard. "Careful, little one. You don't want to tumble down."

"I don't want you to go, Hannah."

Hannah patted the little girl's back as she began to cry. "It's okay, Emma. I still love you. And I won't be far away—just at Esther's house."

"But that's not here."

Hannah couldn't argue with that. "That's true, but I will still see you and tell you stories." Hannah carried Emma up the stairs. "Do you want to help me?" Emma sniffed and nodded.

Just as she set Emma on her feet, Elizabeth toddled into the room. Upset by her sister's tears, Elizabeth's little bottom lip quivered as her face puckered. "No go!" she wailed.

Hannah bent to scoop her up into a hug as she had done to her sister. "It's okay, sweet *boppli*. I will still play with you." She tickled Elizabeth under her chin until her droopy lip curved upward and a giggle burst forth. "That's better." Hannah deposited the child next to Emma. She caught sight of Eli and Jonas peeking into the room. "*Kum, buwe.*" The boys flew into the room and each hugged Hannah tightly.

"I thought the *kinner* were in bed," Samuel bellowed from below. All four children jumped at the harsh sound of their daed's voice.

Rebecca shuffled into the room, panting after climbing the stairs yet again. "*Kum*, let's get to bed." She attempted to herd them to their rooms.

"Help Hannah," Emma whispered sniffing.

"I will help Hannah." Rebecca smoothed strands of Emma's hair off her cheek where her tears had plastered them. "You all go hop back into your beds. I will be there to tuck you back in soon."

The boys said goodnight and slipped back down the hall to their room. It was obvious they wanted to do nothing to further rouse Samuel's ire.

"Don't forget your doll." Emma handed Hannah the faceless Amish doll.

Once again, Hannah felt a kinship with the doll. Once again, she felt faceless, nameless, and homeless. She clutched the doll to her.

"*Danki*, Emma." She hugged both girls again before Emma grasped Elizabeth's tiny hand and led her from the room.

"I was almost afraid to leave Esther alone with Samuel. No telling what she will say to him," Rebecca said.

Hannah smiled. "I know what you mean, but Esther means well."

"She has a heart of gold, but her tongue can get her into trouble.

Hannah stuffed her personal belongings and clothes into her duffle bag while Rebecca gathered up Hannah's quilting and crocheting materials. Her school bag, still packed, sat near the door.

"Are you okay?" Hannah knew Rebecca didn't need this additional stress.

"*Jah*." Rebecca patted her expanding belly. "Just some extra aches and pains since there are two of them in there."

"If you need me, just send for me—anytime. Promise?"

"Promise." Rebecca nodded, obviously struggling to hold back tears. "Carrying these *bopplin* sure makes me cry easily."

"I don't have that excuse." Hannah swiped at her own tears. The women embraced again.

"You need help bringing things down?" Samuel called from the bottom of the stairs. Hannah knew the offer was more to get her out of the house quickly than an act of consideration.

"Just move, Samuel. I'll help," Esther muttered.

Hannah could picture the slender woman nudging big, brawny Samuel out of the way and trouncing up the steps. She could tell Rebecca imagined the same scenario. They shared a private chuckle before Esther clomped into the room.

"Kiss the *kinner* for me," Hannah whispered. Rebecca nodded as she lumbered out into the hallway to once again tuck her children into bed for the night.

Hannah and Esther lugged Hannah's belongings downstairs, each loaded with bags. Hannah's doll peeked out from under her arm.

"*Gut nacht,* Samuel," Hannah whispered. "*Danki* for sharing your home with me." She sniffed again and stepped outside hastily without waiting for a response. She glanced back briefly to see Samuel rub his big weathered hand across his furrowed brow. He didn't utter a word.

"I don't think I could have done that," Esther said once they were settled in the buggy and on their way.

"Done what?"

"Thanked him or even wished him a *gut nacht.*"

"Sure you would."

"Hmm. I don't know."

"He did open his home to me. I did feel like part of the family. Now, I don't have a family again." She pressed the doll more tightly to her chest.

"You have me," Esther offered.

"What would I do without you? You are a great *freind*. I hope you weren't too hard on Samuel."

"I just said what needed to be said."

"That's what I was afraid of."

Chapter Twenty

Hannah threw herself into teaching with abandon. She sat up nights after Esther and her parents retired to either devise creative lesson plans or crochet baby blankets for Rebecca. She had spoken with Bishop Sol and would begin instruction after the holidays so she could be baptized with the next group of young people joining the church.

Hannah was thankful Esther and her parents welcomed her into their home. They did everything possible to make her feel at home, but she still longed for the busyness of the Hertzler household.

She missed helping Rebecca prepare meals, do chores, and care for the children. She missed the talks they shared as they worked. She missed Eli's and Jonas' pranks and lively chatter. She missed Elizabeth's sweet, slobbery kisses and Emma's devotion and gentle nature. Funny, she even missed the wringer washer, struggling to hang tons of heavy wet pants on the line, and that cantankerous old rooster.

Hannah sighed deeply. At least she was able to see the boys at school. Samuel apparently trusted her enough to teach them or else he would have removed them from the school. Emma sent her hand-drawn pictures via the boys. The four-year-old seemed to have a special knack for drawing and coloring. Hannah sent small gifts or notes to the girls in return whenever she could.

The old-timers had been reminiscing about the past and decided this was the coldest Southern Maryland December they could remember, and winter hadn't even officially arrived yet. Old Silas and the almanac were proving correct. Cherry Hill had even experienced several dustings of snow, to everyone's surprise and the children's delight. They were all excited with each flake that fell and hoped this would be the winter they could drag out their sleds. Maybe their daeds would even be able to hitch up sleighs this year.

Hannah would be just as happy if the snow never amounted to more than an occasional flake and if the caterpillars had extra fuzzy brown coats for no special reason. Since the Stauffers' house sat closer to the school, Hannah made the morning and afternoon trek by foot each day. She would be quite happy not to have to wade through knee-deep snow, though a little snow on Christmas Eve might be nice.

Christmas had always been Hannah's favorite season—singing all the old carols, gazing at twinkling lights in store windows, inhaling the fresh crisp scent of spicy apple cider, gathering with family and friends. This year, there would be no multi-colored lights and no family gatherings. She would still sing carols, though they may be different. She would still smell heavenly scents of fresh-baked cookies and cinnamon-spiced cider. She would still marvel over the birth of the Christ child.

But instead of the usual warm, cheery feeling, she had an ache in her heart, a void that could only be filled by a certain tall blond, blue-eyed Amish man. From the looks of things, that void was going to be permanent. Saturday evenings were especially hard. No light flashed into her window. No late-night visitor shared his thoughts and dreams.

"Ach, Jacob," Hannah whispered into her dimly lit room two Saturdays before Christmas. "Will you ever forgive me?" It didn't look very promising.

Hannah crocheted with the green, yellow, and white yarn until her eyes burned and watered and she ended up pulling out more stitches than she created. She wondered if Jacob would attend the children's Christmas program at the school. It was normally a community event. Everyone attended, whether they had school-age children or not. She wouldn't hold her breath waiting for Jacob to put in an appearance.

The children grew more and more excited as the holiday approached. Though never an occasion to show off or appear prideful, the school program did give the children a chance to let their parents and the community see some of their school work and hear their recitations. They would sing Christmas songs, recite Bible verses, and re-enact the Christmas story.

Their best handwriting, math, and spelling papers already hung on the walls beside the national and world maps. Handmade construction paper snowflakes, some lopsided and misshapen, dangled from the ceiling. The children had arranged pine boughs and pinecones around the room to lend fragrance and a festive appearance. The mothers would bake cookies and brownies and other delicious treats for everyone to enjoy.

Hannah's nerves threatened to overtake any excitement she may have anticipated. She knew some of the parents had been leery of her taking Sarah's place, not because they knew the real reason she had joined their community but because she was a newcomer. She certainly wasn't trying to impress anyone. She simply wanted the parents to know she truly cared about their children and provided the very best learning experiences she could.

"Relax, dear." Leah Stauffer reached out to stop Hannah from wringing her hands. "Everything will be fine. The *kinner* adore you, and the parents will be pleased with their progress. Trust *Gott*."

"I'm trying to do that. I just want the parents — and the community — to know I care and want the best for each scholar."

"They know, Hannah. Here, fill this tin with snickerdoodles. It will give your hands something to do."

Hannah unclasped her white-knuckled hands to do as Leah requested.

"Hey, teacher, are you ready for the big evening?" Esther burst into the warm kitchen, her cheeks rosy from the cold. She crossed the room swiftly and placed an icy hand on the back of Hannah's neck.

"Ach, Esther! You're frozen!" Hannah jerked away.

"*Jah*, it is a bit nippy out."

"Nippy? More like arctic, I'm thinking. I better go make sure the school house is warm."

"Not to worry, Hannah," Leah interjected. "I'm sure Henry has seen to that. Everyone will go to the program tonight, so Henry will make sure the school is comfortable."

"Okay. If you say so." *Not everyone will be there, I'm sure*. Hannah tried, not very successfully, to quash sad thoughts.

"She says so!" Esther said. "*Kum*, let's get mamm's goodies loaded in the buggy since you want to arrive early to make sure the scholars are ready and to greet all the families and *freinden*."

"*Jah*." Hannah nearly choked on the single word.

"Everything will be fine. You'll see." Esther squeezed Hannah's hand and helped herself to an oatmeal raisin cookie before Leah whacked her with a spatula.

"Trust *Gott*. Trust *Gott*," Hannah chanted under her breath. Esther and her mamm exchanged smiles.

Hannah and Esther did arrive early—before anyone else even left their homes. They didn't pass a single buggy along the short drive. Since Hannah normally walked to school, being chauffeured was a nice change. It would not have been remotely possible for them to carry all the sweet treats in their arms. Besides, the cold and dark made the idea of walking a lot less appealing. Hannah hopped from the buggy as soon as Esther hollered, "Whoa!"

"You're going to make yourself sick being such a Nervous Nellie," Esther observed.

"I'm trying to calm down. It's just that it's my first program as a teacher, and my first Amish program ever. I'm sure Sarah was always so efficient and successful"

"So are you. I'm sure you don't do things quite the same, but that's *gut*. It makes the scholars think."

"Your mamm made so much food that no one else will need to bring anything." Hannah filled her arms with containers of cookies, brownies, and cake slices and trudged up the steps to the front door of the school house. "She and your daed are coming, ain't so?"

"Of course. They just didn't need to come this early. *We* didn't need to come this early."

"Complain. Complain. I just wanted to make sure everything is organized and ready for when our guests arrive."

"Whew!" Esther nearly dropped her load onto the long table set up in the back of the room for refreshments.

Hannah rescued a tin of cookies before it slid to the floor. "Mary Beiler is acting as Mary, the mother of our Lord. Do-do you think Jacob will come?"

Esther shrugged her shoulders. "I can't imagine he wouldn't come see his sister and the other *kinner*."

"He'll probably stand by the door and slip out right afterward."

"My offer to talk to him still stands."

"*Nee*. I'll keep praying."

"Better pray for a miracle then," Esther mumbled half under her breath. "He is one mule-headed man."

"What?"

"Nothing. Just talking to myself."

"Uh huh."

The sound of a horse clip-clopping drew Hannah's attention to the window. "Someone else is early."

Esther slid over to the window, flattened herself against the wall, and leaned slightly to peek out the window as though spying on whoever drove up.

Hannah giggled. "You're *narrisch*!"

"I know, but I made you laugh."

The door flew open and little feet ran across the floor. "Hannah! Hannah!"

"Emma!" Hannah knelt to scoop the child into her arms. "It's so *gut* to see you." Emma hugged her neck. Before she could set Emma down, Elizabeth hugged her knees and begged to be lifted up. Hannah held out her arms to hold both girls.

"It surely is cold." Rebecca crossed the room to set two huge plates on the refreshment table. "*Kum*, Emma and Elizabeth," she said. "It's mamm's turn." Hannah stood and Rebecca hugged her as tightly as the two babies she carried allowed. "*Wie bist du heit*?"

"I'm fine," Hannah answered. "I miss you. Have you been feeling well?"

"Fine. Carrie had me see the doctor for another opinion, but everything is normal. Carrie is planning to do the delivery at her center instead of home."

"That's probably best," Hannah said.

"I suppose. I'd like to be home, but I want what's best for the *bopplin*."

"W-where's Samuel?"

"Outside. He and the *buwe* will help with the other buggies and horses until you need Eli and Jonas inside."

"Are you and Samuel, uh, okay?" Hannah ventured.

"*Jah*. We just disagree on a few things, but no couple agrees on everything." Rebecca sighed.

"I'm sorry, Rebecca." Tears glistened in Hannah's eyes. She hated to be the cause of problems for Rebecca.

"It's not your fault." Rebecca squeezed Hannah's hand to reassure her.

"I feel like it is."

"Don't you worry about a thing. We're fine." Rebecca paused to look around the room. "The school looks real *gut*."

"*Danki*. The scholars worked very hard."

More horses clip-clopped into the school yard. Children's excited voices carried into the building despite the closed door and windows.

"Esther and I can see to the refreshment table if you want to get the scholars organized."

"*Gut* idea. *Danki*."

The program progressed without a hitch. Some of the younger children were a little nervous and got distracted easily. Once they looked into their teacher's smiling face, they were encouraged and continued with their recitations. Mary Beiler did a fine job. Such a bright, sweet girl, Hannah thought.

Mary invited the audience to sing a few songs with the children at the conclusion of the program. Only then did Hannah allow her gaze to stray from her scholars to the crowd of people packed into the room.

The entire community must have attended! Hannah immediately spotted Jacob standing near the door, his eyes fixed on her. She stumbled over the words of the hymn as her heart lurched. When her eyes met his, he looked down quickly and slipped silently out the door. Just like she'd said to Esther. When Hannah turned her attention back to her scholars, she discovered Mary had taken in the entire silent exchange between her and Jacob.

As the notes of the last song faded, the scholars joined their parents to look at the school work on display before Bishop Sol signaled for prayer. Hannah saw Mary disappear the same way her brother had. What was she up to?

Hannah bowed her head and closed her eyes for the silent prayer. At the end of the prayer time, conversation escalated and people descended upon the refreshment table. Hannah scurried to the table to help Esther and Rebecca. Before she took more than five steps, a hand on her arm halted her.

"The program was *wunderbaar*." Sarah grinned broadly. Her doting new husband nodded beside her. They were obviously blissful newlyweds.

"*Danki*, Sarah. That means a lot coming from you."

"I just knew you'd be the perfect teacher."

"I don't know about that, but I'm doing my best and truly enjoy teaching."

Sarah squeezed her arm before she and Zeke moved off to chat with other folks. Hannah resumed her journey to the refreshment table to offer her assistance.

"You go mingle with the parents and guests," Rebecca urged when Hannah sidled up to the heavily-laden table. "We can handle this."

"For certain," Esther agreed. "I can always recruit mamm if we need help."

"The program went well, I'm thinking," Rebecca commented. Esther nodded in agreement.

"*Danki*. The scholars are all good *kinner* and have worked very hard."

"It's obvious they like their teacher and want to please her," Rebecca added.

"I agree. Now shoo, Teacher!" Esther said.

Hannah breathed a sigh of relief that the program had gone well. The children were all wonderful. She would like to compliment them more but had to be careful not to instill prideful thoughts in their impressionable minds.

The school board would undoubtedly be scrutinizing her every move, so she had to be sure she followed the Ordnung and the school curriculum to the best of her ability. There was no room for slip ups. Though she had tried to keep it tamped down throughout the evening, the fear of the school board's decision threatened to steal the joy of the celebration. Bishop Sol had promised an answer by tonight. "Trust the Lord," Hannah whispered to herself.

That thought still swirled in her head when the door opened to let Mary sneak back inside, dragging her older brother by the hand. Jacob looked as if he would rather be anywhere but in the school house right now. Doting on his little sister as he did, Hannah knew he had great difficulty refusing any request from Mary.

The frown on his face deepened, but he allowed Mary to propel him toward the refreshment table. Hannah considered disappearing into the crowd to save him from having to exchange pleasantries with her, but her shoes seemed to be cemented to the wood floor. She stared at Jacob's handsome face and could not will her feet to move even one inch.

Hannah's hand trembled so violently she had to set the Styrofoam cup of hot cider she had been sipping on a nearby desk. She feared if she attempted even a tiny swallow to moisten her suddenly dry throat, she would dribble the hot liquid all down the front of her body.

Unconsciously she began shredding the paper napkin she still clutched in her hands. Jacob's clear blue eyes found her own for just the briefest of moments, and then he abruptly dropped his gaze to the floor. Through tear-filled eyes, Hannah saw Mary nudge her brother none too gently.

"Hello, Hannah. Nice program." Jacob mumbled, trying to extricate himself from the arm Mary had looped through his.

"*Danki*, Jake," Hannah murmured. "I'm glad you could come."

Jacob nodded and practically towed Mary to the refreshment table.

"What's wrong with you, *bruder*?" Mary admonished loud enough for Hannah and probably anyone else in the county to hear. "Talk to her," she commanded a bit more softly.

"Mind your own business, Mary."

"You are my business." Mary stood firm. "You're my *bruder*, and you're miserable."

"Says who?"

"Says me!"

"You don't know what you're talking about." Finally shaking free of his meddlesome little sister, Jacob quickly chose a handful of cookies from the table.

Not to be brushed off so easily, Mary rushed to Jacob's side. As she took a breath to continue the conversation, Jacob shoved a snickerdoodle into her mouth. When Mary released her hold on Jacob's arm to remove the over-sized cookie, Jacob used the opportunity to slip into the crowd and head for the door. Mary searched out Hannah's gaze, shrugged her shoulders, and rolled her eyes. Hannah offered her a wobbly smile.

Hannah reined in her emotions and turned to greet other guests, almost colliding with Bishop Sol. His grim expression did nothing to lift Hannah's spirits. Had the school board decided to fire her or dismiss her or whatever they wanted to call it? She gulped and watched as the bishop straightened the cup in his hand before it overflowed onto his beard and chest. "A word, please, Hannah?"

"O-of course, Bishop." Why did she feel like a naughty child about to be hauled out to the wood shed for a good paddling?

Bishop Sol led her to a corner of the room unoccupied by children or groups of socializing adults. He cleared his throat twice and looked down at the trembling young woman. "The school board has met." The bishop paused and took a sip of his cider.

Why did he prolong her agony? Hannah wanted to scream. She counted silently to ten. When the bishop still didn't continue, she prodded, "Did they reach a decision?"

"That was a bit hot," Bishop Sol remarked when he swallowed noisily and found his voice. "*Jah*. We have decided that you may continue to teach."

Hannah exhaled louder than she had intended. "Truly? That's *wunderbaar*!" She knew her voice had risen in her excitement. She tried to calm down and behave in a more mature manner befitting of a school teacher. "I-I mean, I'm very happy to continue teaching."

"It's all right to be excited, Hannah." Bishop Sol's lips curved upward slightly. His eyes actually crinkled in amusement. "Your enthusiasm encourages the scholars to learn."

"*Danki*, Bishop Sol, and please tell the other school board members how happy I am to teach." The bishop nodded and, without another word, stepped away to join a nearby group of men.

Strange man, but not nearly as formidable as I thought. He almost chuckled aloud.

Hannah coerced Rebecca into leaving the mess for her and Esther to clean up. Rebecca looked about done in, though she would never admit to her fatigue. Hannah hugged her and the children and sent them on their way with a promise to visit them soon.

The crowd had thinned. Only Naomi, Leah, Esther, and Hannah remained to finish tidying up the school house. The older ladies' menfolk readied their buggies as the women completed their tasks.

"Go ahead, mamm," Esther said. "Hannah and I will lock up and be home soon."

"*Danki*, Naomi and Leah for all your hard work," Hannah said. She was beginning to feel as tired as Rebecca had looked. She, too, would be happy to arrive back at Esther's home and to slide into a waiting bed. The day had been fraught with physical and emotional strain. It was time to de-stress and rest.

Hannah and Esther continued chatting as they locked the door and hurried to the buggy Daniel had hitched for them. The horse stomped and snorted, eager to get moving and return to a warm stall and oats. In the moonlight, the horse's breath looked like smoke rising into the sky. Esther's horse undoubtedly wanted to follow Daniel and Leah as quickly as possible. Naomi and Mary were still situating themselves and their many empty dessert containers in their buggy. Esther fumbled around under the buggy seat.

"*Was ist letz?*"

"I'm trying to find my flashlight. I thought I saw something white. Ugh, the light must have rolled to the back." Esther grunted. "Got it!"

"Why…?" Hannah began. Her voice trailed off as soon as Esther clicked on the flashlight. The beam of light landed on a white slip of paper that had been tossed on the seat. Hannah gasped and reached out a shaky gloved hand to snatch the note before Esther could grab it. She quickly read the sloppy words printed in black: "You can't hide." She scrunched the note and clamored into the buggy.

"What was that?"

"N-nothing."

"If it's nothing, why did you squirrel it away so fast?"

Hannah sniffed. She didn't want to cry. The evening had been too emotional. And now this. She wanted to scream but knew she had to calm herself. "Let's go — quickly!"

"Hannah, tell me. What are you afraid of? Was — is this linked to, you know, the crime?" She finished in a whisper.

"I think so."

"I'm going to ask John and Naomi to follow us home."

"*Nee*. Let's just go — now!"

"John!" Esther yelled, ignoring Hannah's request.

The man jumped from his own buggy and rushed over. Only it wasn't John who peered into Esther's buggy where Hannah sat weeping quietly.

Chapter Twenty-one

"*Was ist letz?*" Jacob demanded. "What happened? Is she hurt?" Jacob nodded toward Hannah.

Hannah pulled her hands away from her face. Even in the thin beam of the flashlight, she could see concern scribbled across Jacob's handsome face. "N-nee. N-not hurt." Hannah sniffed and tried to get control of her tears.

"I think she got some kind of threatening note," Esther explained.

"Someone threatened you?" Jacob tried to act unconcerned but couldn't quite pull it off. He clenched and unclenched his fists.

"Could you just follow us home?" Esther knew Hannah wouldn't make the request, so she did it herself.

"I d-don't want to bother Jake," Hannah mumbled.

"No bother. Why don't I drive you two? I'll just tell Daed to pick me up at your place, Esther. Be right back." Jacob sped away.

"Esther, Jacob doesn't want to be b-bothered with me. H-he's washed his hands of me."

"I wouldn't count on that. Didn't you see his face? Even in this semidarkness, I could see he cared."

"I—" Hannah tried unsuccessfully to interrupt.

"Besides, this even gives *me* the creeps in the dark of night. I want Jacob or John to see us home." Esther almost fell over Hannah in her haste to change places.

"What are you doing?" Hannah grunted, trying to move out from under Esther.

"Changing places, of course. You sit next to Jacob."

"Ach, no you don't! No matchmaking, Esther. You can't fix this relationship."

"We'll see. Move over!"

Hannah either had to move or let Esther sit on her lap. She scooted over a bit.

"Give me some room," Esther said, wiggling on the seat.

"You have room. You aren't that big," Hannah replied through gritted teeth.

"Shhh. Here's Jacob."

"Ready?"

A look of surprise crossed his face when he now saw Hannah sitting in the middle of the seat. She lifted her shoulders in a shrug. Jacob climbed in and settled himself as far away from Hannah as he could on the crowded buggy seat. Taking her cue from him, Hannah pulled her arm and leg over as far as possible to keep from touching this man who used to like her nearness. Now, he did everything in his power to avoid her. Jacob clucked to the horse which set out at a brisk pace.

"I'm squished!" Esther squealed, pushing against Hannah who collided with Jacob.

"Esther, sit still!" Hannah felt like she was admonishing one of her scholars. "Sorry, Jake."

"It's okay."

Hannah wondered if he felt the same burning sensation when they touched and if his heart pounded as hard in his chest as hers did. Did he want to clasp her hand as much as she wanted that connection with him? She longed for his reassurance but knew she had destroyed everything that was good between them. He thought she just like his old girlfriend, Anna.

They reached the Stauffer house in record time, or so it seemed to Hannah. No doubt Jacob wanted to spend as little time as possible in her presence. Her eyes ached from straining to make out any danger lurking in the darkness. Her throat ached from holding back sobs. Her heart ached because it had shattered like fragile glass.

"Here we go, ladies," Jacob said when they reached the Stauffers' house. He looked over his shoulder. Seeing only his daed's buggy lights approaching, he felt confident in telling the women to get out of the buggy. "I'll see to the horse and buggy, Esther."

"*Danki*, Jake." Esther hopped out.

"*Danki*, Jake." Hannah raised her eyes to meet his. As she slid across the seat to follow Esther, Jacob reached out his hand. Before making contact, he withdrew his hand quickly as though he'd been about to plunge it into a nest of vipers. Hannah sniffed as she climbed from the buggy.

"I have half a mind to go right back over there and talk some sense into that mule!" Esther fumed.

"Don't you dare!" Hannah grabbed Esther's arm. "Let's take your half a mind and go inside."

Hannah danced around on the cold wooden floor, changing into her night clothes and loosening her hair. She was about to dive beneath the quilt and blankets when a soft tap sounded at her door. Before she could call out, the door cracked open and Esther's head of dark hair poked through the gap.

"Can I *kum* in?"

"*Jah*." Hannah crawled onto the bed, pulled the thick blue and purple log cabin quilt around her shoulders, and patted the spot beside her.

Esther hopped across the room, her own quilt draped around her shoulders like a queen's cape. Hannah thought her friend looked rather regal. She just needed a crown and scepter to complete the image. "*Was ist letz?*"

"I can't stop thinking about your note. Tell me about it."

"There's nothing to tell." Hannah sought desperately for some topic of conversation to distract Esther. Most likely, the less the other young woman knew, the better.

"I saw you crumple up that paper, you know. What did it say?"

"Nothing important."

"Really? Then why were you so upset?"

"I wasn't...uh, upset. Startled, maybe. *Jah*, startled."

"Good try. But I'm not buying that."

"Are you always so persistent?" Hannah drew the quilt even tighter around her.

"Hmm, let's see. *Jah*. Pretty much."

"I was afraid of that."

Esther chuckled and reached out to pat Hannah's shoulder. "I only want to help, you know."

"I do know. And I appreciate that. I just don't want to involve you any more than I already have. It's bad enough that I'm living in your house."

"Pshaw! I'm not afraid!"

"You certainly seemed so when you called for John to see us home."

"*Nee*, I wanted to get you and Jacob together."

"You fib! You didn't even know he was out there. You called John."

"But I thought maybe Jacob was there."

"Uh huh. Maybe you should take up writing fiction."

"Hey, that could be fun. I'd write whodunits."

Hannah bashed her with the fat feather pillow.

"Please, Hannah, fill me in. Maybe by being outside looking in, I can put some clues together. I'm pretty good at it, if I do say so myself."

Hannah laughed softly. "That's for sure." Should she clue her *freind* in? She wanted Esther's opinion, needed fresh eyes to look at the puzzle pieces, but she wanted to protect Esther from any remote possibility of harm. She let the silence grow between them.

"Whew! Why is it so hard to drag information out of you?" Esther groaned.

"I-I just don't want you to be hurt in any way. I'd hate to think I caused you or your parents any harm."

"I don't think you have to worry. Besides, no one will know you told me anything. There aren't any microphones or cameras in this room."

Hannah burst out laughing then clapped her hand across her mouth to muffle the sound. She didn't want to awaken Leah and Daniel, even though Esther had assured her they could sleep through an earthquake and tornado occurring simultaneously. The image of a bugged Amish bedroom caused another spasm of laughter that she tried unsuccessfully to suppress. "I'm sure you're right about that," she gasped, holding her side.

"So spill. I won't squeal. Pinky swear."

"You are too much, Esther Stauffer. And you've read too many cheap mysteries or spy novels."

"Hey, they weren't cheap—well…actually, they were free since they were library books—but they were good books!"

"Okay. Okay. I'll tell you what the other notes said."

"Other notes? How many? Wait!" Esther jumped off the bed, dashed out of the room, and returned before Hannah could even wonder what she was up to. She pounced on the bed and pulled a tablet of paper and a pen out from under her quilt. Pen poised over the paper, she announced, "Let's get started."

"Aren't you tired?"

"Not in the least, but ach, I'm sorry. I guess you've had a stressful day. Do you want to go to bed?"

"*Nee*. I probably wouldn't be able to sleep, anyway." Despite the heavy quilt, Hannah shivered, recalling all the messages she had received.

"All right," Esther said. "How many notes have you received?"

"This was the fifth one."

"Fifth! Have you told anyone? Do you have a way to let any detective know?"

"I tried to use the phone near Rebecca's house after the first note, but the phone wasn't working. I mailed a letter to Liz—the former Amish woman Bishop Sol told you about—but I haven't heard back from her. I don't know if she got my letter or not. I had to mail it to a contact person in Pennsylvania who was supposed to forward it."

Esther whistled softly. "I wonder if that letter was intercepted somehow. That phone hasn't worked in ages. Most people with a business have a cell phone that we can use for business reasons or emergencies. Tell me what the notes said."

"Esther, I'm not sure about getting you involved."

"I'm already involved, and before you say anything, I *chose* to be involved."

"The first note was really strange. It said, 'little man by the window stood'!"

"That is odd. When did you get that?" Esther scribbled details busily on her paper as Hannah revealed them. "Have all the notes been on the same kind of paper?"

"*Jah*. Just scraps of white paper with black ink or marker. Nothing fancy."

"I wish we had them all to compare."

"I know. I sent a couple in my letter to Liz. Samuel destroyed one."

"Okay, what was the next message? Just give them all to me."

"The second one said, 'saw a rabbit hopping by.' Next was 'before a hunter shoots you dead'." Hannah shivered and pulled the quilt even tighter. Esther nodded so she continued. "Then came 'don't bother going inside, little bunny.' And this is the last one tonight. Hannah produced the most recent scrap of paper and handed it to Esther.

"'You can't hide'," Esther read aloud. She scribbled it down then tapped her pen against her chin.

"The words all sound familiar, somehow. I keep wracking my brain." Hannah frowned, trying to force a memory.

"Let me think," Esther replied still tapping her chin. "Who is the little man?"

"I don't know. I've wondered about the guy on the bicycle with the red baseball cap. He keeps showing up. Have you seen him?"

"Hmm. Now that you mention it, I have seen him in a few different places."

"Do you know him?" Hannah turned a hopeful expression on her friend. Maybe Esther had some knowledge of this guy.

Finally, Esther shook her head. "I don't know who he is, but I think I'll keep an eye out for him. I think he's a 'person of interest,' as they say. I'll try to ask around about him. That won't seem strange. Everyone knows I'm nosey."

Hannah laughed. "Curious, not nosey."

"Right. That sounds better."

"Don't go getting yourself into trouble, Esther."

"Not to worry about me. I'm a super sleuth."

"You're a nut who reads too much!"

"That, too. I'm going to mull all this over. I'd better let you get some sleep."

"Okay. You too."

"*Gut nacht*, Hannah. By the way, you make a fine Amish woman."

"*Danki.*" Tears sprang to Hannah's eyes. She reached out to hug this friend who never hesitated to champion her cause. "*Gut nacht*, Esther. And *danki* for listening."

Esther hugged her back and slipped from the room dragging her quilt behind her. Did she do the right thing confiding in Esther? Would this cause any problem for her friend? Hannah would never be able to live with herself if any harm came to Esther or her parents because of her. She blew out the oil lamp and crawled beneath the covers to stare into the darkness since sleep evaded her.

Christmas Eve was a flurry of activity in the Stauffer household—as in most other Amish and *Englisch* households as well. Hannah, Esther, and Leah cleaned, baked, and cooked in preparation for the Lord's day of birth and for Second Christmas, the day after. Esther didn't seem to mind in the least when her cooking or baking efforts were interrupted by a customer who wanted to buy a last-minute holiday wreath, poinsettia, or Christmas cactus. She dashed out of the house as soon as any car pulled into the driveway.

"That girl!" Leah sputtered. "Never going to find a husband if she doesn't settle down and hone those cooking skills."

Hannah laughed. "I think she'll be fine when the right man *kums* along."

"Huh! Only if he likes eating cold cereal with milk past its expiration date."

"Are you talking about me, Mamm?" Esther burst into the kitchen out of breath, her cheeks stained crimson by the wind. "I look at the date on the milk. If it still smells all right, I use it anyway."

Leah wagged her head, a look of disgust crossing her face. "Impossible!"

"Besides, Mamm, you're a *wunderbaar* cook. You don't need two such cooks in the same kitchen." Esther sidled up to her mother and gave the older woman a hug.

"No danger of that happening."

Esther elbowed her mother playfully and snatched a peanut butter cookie off the cookie sheet Leah was unloading. Leah swatted at her with the spatula.

Hannah laughed again She wondered if she and her mother would have had such a playful but loving relationship. Although Aunt Genevieve had always been good to her, she couldn't help but miss knowing the love of her own mother.

Christmas was family time with big meals and visits to friends and loved ones. Hannah exchanged small gifts with Esther and her parents and stopped by the Hertzler home on Second Christmas to drop off treats and trinkets for Rebecca, Samuel, and the children.

As usual, the children clung to her and all tried to talk at once. Hannah gave them each candy canes and presents which occupied them momentarily so she could visit with Rebecca.

"Ach, I miss you," Rebecca exclaimed.

"I miss you all, too. I wish I was here to help you."

"I didn't mean I missed your hard work, though it did help me out a lot. I miss talking with you every day. It was fun having another woman in the house."

"*Jah*, it was fun. You have to let me know how I can help you now. How is everything going? Have you seen the doctor?"

"*Jah*." Rebecca patted her large belly. "I did as Carrie asked and saw Dr. Morris. He said everything was fine. Carrie wants me to deliver at the hospital, but I said I'd prefer her birthing center."

"Would it be safer for you and the *bopplin* to be at the hospital?"

"I trust Carrie. I really wanted a home birth like all my other *kinner*."

"I know that's what you want," Hannah soothed. "I'm sure the birthing center will be easier for Carrie since there are two little ones in there."

"I suppose. Carrie's *gut*. I told her she could transfer me to the hospital from her center if necessary, so that satisfied her."

"And me too." Samuel entered the warm kitchen to grab a handful of cookies. He nodded to Hannah.

"Hello, Samuel. *Wie bist due heit*?"

"*Gut*. You?"

"Fine." Hannah felt awkward. She didn't hold a grudge. She knew Samuel only wanted to protect his family, but still, she felt uneasy around him now.

"Have a good visit." Samuel headed for the door. He called over his shoulder, "I'll drive you home so you don't have to walk in the cold—when you're ready, that is."

"*Danki*, but Leah and Esther will stop back by to pick me up on their way home."

Samuel nodded and continued striding to the door. Hannah tried to decide if Samuel was just being polite or if he wanted to get her out of the house as quickly as possible. She chatted with Rebecca a little longer, colored with Emma, played with Elizabeth, and read a quick story to all four *kinner* before the clop-clop of hooves heralded the arrival of her ride.

Not wanting to keep Leah and Esther waiting, she hugged Rebecca and the children, promising to visit again as soon as she could.

"See you in school tomorrow," she reminded Eli and Jonas before making her way out to the waiting buggy where the horse pranced and snorted in the frosty air. Tomorrow would be back to school and work for everyone. No week-long break between Christmas and New Year's like in the *Englisch* world.

Chapter Twenty-two

As far as Hannah was concerned, "Southern Maryland" was a misnomer. Nothing about the weather they were experiencing in St. Mary's County could be considered southern. January's temperatures remained below freezing, and several good-sized snowfalls had already blanketed the fields. The scholars could hardly wait for the school day to end so they could drag their sleds to the big hill behind the Eshs' store.

Miriam and Levi welcomed the *kinner* and always had hot cocoa or cider to offer the chapped-cheeked, half-frozen youngsters when their stiffened fingers could no longer haul the sleds back up the hill.

Hannah practically ran to the school house each morning, just to keep from freezing. On the coldest mornings, Esther drove her the short distance and fetched her when the school day was done. The almanac and Old Silas were proving accurate.

The first Friday of January turned out to be one of those bone-chilling days where even Hannah's eyeballs felt cold. The thick, gray sky threatened to discharge more snow or sleet, or both. Hannah wrapped a scarf around her neck and pulled on the heaviest mittens she owned. Not one for coffee, she filled a thermos with hot tea to sip on throughout the morning. Tucking the thermos and her lunch into her quilted school bag, she braced herself to face the cold on the other side of the door.

"Oh no you don't," Esther called. "You can't walk today. Why, that wind would blow your itty bitty body clear across the river to Virginia, even if you had rocks in your pockets. I'll take you to school."

"I hate to be a bother. Then you'll have to interrupt whatever you're doing to come pick me up this afternoon."

"No problem. Besides," she cupped a hand to her mouth and dropped her voice to a whisper, "it will get me out of the kitchen and away from Mamm's impromptu — though I know she really plans them — cooking lessons."

"You're incorrigible!" Hannah laughed.

"But truthful. Besides, I have an errand or two to run. Are you ready?"

"As ready as I'll ever be to face the brutal cold."

The trip to school was mercifully short. Esther didn't seem too bothered by the cold. Hannah's teeth chattered uncontrollably. "You wait for me when school is over. There is no need to walk home."

"All right, boss." When she saw the smoke curling from the school house chimney, Hannah offered a quick, silent prayer of thanks for Jeremiah Yoder's dedication to the school and the scholars. She waved as Esther drove away and dashed into the building to ready herself and the room for the day ahead.

First order of business, Esther thought, is a little visit to Beiler's Furniture Shop.

"What brings you this way?" Micah Beiler glanced up as the tinkling bell above the shop door announced Esther's arrival. "Looking for some new furniture?" he teased.

"Looking for your mule-headed *bruder*."

"I've got two of those. Just which one might you be referring to?"

"I think you can probably guess."

"I suppose I can. I'll go fetch Daniel for you."

"Micah Beiler!" Esther stamped her foot for emphasis. "You know very well Daniel isn't the *bruder* I want a word with."

"*Jah, jah,* Esther. Don't get riled up. I'll send in your victim—I mean, Jacob." Micah smirked and headed for the back where the sound of hammers, saws, and other tools reached a nearly deafening decibel. Esther paced until Jacob walked through the door.

"*Gut mariye*, Esther." Jacob brushed an unruly lock of blond hair from his face and turned a questioning gaze on his visitor.

"*Gut mariye*, Jacob." He needed to get his mamm to trim his hair, Esther thought.

"Can I help you with a new dining room table or rocking chair or—"

"Wise guy, just like your *bruder*," Esther muttered. "I need to talk to you, Jacob."

"So, talk away. What's on your mind?"

"A certain little blonde who is hurting as much as you are."

"I have work to do." Jacob turned his back and marched toward the door he'd just come through.

"You come back here, Jacob Beiler! I didn't drive over here to have you be rude to me."

"I'm not being rude. I have nothing to say."

"Well, I do, so you'll have to listen." Jacob raised an eyebrow. Esther took a deep breath and tried a softer tactic. "Jake, you and I have known each other all our lives. I consider you a *freind*. I've only known Hannah a short time, but she has already become a dear *freind*. She is bright, kind, funny, and honest, and—"

"Honest! You must have a different definition of honest. Hannah lied to me and to everyone else."

"She had to. Didn't you hear what Bishop Sol explained about her situation? And don't say you didn't. I saw you lurking in the barn after the auction."

"She could have told me the truth all those Saturday evenings. She could have trusted me."

"Have you ever thought she was trying to protect you? That she didn't want you to have knowledge that could possibly cause harm to come to you?"

"That's *gegisch*. I can take care of myself."

"Hannah came upon a crime scene. Those guys murdered someone—or more than one person.

Hannah could identify them. Don't you think they would come after her or anyone close to her?"

"Hannah is safe here. That's why she invaded our community. That's why Bishop Sol allowed her to come without telling anyone—to keep her safe."

Esther chose to overlook Jacob's sarcasm or bitterness or whatever emotion he wrestled with. "Hannah loves it here. She's going to stay. And, though it wonders me why—you're such a *dummchen*—she cares about you. She's been miserable that you've turned your back on her, and I'm reasonably sure you are just as miserable."

Jacob turned away again. "Hannah chose to lie, just like An—"

"No!" Esther exploded, grabbing Jacob's arm. "Not like whoever hurt you in the past. Try not to be so stubborn. Use that brain I know the Lord *Gott* gave you. Hannah's in trouble, but she wanted to protect you, protect all of us."

"Hannah's safe here. She could have been truthful."

"She would have jeopardized all of us and herself. Besides, she's not necessarily safe here."

"What do you mean?" Jacob faced Esther squarely.

"I-I mean things have happened. I shouldn't say more. I've been too much of a *blabbermaul* as it is."

"Don't stop now, Esther. Fear of being a *blabbermaul* has never stopped you before. Is someone after her now? Here?" Jacob's tension was obvious.

"I'm not sure, but possibly. Very possibly." This time, Esther turned to leave. "Think of all I've said, Jake. Please."

She whispered the last word, then pulled open the door to admit a cold blast of air and marched out to her waiting horse and buggy without looking back at Jacob. She didn't see him standing with his mouth agape, an expression of fear mingled with panic on his face.

The thick, dark gray clouds hung so low, Hannah felt she could pluck them from the sky when she dismissed the scholars at the close of the school day. The clouds seemed ominous, a harbinger of evil, and were making good their threat by spitting ice pellets mixed with snowflakes. The scholars, oblivious to the wind and dampness, danced and laughed as they headed home in different directions, shouting out plans to meet at the Eshs' hill for more sledding if the snow kept up.

Hannah shivered and closed the school house door after the last scholar left. She was cold, but it was more than the freezing temperature that made goosebumps erupt all over her body. She couldn't exactly put her finger on it, but something felt different today. Something felt odd, expectant…creepy. A vision of eyes watching her every movement haunted her thoughts.

At recess, her eyes had continually searched the parameters of the school yard, looking for anything out of the ordinary. Her heart plummeted to her toes, and her stomach tried to churn out the few bites of lunch she had forced herself to eat when two of the third graders pointed to something on the road.

The same bicyclist, his red cap pulled low, shielding his face, pedaled slowly past the school. He seemed to be scanning the school yard. Hannah almost yelled for the *kinner* to run inside when he cycled on down the road. She had never been able to get a clear view of the man's face, but something seemed awfully familiar about him.

Now, she was alone. Did those watching eyes know that? What had happened to Esther? She had promised to pick her up after school. Maybe she should go ahead and start for home. It wasn't that far. If she walked on the road, she'd probably run into Esther, anyway — or the bicyclist.

Hannah rubbed her hands up and down her arms, attempting to erase the goosebumps that had taken up permanent residence there. *Calm down. Just do some work. Esther will be here soon.*

She crossed the room to the blackboard her helper for the day had cleaned a short time ago. She picked up a long piece of yellow chalk that snapped in two with her tense grip. She relaxed her hand and using the larger fragment of chalk, wrote Monday's assignments on the board. She tidied her desk and banked the fire. Jeremiah would no doubt be by later to check that the fire had gone out and everything was okay for the weekend.

Hannah shuffled to a window facing the road, hoping to see Esther's buggy driving in. Her sigh turned into a gasp when she spotted the red cap bobbing along the road. She stood transfixed as the bicycle wheeled onto the school property and sat at the end of the roadway. Was he going to come all the way up to the building? Did he know she was still inside? What should she do? A cell phone would sure come in handy.

Hannah backed away from the curtainless window, her gaze darting around the room. She could find nothing to use for a weapon. Besides, the Amish didn't fight. Should she hide? The cloakroom was the only place not in plain view of the entrance. It was, of course, the first place anyone up to no good would search for a scared victim.

She had to do something. Crawl under her desk? Her blue dress would be a dead giveaway. She shivered again.

"Poor choice of words, Hannah," she mumbled aloud.

How many minutes had ticked past? Was he ready to mount the steps and push open the door? She scurried soundlessly toward the cloakroom. With trembling fingers, she wrapped a scarf around her neck and fumbled to fasten her cloak and tie her bonnet. Heavy footsteps stomped up the steps. Her heart pounded in her ears blocking any other sound. Her breath came in short, strained pants. The door flew open. Hannah screamed.

She slipped through the tiny cloakroom window and sprinted for the woods as fast as she could while battling the wind. She strained to hear if footsteps clomped behind her, but could hear nothing over the noise of the wind and sleet. She feared she wouldn't hear a bullet whiz past her either.

Already wet and cold, Hannah forced herself to run at top speed. *Thank goodness I've been a runner and haven't gotten out of shape.*

The only immediate plan that came to mind involved somehow making it to the cover of the trees. Then she hoped she could find her way out to some public place to call for help. The major flaw with this plan was that she was not familiar with the woods. She didn't know how deep the forest was or how far she would have to travel, provided she didn't get lost.

For now, she had to keep running, keep panting for each frosty breath, keep her feet from slipping on the sleet and snow-glazed ground, and mainly, keep from becoming hysterical. That last part was probably the hardest of all. "Trust *Gott*. Trust *Gott*," she gasped with each breath.

Hannah slowed her pace just slightly a few yards into the woods. A quick look over her shoulder told her no one followed her just yet. She stopped for just a moment and bent at the waist to catch her breath and to ease the stitch in her side. She was thoroughly chilled, soaking wet, and miserable. But she was alive.

She gulped in a deep breath and took flight again, deeper into the woods. The howling wind wasn't such an issue now. The trees offered some measure of protection. Hannah strained to hear if a twig snapped but could discern no sound other than her ragged breathing. She turned in a circle to survey her surroundings.

The trees in any direction looked the same to her—tall, leafless hardwoods and crystal-coated evergreens. Nothing looked familiar. Hannah had no idea where she was or if she had been running in circles. Somewhere, there had to be a clearing. She prayed she found it before darkness closed in or before she froze to death.

At least the sleet had stopped. Big, fluffy snowflakes still floated from the sky and adhered to her cape, bonnet, and eyelashes. Hannah rubbed her arms, shook her nearly numb hands, and trudged off in the direction she hoped would lead her out of the shadowy, menacing woods where every squirrel or rabbit incited panic.

Where was she? He'd heard her scream as the wind snatched the door from his hand and banged it open. Had someone already gotten to her? But they would have had to pass him to get out of the building. Was someone in the cloakroom, the only cubbyhole he couldn't see into from the doorway of the one-room school house?

"Hannah! Are you here?" The room was tidy, as always. Every desk sat in perfect alignment. There was no sign of any scuffle. Hannah's bag rested against her desk.

Jacob crossed the room in long strides, leaving a trail of snowy footprints. He paused at the alcove, almost afraid of what may await him in the cloakroom. He stiffened his spine, conjured up his courage, and rounded the corner. Empty. He knew he heard Hannah scream. His heart pounded harder.

The hooks on the wall were all empty, and there was no place to hide. A gust of wind caught Jacob by surprise, and that's then he noticed the open window.

He ran the few steps to the small window and looked out just in time to see a dark cloak and bonnet-clad figure disappear into the woods. Hannah! Where on earth was she going? Someone must really be after her. Could he catch her?

Jacob raced out of the building, leaped off the steps, and ran for the woods, shouting Hannah's name. The wind caught his voice and threw it back in his face. She couldn't hear him.

He was too late. He should have stopped by Esther's place sooner. Esther's words had finally sunk into his brain. Hannah was the same person he knew from the beginning. She was the same woman he fell in love with.

He stopped abruptly at the edge of the woods as the realization of that last thought struck him like a heavy weight crashing into his skull. *Jah*. He loved her. He loved Hannah. Would he get a chance to tell her? Would she forgive him? He had to find her, but the woods had swallowed her without a trace. Would someone grab her in the woods or would she be able to find her way out?

He would have to get help. Jacob made a U-turn. Bishop Sol would help him. He willed his legs to pump faster than he'd ever run in his life.

Chapter Twenty-three

Hannah's teeth chattered. Her fingers and toes no longer tingled. Now, they were just numb. It looked like the woods thinned at the top of the next hill. If she could just scramble up that embankment, maybe she could reach safety. She paused in her wandering to listen again.

Was that a deer rustling the bushes? Did the wind cause the snapping twigs? Hannah's breaths came faster. Frantically, she searched for a hiding place. She mentally repeated a Bible verse she had memorized years ago.

Fear not, I am with thee. Be not dismayed for I am thy God. I will strengthen thee; yea I will help thee.

Help me now, Gott. Strengthen me.

She wiggled under a prickly bush, ignoring the scratches to her cheeks. Her heart thudded, and she seriously considered throwing up. She breathed so shallowly and quietly, she feared she would faint. Out of the blue, a children's rhyme sing-songed through her mind:

In a cabin in the woods
Little man by the window stood
Saw a rabbit hopping by
Knocking at his door
"Help me! Help me! Help me!" he cried
Ere a hunter shoots you dead,
Little rabbit come inside
Safely you may hide

That's it! The notes. They make sense. I'm the rabbit!

Heavy footsteps drew closer. Hannah fought not to scream.

"Lookee here," a gruff voice yelled. "I think I found our little bunny."

Hannah recognized the voice—the voice that hollered, "We'll get you," as she ran from the crime scene in Virginia. The man reached through the brambles and grabbed for Hannah's arm. She drew her arm back but not quickly enough. He dragged her out of her hiding place, a long thorn tearing a jagged gash on her cheek.

Tears sprang to Hannah's eyes—tears of pain, tears of frustration, tears of regret. She knew in a matter of moments, her life would be snuffed out. She would never see Rebecca and the *kinner* again. She would never know if Rebecca's twins were boys or girls. She would never tell Jacob she loved him even if he could never love her in return. Tears mingled with blood trickled down her face. She peered through them at the tall, thin man with the baseball cap. She gasped when she realized he wasn't the bicyclist after all. This man was a lot thinner.

"Hey, hey!" the paunchy, balding man called.

So they were both here. How had they found her? How many cronies did they bring with them? How could she get away? She would not give up easily.

"Nice disguise," the first man said, looking Hannah up and down. She shuddered under his scrutiny.

"Not quite good enough, though." The heavier man guffawed as if he cracked the funniest joke ever.

Hannah squirmed to free her arm from the vice-like grip.

"Where ya going, bunny? We just got here?" the skinny man said. Both men snorted.

Twigs snapped again. Hannah prayed for assistance. She jerked her head to look in the direction of the sound and nearly collapsed in relief. "O-Officer Kade. You found me. Thank goodness." She sighed in relief as she took in the welcome sight of the tall, young officer from Virginia. "How did you f…"

"Shut up!"

Hannah turned wide, shocked eyes on the man she assumed would be her rescuer. "What? You're one of them? No wonder they knew where to find me."

She took a deep breath, ready to scream for help. As if able to read her mind, Kade took two giant steps and backhanded Hannah across her unbloodied cheek. She sagged and struggled to stay on her feet. Pain, fear, and disbelief vied for top billing.

"No!" a distant voice shouted. "Don't hurt her!"

Hannah strained to make out a face in the waning daylight. "*Nee*," she whispered. "Jacob, go away!" she yelled at the big man in the distance. She couldn't let him come down from the embankment where he stood. He would not fight them, and they would surely kill him. She would rather they kill her than witness Jacob's death. "Please, Jacob," she pleaded.

"Shut up!" Kade snapped. He raised his hand to strike again, but Hannah ducked, avoiding the blow. Her cheek still throbbed, but fear overshadowed all pain. She willed Jacob to stay put and not endanger himself further. She had to draw attention away from him.

Jacob lurched forward. He could not let that man hurt Hannah again. He hesitated momentarily. Would his presence make things worse for Hannah or would he be able to shield her from harm? He started forward again.

"Better tell your hayseed boyfriend there to get back up that hill unless he wants to witness a crime," Kade ordered.

"Or be part of one," the lanky thug chimed in.

"Jacob, please go back." Hannah tried to shout. Her throat felt coated with sawdust. Why didn't they just kill her and get it over with?

Hannah concentrated on Jacob, praying he would turn back. In her mind, she saw his brilliant blue eyes and easy smile. This was what she wanted to remember—the caring, happy, wonderful man he had always been—not the angry man who had lost faith in her.

Please, Jacob, she mouthed silently. She didn't think he could see her eyes, but she hoped he could feel her love. She wanted to leave him with that.

Jacob remained rooted to the spot, seemingly unable to move forward or backward. His eyes locked on Hannah. How could he help her? There had to be a way. He knew these woods like he knew his own bedroom. Silently, he backed away, knowing Hannah watched him, fearing she would think he was deserting her—again.

"Please forgive me, Hannah, for everything," he whispered. Exaggerating the words in case she could see his lips, he mouthed, *Trust.*

Please spare her, Gott, and please show me how to help her, Jacob prayed over and over as he scrambled back up the embankment.

Hannah saw Jacob's retreat. She felt relieved that he would be out of harm's way and would not have to watch whatever happened to her. But now she was completely alone with these evil men. "Help me, *Gott,*" she whispered.

Kade jerked his head and the balding thug pulled Hannah in the indicated direction. Hannah would not make this easy for him. She locked her knees and attempted to root herself to the spot, taking the heavy-set man off guard.

"Come on," he grumbled yanking her arm hard.

She stumbled forward. "W-Where are you taking me?"

"Shut up!" She wondered if Kade had any other words in his vocabulary. "Why are you doing this? The police already know who you are. I don't have any other information to give them."

"You talk too much," the tall, skinny thug said. "If you'd kept your mouth shut before and not gone to the police the day we dumped Miss Judy, you might not be in the fix you're in right now. Your mouth gets you in trouble."

Judy. Why did that name ring a bell? Hannah searched her memory. "Judy was the name of the jogging victim."

"Well, you're a real bright one, aren't you?"

"You guys are the ones that kidnapped and killed the three joggers?"

"Make that four." The stout guy sounded proud.

"Soon to be five." The other man snickered.

"That b-bag you dumped the day I saw you looked too big to be Judy. I saw her picture on the news."

"Judy was the first one down the hill that day. The one you saw was one of Kade's drug buddies who got too lippy. Kade here was too chicken to take care of him. Left the dirty work to us."

Hannah gasped. How many people had these guys killed? "You're a police officer, Kade. How could you be associated with these guys? You're supposed to protect people."

"Huh," Kade grunted.

"He wouldn't get the money for his little drug business if he didn't help us. Ain't that right, Kade?" Kade remained silent.

"Where are you taking me?" She knew after all they confided there would be no chance she'd be allowed to live. Why didn't they just get it over with?

"We don't usually kill right away," the heavy man said. "We like to see people squirm a little first." He threw back his head and laughed. "She is uncommonly pretty, even in this Halloween getup, ain't she, Kade?" He tugged at Hannah's bonnet. She jerked her head away.

"Leave me out of this," Kade snarled.

"Oh, you're already in it, buddy, whether you like it or not."

"I'm not into torture." Kade spat on the ground as if the whole conversation was distasteful. Hannah's only hope was that he wasn't as heartless as the other two.

"You know, we were kind of thinking you'd be next, even if you hadn't seen us. We knew your ten-mile routine," the lean man said.

Hannah shuddered. She had been stalked as she ran and never knew it. "So Kade told you how to find me here?"

"Ding, ding, ding! Give the lady a prize!"

There went her hope that maybe, just maybe, Kade would help her. She had to get away. She didn't want to be dragged off with them. There would be no chance anyone would find her if she left this spot. She pretended to trip over a root and stumbled, hoping to pull her captor down with her. Despite his short stature, Hannah underestimated his weight. He was like a tank and didn't even miss a step. He jerked her upright.

"Careful there, hon. We wouldn't want you to get hurt now." He laughed raucously.

Tears of frustration and fear again filled Hannah's eyes. She tried to blink them away. She wouldn't give these creeps the satisfaction of knowing the extent of her fear. She would not admit defeat—not yet.

Please, Gott, show me what to do.

An ever so tiny rustling sound caught Hannah's attention. She glanced sideways at the thug clutching her arm. He didn't appear to have noticed any sound. When had it stopped snowing? Hannah hadn't even paid attention. The snow shower had dwindled to just an occasional flake. The *kinner* would be so disappointed if there wasn't snow to go sledding this weekend. Funny how she could still think of that when her very life would soon be snuffed out.

There came that slight rustling sound again. Hannah turned her head slightly to the right. Her captor still stared straight ahead. She ventured a quick peek to her left and barely kept from gasping. Not more than a few feet away, something wiggled and eyes peered at her from a bush. Jacob! He put a finger to his lips. What was he doing? He was going to get himself killed. She had to keep any attention off of him.

Hannah feigned a hacking cough. Kade and the thug beside him looked over their shoulders. Hannah continued to cough, hoping her noise covered any sound Jacob may make as he moved stealthily through the underbrush. She had no idea what he planned to do, but she couldn't let them hear him.

"Coughing up a lung?" the tall guy called from a few feet in front of her.

"Probably pneumonia," Hannah mumbled.

"Won't matter soon." The man beside her laughed, pulling her forward again.

"Kade, how can you kill people when everyone has always looked to you for help?" She had to try to get through to him again.

"Kade ain't never killed anybody," the man holding her arm explained. "Kade's just in the drug business. Drugs are kind of a side line for us two." He nodded at his buddy in front of him.

"Shut. Your. Mouth." Kade dropped his hand to his hip, most likely reaching for his gun. Hannah's panic nearly swallowed her.

"Who's she gonna tell, man?"

"Just keep quiet and keep your eyes open."

Hannah struggled to keep her balance and to catch her breath as she struggled up the embankment. Kade stopped to scan the area before signaling the others to continue their ascent. Hannah's mind whirled. She couldn't get in a vehicle with these guys. She knew she would never have a chance at survival then. And no one in the community would ever know what happened to her—except Jacob. That is, if he lived to tell.

"Stop!" a voice bellowed.

Nearing the top of the hill, the thug gripping her arm jerked Hannah to a halt. A red-capped man stood with a gun drawn. The bicyclist! He was in on this too? Why hadn't he grabbed her all these weeks? Kade reached for his gun.

"Drop it, Kade," the cyclist shouted, his gun aimed at Kade's head. "All of you, stop right where you are." He was telling Kade to drop his gun?

Confused, Hannah squinted at the man. Loudon? The pimply-faced young cop from Virginia? He had been in St. Mary's County all this time? Was he a bad cop, too?

From out of nowhere, state and county police officers converged on the area, guns drawn. Kade threw his gun away from him.

"You two! Throw down your weapons. Now!" Loudon jerked his head toward the other two thugs.

Two guns and a hunting knife joined Kade's gun a few feet away from Hannah.

"Take your hands off the lady," Loudon commanded. Two officers trained their guns on Hannah's guard and the other thug. The man released his grip so suddenly, Hannah nearly collapsed. Relief flooded her. Was she really going to be freed?

"And to think you were my partner!" Loudon spat out. He looked in disgust at Kade. "You fooled a lot of people, but I had my eye on you."

Hannah ventured a good look at Loudon. Gone were the little boy look and the bright red pimples. Were they all a disguise? He only had a hard scowl for his former partner who stared at him in surprise.

"Loudon, how did you—" Kade began.

"I'm not as dumb as you thought, Kade. Just for your information, I wasn't a green, rookie cop. I've been working undercover for years. Even the captain thought you could be trusted. He thought you were a fine, dedicated cop. I had my doubts. Turned out I was right." Loudon's expression softened as he turned to Hannah. "Are you all right, miss?"

Hannah could only nod and whisper, "*Jah*," before breaking into gulping sobs. She covered her face with her frozen hands. Her body shook convulsively.

"Shh!" Strong arms enveloped her, pulling her close. "It's okay, *liewe*. You're safe now. I will make sure you stay safe—if you will let me."

Hannah sniffed and pulled back to find Jacob's blue eyes searching her face. He reached out to touch her bruised, swollen cheek gently. "I'm so sorry," he whispered.

Hannah broke into fresh tears—tears of relief, tears of gratitude, tears of joy. Jacob continued murmuring to her and patting her back. Hannah wanted nothing more than to stay securely ensconced in Jacob's arms forever but the surrounding shouts and commotion forced reality upon her. She drew away to see what was happening. Uniformed officers fastened handcuffs on the three criminals and led them the rest of the way up the embankment.

With his arm firmly around Hannah, Jacob helped her up the steep hill. "You are the most courageous person I've ever met, and probably the most forgiving," he murmured. "Even after the way I treated you, you were willing to do whatever you could to protect me. I'm so ashamed of myself. I don't deserve your forgiveness."

"Don't, Jacob." Hannah raised a hand to stop his words. "Don't feel ashamed. I was deceitful even though I didn't want to be. Honesty and trust are very important and I violated those things. I can't fault you for your reaction. And here you were today, willing to sacrifice your life for me. I'm not worthy of you."

"You are all I could ever hope for."

At the top of the embankment, the woods gave way to a paved road unfamiliar to Hannah. It must have been one of the little side roads she had not yet explored. She had been so close to freedom. White and black county police cars mingled with brown and black state police cars, all with red, white, and blue lights flashing.

To the side of the police cars stood Bishop Sol, Jeremiah Yoder, Henry Zook, and Samuel Hertzler. All four men converged on Jacob and Hannah at once, all speaking rapidly in Pennsylvania Dutch. Hannah turned a questioning look on Jacob, her numb brain unable to comprehend the rapid words. She fumbled to push stray strands of pale blonde hair back under her bonnet, but her hands were as numb as her brain.

"It's okay," Jacob whispered, capturing her small hand in his larger, only slightly warmer hand. He didn't let go of her despite their onlookers.

"Hannah. Jacob." Bishop Sol sounded relieved. "Thank *Gott*." He bowed his head briefly. Snow crystals still clung to his bushy beard and brows. Tears shimmered in his dark eyes when he lifted them to look at Hannah and Jake. Henry, Jeremiah, and Samuel also whispered prayers of thanks before crowding around the missing couple.

"How-how did you know to be here?" Hannah wondered aloud.

"Jacob," Bishop Sol replied. Hannah turned to look at Jacob.

"I had...uh, a little...uh, talk with Esther today," Jake began.

"She didn't—" Hannah began.

"Esther gave me the talking to I needed. She made me think."

Hannah shook her head. "I specifically told her not to corner you, not to get involved."

"I'm glad she did," Jacob said. "This time, anyway, her meddlesome way was a *gut* thing. She helped me see how wrong I was. I drove over to her place this afternoon to tell her I would pick you up after school."

"You came to the school house?"

"*Jah*. When I got there I couldn't find you. I thought you'd been kidnapped. Then I saw you run into the woods. I ran after you and hollered for you. You couldn't hear me over the wind. You had disappeared without a trace by the time I entered the woods. I was afraid you'd get lost. I drove faster than my poor horse has ever trotted to Bishop Sol's." Jacob broke off and sniffed, obviously overcome with emotion.

"*Jah*," Bishop Sol took up the story. "I told Jacob I'd round up some help and for him to wait at the edge of the woods for us." The bishop scowled at Jacob. "Of course, this stubborn man would not heed my advice—which for once, was a good thing. He took it upon himself to rescue you."

"You could have gotten killed," Hannah squeezed Jacob's hand as much as she could with her stiff fingers.

"It was a chance I was willing to take—for you."

Hannah lowered her gaze and fought to keep fresh tears at bay. She looked up quickly at a scuffling sound. The tall thug was giving his arresting officer a hard time. The other man had already been locked inside a state police cruiser. Kade, his head hung low, climbed willingly into another state police car. A second officer hurried to help subdue the unruly man. As soon as all three criminals were on their way to jail, Loudon jogged over to Hannah and the men. "Are you all right, Ms. Bra—uh, Ms. Kurtz?"

"I am now. *Danki*...er, thank you."

"She's about frozen solid, though, and has a nasty bruise and scratch." Jacob pointed to Hannah's face.

"Do you need an ambulance?" Loudon pulled out his cell phone.

"I don't think so." Hannah had no desire to be carted off to the hospital.

"Can we get her home?"

"Sure, but I'll need to come by to get statements from both—make that all of you."

Jacob started to rattle off the Stauffers' address.

"That's okay," Loudon interrupted. "I know where she's been staying."

Thankfully Hannah didn't have to say anything right now since her brain felt like it was wrapped in ice. She sagged against Jacob, ready to collapse from exhaustion and relief. Instantly, his strong arms encircled her. She wanted only peace.

Chapter Twenty-four

"*Kum*, Jacob," Bishop Sol said. "You are not fit to drive right now, I'm thinking. I will take you and Hannah to the Stauffers' house. Jeremiah and Henry will take your horse and buggy home and update your folks.

"*Danki*." Jacob looked at Hannah whose shivering had increased. Even in the near darkness illuminated by the spinning lights of the police cars, he could see the paleness of her face and the bluish tint to her lips. He feared she may suffer dire consequences from her exposure to the cold and the shock she'd experienced. He had begun to shake with cold and emotion himself.

"Are you sure you don't want to go the hospital to be checked out?" a policeman called out. "Or at least a ride home?"

Hannah shook her head. Her eyes felt glazed over and her mind seemed unable to comprehend everything going on around her. She tried to follow Bishop Sol, but her leaden legs refused to cooperate. She saw the police cars gradually pull away from the scene. She saw Loudon slide into one of the state cruisers and signal that he would meet them. Still, she could not make her body obey.

"*Kum*, Hannah," Jacob crooned. "Let's get you warm."

"And you, too," Bishop Sol added.

Jacob wrapped a strong arm around Hannah's waist and half carried her to the bishop's buggy. He lifted her inside and helped her slide to the middle of the seat. He jumped in beside her and sat as close as he dared.

"Here." Bishop Sol tugged out a blanket. "Wrap her up well."

Jacob wrapped the heavy blanket around Hannah, drawing it up under her trembling chin. "We'll be home soon," he whispered, his own teeth beginning to chatter.

Bishop Sol shook the reins and urged his horse into a trot. "Hold on, Hannah. We'll get you there as fast as old Stockings can take us." He looked over at Hannah and then mumbled, "Should have let the policeman drive her home."

Hannah heard the bishop's voice seemingly from a great distance. She wanted to respond, tried to respond, but could only manage a very slight nod. She was slipping away and could do nothing to prevent it.

Sol glanced at Hannah again and encouraged Stockings to trot faster. "Talk to her Jacob. She looks barely conscious. Don't let her slip away."

Jacob jerked alert. He nudged her gently.

"Hannah, talk to me. Are you hurting anywhere?" He knew her bruised, swollen cheek must ache, if she could still feel it at all. The blood from her scratches had long since dried or frozen on her face. Jacob used a corner of the blanket to gently wipe a tear that trickled from her eye. "It's okay. Can you look at me?"

Hannah turned her head. "*Danki.*" The single word came out as a croak. Tears again shimmered in her cloudy blue eyes.

"Shh." Jacob took her gloved hands in his. Even though his hands were cold, they were nowhere nearly as frozen as Hannah's. He pulled off her soaked gloves and gently but briskly rubbed her small hands between his much larger ones. He had to warm them, at least a little.

He prayed her hands weren't frostbitten. There would be more pain when the feeling returned. He vividly remembered playing in the snow as a child long after his mamm cautioned him to come inside. Pain like he'd never before experienced shot through his frozen hands as they thawed. He remembered crying and promising to listen to his mamm next time. He didn't want Hannah to go through that.

Bishop Sol reached the Stauffers' house in record time. He stopped the buggy as close to the back door as possible so Hannah would not have far to walk. Before Jacob could slide halfway out of the buggy, the back door of the house flew open. Esther, not even wearing a cloak or bonnet, bounded down the steps ahead of the other women.

"Hannah? Jake, do you have Hannah?" Esther grabbed Jacob's arm and tried to peer around him into the dark buggy.

Jacob shook off Esther's hand. "*Jah, jah*, Esther. Just give me a minute—"

"Is she all right?" Esther clutched Jacob's arm again.

"I was going to say, let me help her out. Then you can see for yourself."

"Ach, sorry Jacob." Esther pulled her hand back.

"We've got to get her warm. She's nearly frozen." With his head inside the buggy, his voice was muffled.

Other women poured from the house. Naomi rushed to the buggy. "Ach, Jacob. You are all right. *Danki, Gott.*" She obviously wanted to hug her son but knew she would have to wait.

Jacob lifted Hannah from the buggy and helped her stand. "Can you walk?"

Hannah nodded. "I-I think s-so." Her words came out slurred.

Esther took charge. "Stand back, ladies, we've got to get this *maedel* warm." She raced around to grab Hannah's other arm and helped Jacob steer Hannah up the steps and into the house.

"Our prayers have been answered," Leah murmured. "They are safe."

"The other men?" Barbara ventured.

"Henry and Jeremiah are taking Jacob's horse and buggy home for him," Bishop Sol informed her.

Barbara breathed a sigh of relief. "*Kum* in, Bishop, and get warm. Your *fraa* is here, too. I brought her with me. We've been praying since you gave us the news."

"*Danki*. Our Lord has been merciful."

Esther and Jacob led Hannah to a chair as close to the wood stove as they could get. Jacob removed Hannah's cloak and bonnet and handed them to Leah,

"I'm going to run get her some dry socks. Take those wet things off of her," Esther ordered.

Jacob looked flustered. He'd do anything for Hannah, but this was a rather personal matter. He hesitated, not sure if it would be proper even given these extreme circumstances.

"Here, Jacob, let me." Sophie Hostetler apparently noticed his distress. Gratefully, Jacob moved aside and turned away to spare Hannah any embarrassment.

Naomi took advantage of the opportunity to hug her son. She wrapped her arms around him and stood on tiptoes to kiss his cheek.

"Ach, Jacob. I was so worried."

Her voice quivered and she blinked back unshed tears. Jacob patted his mamm's back and whispered soothing words to her. He let her peel his damp jacket from his cold, weary body and smother him with a little motherly love. It was obvious he longed to be at Hannah's side but would have to allow the women to tend to her.

"Hannah, dear, let's get these wet shoes and socks off." Sophie's hands removed the wet items quickly. She rubbed each foot gently to restore the circulation. "I have some herbs steeping for you."

After warming each foot, Sophie wiped the dried blood carefully from Hannah's face and pressed a cool cloth to her blackened, puffy cheek. She was as loving and gentle as Hannah believed a mother would have been.

"Can you hold this here, dear?" Sophie moved one of Hannah's hands to hold the cloth so she could continue her ministrations. She smoothed Hannah's hair and tucked loose strands beneath her *kapp*. "Looks like we're too late to prevent bruising, but this should help the swelling and pain."

Hannah nodded and tried to thank the kind woman for her caring and help. Sophie patted Hannah's unbruised cheek and attempted to lighten the mood.

"We need our teacher fit and ready to take on these rambunctious scholars, ain't so?"

Hannah tried to smile. "*Danki*," she finally managed to whisper.

"Warm socks!" Esther announced, passing soft, woolen socks to Sophie who pulled them onto Hannah's cold feet.

"You're warming up nicely," Sophie observed. "Would you like some tea now?"

"P-please," Hannah croaked. Her throat felt like it had been scraped with broken glass.

"I'll bring you tea, too, Jacob," Sophie said.

"I'd rather have *kaffi*."

"*Nee*. You need my tea, too."

"*Danki*, then," Jacob conceded. No one argued with the medicine woman.

Hannah sat as close to the stove as she could without actually touching it, her hands wrapped around the steaming mug of herb tea Sophie had prepared for her. Her brain had gradually thawed so she could comprehend the conversations and actions around her. She winced in pain as the feeling began to return to her fingers and toes.

A flurry of activity near the door caught her attention, and she tried to focus her glazed eyes in that direction. She felt a smile tug at the corners of her still slightly frozen lips as Rebecca rushed into the room with all four children in tow.

"Samuel wanted me to stay home, but I just couldn't. I have to see for myself if Hannah is all right. Where is she?" Rebecca's eyes followed Leah's gaze until she spied Hannah by the stove. "Let's go," she said to Emma and Elizabeth who had clung to her.

Jonas and Eli hung back near the door shuffling their feet and staring after their mamm.

"Ach, Hannah!" Rebecca cried, dashing across the room. She dropped to her knees in front of Hannah. Tears spilled from her eyes as she gathered the younger woman in her arms. "I-I'm so g-glad you are safe." Rebecca gave up trying to hold back her tears and wept openly.

"Mamm! Mamm!" Emma and Elizabeth wailed, upset by their mother's weeping.

"Your mamm is fine," Esther soothed the girls. "She is crying happy tears."

Hannah hugged Rebecca and then held out a hand to the frightened little girls. "*Kum*," she said.

Instantly, Emma and Elizabeth ran to Hannah, followed closely by Jonas and Eli who summoned up the courage to enter the room. Hannah hugged each one, reassuring them everything was all right. The brief distraction allowed Rebecca time to pull herself together.

"Let's go find a cookie," Esther said to divert the children's attention. "If it's okay with your *mamm*, that is."

Rebecca nodded and mouthed her thanks as Esther hustled the little ones out of the room.

With the children happily accompanying Esther to the kitchen, Hannah turned her attention to her friend. The hot tea had soothed her raw throat so her voice wasn't quite as raspy.

"Rebecca, you shouldn't upset yourself so. Here, sit with me. Tell me about the *kinner* and the *bopplin*." Hannah wanted to erase the worry from her dear friend's brow.

"We're all fine. Carrie says everything is going well. Ach, Hannah! I've been so worried." Tears threatened again. Rebecca sniffed them away. "You know I think of you as a *schweschder*. I thought I'd lost you." Now, another tear did escape.

Hannah wiped a tear from her own eye. "I wondered for a while there myself, Rebecca. I kept telling myself to trust *Gott*. And He sent Jacob to find me and to get help.

"Are you sure you are all right? Your poor cheek." Rebecca reached up to touch Hannah's cheek but drew her hand back. "I don't want to hurt you further. I'm so sorry this happened." Rebecca's voice broke again.

"My cheek will heal, Rebecca. Please don't cry. I'm sure I have scrapes and bruises, but they will mend." Hannah sucked in a sharp breath.

Instantly at attention, Rebecca exclaimed, "Are you in pain? What? Where?"

"Oooh! My hands and feet." Hannah dropped the cloth and shook her hands.

"Sophie!" Rebecca called.

"I'm right here," the older woman replied. "It's just the feeling coming back. I know it hurts, but 'tis a good thing. We want the feeling to come back, ain't so?"

"It hurts." Hannah bit her lower lip and tried not to howl in pain.

Sophie rubbed Hannah's feet again, ever so gently. She motioned for Rebecca to massage Hannah's hands.

"*Danki*," Hannah whispered.

Across the room, Jacob observed every move Hannah and the women made. He winced as Hannah winced, her pain almost as real to him as it was to her. He wanted to rush across the room to her. He wanted to be the one to warm her hands and feet. He wanted to hold her and never let her go.

"She'll be fine, son." Naomi wrapped an arm around her big, strong son. With her free hand, she brushed the hair off his face. "I know you want to go to her. Let the women take care of her—for now."

Jacob nodded. He understood his mamm's unsaid words. Later, he would have time with Hannah. He needed to be patient a while longer, then he could tell Hannah his feelings.

Hannah relaxed visibly as the pain in her hands and feet subsided. Jacob heard her thank the women again. He let out the breath he didn't remember holding and relaxed his tense shoulders as he saw the lines of pain flee from Hannah's lovely face.

Mamm was right. She was always right. Hannah will be fine. She has to be fine.

"Here, Rebecca, sit." Leah pulled a chair over beside Hannah. "You shouldn't be down there on the floor."

"I had to hug Hannah," Rebecca explained. "I'm not sure I can get up now."

"Let me help you." Leah grasped an arm and helped Rebecca to her feet. "You aren't that big, you know, especially for expecting twins."

"I feel as big as a heifer." Rebecca grunted as she rose and then dropped down onto the offered chair.

"Are you really okay?" Hannah reached out a shaky hand to her friend.

"Of course. No more morning sickness. I'm probably no more tired than any other mamm with four young ones."

"I will still help you however and whenever I can."

"Let's get you recovered first. Drink Sophie's tea. It will be good for you. It will warm you up inside. We don't want you getting sick from this."

Obediently, Hannah raised the cup to her mouth and took a sip of tea. Her hands felt a little steadier now so she had more success at actually getting the cup to her lips.

"Samuel and I would like you to move back into our home," Rebecca murmured, "if you'll forgive us."

"Really? Samuel too?"

"*Jah*. It was his idea, actually. Can you forgive us, and can you live with four rowdy *kinner* again after the peace and quiet here?"

"Ach, Rebecca, there's nothing to forgive. I understood that Samuel wanted to protect his family. And you know I love the *kinner* and being surrounded by a big family. It's been a little too quiet here."

"Think on it, then," Rebecca patted Hannah's arm.

Hannah caught movement in her peripheral vision and swiveled slightly to see Sophie leading Jacob nearer the wood stove. "You've got to warm up, too, you know." She handed him the tea he had set down on a side table. "And drink your tea!"

"Okay, Sophie, I will."

Rebecca hoisted herself up from her chair. "Here, Jacob, sit. I need to check on my little ones."

She shuffled off before Hannah could call out to her. Hannah knew full well the real reason Rebecca pulled a disappearing act. She'd probably tell the other women to leave them alone, too. Hannah gazed into Jacob's face, noting the concern, tenderness, and caring etched there.

"*Danki* again, Jacob," she whispered.

"Ach, Hannah, I'm so sorry you had to go through that. I'm so sorry I didn't reach you in time."

"*Nee*, Jacob, if you had been there any sooner, you might have been hurt or-or killed. I would never have been able to forgive myself if that happened. You found me. You led the others to me. I'm so glad you are safe and unharmed."

"You saved me, Hannah." Jacob took one of Hannah's hands. "I read your expression even from a distance. Your eyes and unsaid words warned me."

"But you tried to reach me anyway."

"I couldn't leave you there alone with those men, Hannah. I wouldn't let them hurt you again. I couldn't bear that. I wish I could have kept this from happening." Jacob paused to caress Hannah's injured cheek gently. "I had to make them think I was leaving so I could sneak around and try to get to you."

"I was so afraid for you, Jacob. I didn't want to be alone with those men, but I wanted you to leave so you'd be safe."

"I know, Hannah."

"You were so brave."

"*Nee*. Just determined not to let them take you away."

"Jacob—"

"Hannah—"

They spoke at the same time and laughed.

"You first," Jacob said.

"I-I wanted to tell you how sorry I am that I was not truthful with you from the beginning I wanted to be. I should have been. Can you forgive me?"

"*Nee*, Hannah. I need to ask your forgiveness for being—as Esther calls me—mule headed." Jacob paused and smiled as Hannah smiled and patted his hand. "I understand why you couldn't tell me. I'm glad you didn't because it kept you safe—until today, anyway."

"You don't know how awful I feel, Jacob, for deceiving you and for hurting you, especially after—well…after what you'd been through before. I-I didn't want to be like Anna." Hannah's voice dropped to barely above a whisper.

Jacob squeezed Hannah's hand. "You are not like her. You could never be like that. I know that you are a good, honest person. I really understand now. I'm just a little dense." Jacob knocked at his head, bringing another smile to Hannah's face. "Besides, Hannah, the past is just that. It's over and done with. We have the future."

Hannah gave a slight nod of her head, not letting on that the movement caused her head to ache.

Hannah and Jacob sat silently for a few moments, looking at each other, marveling at the wonder of their unspoken feelings. Jacob cleared his throat.

"Hannah, maybe this isn't the right time or place, but…uh, I have to tell you—"

A knock at the door interrupted Jacob's speech. They both looked toward the door to find Loudon and two other officers stamping off their boots and greeting Leah.

"Sorry to interrupt, ma'am" Loudon said. "But we need to talk to some folks."

"*Kum* in." Leah stood back and allowed the men to enter her home. They crossed the room to where Hannah and Jacob sat.

"Ms. Br—uh, Kurtz, how are you feeling?"

"It's Hannah, please. Except for a headache and other assorted aches, I'm better now that I'm thawing out." With a trembling hand, she brushed at a stray strand of hair. Why was she suddenly so nervous?

"Your cheek looks pretty bad. Are you sure you don't want me to run you up to the hospital to get it checked out?"

"*Nee,* Officer—or is it Detective Loudon?"

"I am a detective, but I'll answer to either." He smiled. Hannah knew he tried to ease her nervousness.

"You were the cyclist in the red hat. You've been here all this time?" Hannah ventured.

"Most of the time. I had to keep an eye on you."

"Did you suspect Kade of being involved all along?"

"No, at least not involved in all he really is mixed up in. I just got bad vibes from him and wasn't sure what he was up to. I hadn't worked with him too long, but I didn't completely trust him. It's not good if you can't trust one of your own. I just wanted to keep an eye on him. Our superiors, Kade, and I—and, of course, the marshals—were the only ones who knew your whereabouts."

"And Liz."

"Yes."

"She never answered my letters."

Loudon coughed slightly. "I'm sorry, but she...uh, didn't receive your letters."

"Why — oh, did you take them?"

"I'm sorry, but I had to intercept. I know she meant well, but she shouldn't have contacted you. Too risky."

"Yet you left those other notes — the threatening ones — in the mailbox."

"I was busy keeping tabs on you when they were delivered. Besides, I couldn't run the risk of Mr. Hertzler seeing me taking things from his mailbox."

"You certainly look and act different," Hannah blurted out and then clapped her hand over her mouth.

Loudon chuckled. "That bumbling, immature, inept act was pretty good, huh?"

"It sure fooled me."

"And your skin..." she began. "Oops, sorry. I don't mean to be offensive."

"That was fake acne. I wasn't real sure about Kade, even before we left Virginia."

"Then why did you let that man bring Hannah here?" Jacob interrupted.

"My bosses trusted him. They thought he was a good cop. They had no evidence otherwise, but they knew I was honest and let me do some surveillance. I'm afraid it was a chance we had to take."

"It seems pretty risky when lives were involved," Jacob persisted.

"Unfortunately, yes. But we got our men. More young female joggers are spared, and we should be able to break a big drug ring in our area. I'm pretty sure Kade will talk. Thank you, Mr. Beiler, for your quick thinking and for helping us get to Hannah in time."

"It's Jacob, and I'm just thankful I was there to help."

"Now, we need to get statements from both of you, please. We'll try to make it as quick and easy as possible. These two fellows"—he nodded to the officers with him—"will take notes and ask any questions they can think of. Okay?"

"Okay," Hannah and Jacob both replied.

"That about wraps it up," Loudon announced. The officers snapped their notebooks closed. "Do either of you have any questions?"

"Can you tell my aunt and uncle and cousins that I'm all right?"

"You are free to tell them yourself. You can go home and resume your normal life."

Jacob's heart dropped to his knees. Her normal life. How could he have forgotten that this wasn't Hannah's normal life? She had a whole different life apart from St. Mary's County—apart from him. He felt like he'd been kicked in the stomach by his grandfather's old mule. He struggled to suck in a breath. It seemed like everyone in the house—from the quietly chattering women to the playing children to Bishop Sol and the other men who had slipped into the house—stopped breathing. Only the wind-up mantel clock ticked noisily, filling in the silent gap.

Hannah, tears glistening in her eyes, looked around the room. Her gaze settled on Jacob, and her eyes locked on his. "I am home, Detective Loudon. This is my normal life. I want to stay here, if they will still have me."

The whole room erupted in cheers and a flurry of activity. Throwing propriety to the wind, Jacob pulled Hannah into a quick embrace, regardless of a room full of onlookers. Rebecca, Leah, Naomi and the other women waited in turn to hug Hannah. Esther grabbed Hannah in a bear hug, eliciting a groan from her petite, slender friend. "No more hiding," she said. "You're safe now."

"*Jah*," Hannah agreed. "Safely you may hide." At Esther's questioning look, Hannah explained. "I finally remembered that silly rhyme."

Across the room, Bishop Sol stood with Jeremiah and Samuel. The bishop stroked his beard, nodded, and said loud enough for everyone to hear, "*Wilkom*, Hannah Kurtz."

EPILOGUE

Hannah's knees knocked together as she followed the other baptismal candidates into the Eshs' big barn where the Sunday service was being held. While the congregation sang hymns from the Ausbund, the four young women and two young men spent forty minutes secluded with Bishop Sol and the ministers, reviewing the Dordrecht, the Confession of Faith.

They had spent the last two months learning about the eighteen articles and the specific details of their local Ordnung. Now, having just been asked a final time if they were ready to take their baptismal vows and be bound to the Amish faith for the rest of their lives, the six candidates took their places near the ministers' bench.

Hannah had the urge to reach up to ensure her baby-fine hair was behaving but resisted and kept her trembling hands folded in her lap. Rebecca had helped her secure every wisp of hair and made sure her *kapp* was straight. Her dress, cape, and apron were as wrinkle-free as possible. Hannah licked her dry lips. She forced herself to sit still and listen to the sermons.

After two hours of sermons and a lengthy prayer, the candidates were called forward to kneel before the bishop and ministers. The bishop asked each of them to confess their belief that Jesus Christ is the Son of God, to submit themselves to the church, to renounce the world, and to promise to support the teachings and regulations of the church. Despite her bad case of nerves, Hannah's "*Jah*" in response to each question resounded clear and strong.

The bishop cupped his hands over each candidate's head as one of the ministers poured water into his hands. As Bishop Sol pronounced her baptized in the name of the Father, Son, and Holy Spirit, Hannah felt tears run down her face to mingle with the water that dripped from her hair.

After the six young people were baptized, Bishop Sol shook their hands and offered a holy kiss to the young men. His wife kissed the young women and helped them readjust their *kapps*. The six were now full church members, bound to the Amish faith for the remainder of their lives.

Hannah smiled broadly. Excitement and relief replaced her anxiety. She was truly Amish now. For the first time in a long, long time, she felt totally at peace. She belonged—to these people, to this way of life, to God. She had chosen this life. She had been accepted and welcomed by the community. She sighed in contentment.

The service continued as usual and concluded with prayers, the benediction, and a hymn. Hannah could hardly wait for the common meal. Her happiness bubbled up and threatened to spill over.

She struggled to rein in her emotions until the solemn service ended.

Hannah filed out of the service with the other new church members. She received hugs from Rebecca, Esther, Leah, Naomi, Sophie, and the other women. Jacob smiled and winked at her from across the way where the men had gathered, awaiting the meal. Hannah returned his smile and could tell her cheeks now sported a pink tint. Women hurried to set out plates of meats, breads, salads, and desserts.

The thinning crowd left two red-haired women and two brunette men standing on the fringe. "Be right there," Hannah called to Rebecca. She squealed in delight and rushed to join the four *Englischers*. "Aunt Vee, Uncle Ted…Michael, Rennie, I'm so glad you came."

"We wouldn't miss being here for anything," Rennie said hugging her cousin hard. "I've really missed you. I'm so glad you're safe and happy, but I'm sure going to miss having you close by."

"I've missed you, too. And I'll miss seeing you and talking to you often. We can write, though, and you are welcome to visit anytime."

Rennie tugged gently on Hannah's sleeve. "Is that blond guy with the gorgeous blue eyes over there—the one who keeps staring at you—someone special?"

"You might say that." Hannah felt her cheeks grow warmer.

"Hannah, dear, we are so relieved you are safe. Are you sure you're happy here?" her aunt inquired.

"*Jah.* This place was my haven and is now my home. I'm very happy here. For sure and for certain."

ABOUT THE AUTHOR

Susan Lantz Simpson's love of words and books led her to earn a degree in English/Education. She has taught students from prekindergarten to high school and has also worked as an editor for the federal government. She also holds a degree in nursing and has worked in hospitals and in community health.

She writes inspirational stories of love and faith and has published a middle-grade novel (Ginger and the Bully). She lives in Maryland and is the mother of two wonderful daughters. She is a member of ACFW and Maryland Christian Writers Group. When she isn't writing, she enjoys reading, walking, and doing needlework.

Acknowledgements

Thank you to my family and friends for your ongoing support.

Thank you to my daughters, Rachel and Holly, for believing in my dream along with me and for all your help. (Rachel, you've been a very patient listener, and Holly, I couldn't have done any of the tech work without you!)

Thank you, Mom. You encouraged my writing ever since that first childhood poem I wrote. I know you're smiling down from Heaven.

Thank you to Greta Martin, Mennonite friend, for all your information.

Thank you to my wonderful agent, Julie Gwinn, for believing in me from day one and for all your tireless work.

Thank you to Dawn Carrington and her staff at Vinspire Publishing. I appreciate all your efforts to make my dream a reality.

Thank you most of all to God, giver of dreams and abilities and bestower of all blessings.

Dear Reader,

If you enjoyed reading *Plain Haven*, I would appreciate it if you would help others enjoy this book, too. Here are some of the ways you can help spread the word:

Lend it. This book is lending enabled so please share it with a friend.

Recommend it. Help other readers find this book by recommending it to friends, readers' groups, book clubs, and discussion forums.

Share it. Let other readers know you've read the book by positing a note to your social media account and/or your Goodreads account.

Review it. Please tell others why you liked this book by reviewing it on your favorite ebook site.

Everything you do to help others learn about my book is greatly appreciated!

Susan Lantz Simpson

**Plan Your Next Escape!
What's Your Reading Pleasure?**

Whether it's captivating historical romance, intriguing mysteries, young adult romance, illustrated children's books, or uplifting love stories, Vinspire Publishing has the adventure for you!
For a complete listing of books available, visit our website at www.vinspirepublishing.com.
Like us on Facebook at
www.facebook.com/VinspirePublishing
Follow us on Twitter at
www.twitter.com/vinspire2004
and join our announcement group for details of our upcoming releases, giveaways, and more!
http://t.co/46UoTbVaWr

We are your travel guide to your next adventure!

71339716R00200

Made in the USA
Columbia, SC
29 May 2017